THE GERMAN AGENT

THE GERMAN AGENT

J. Sydney Jones

This first world edition published 2014
in Great Britain and 2015 in the USA by
SEVERN HOUSE PUBLISHERS LTD of
19 Cedar Road, Sutton, Surrey, England, SM2 5DA.
Trade paperback edition first published
in Great Britain and the USA 2015 by
SEVERN HOUSE PUBLISHERS LTD

British Library Cataloguing in Publication Data

Jones, J. Sydney author.
  The German agent.
  1. World War, 1914-1918–Secret service–Germany–
  Fiction. 2. World War, 1914-1918–Diplomatic history–
  Fiction. 3. United States–Politics and government–
  1913-1921–Fiction. 4. Washington (D.C.)–Fiction. 5. Spy
  stories.
  I. Title
  813.6-dc23

ISBN-13: 978-07278-8436-7 (cased)
ISBN-13: 978-1-84751-544-5 (trade paper)
ISBN-13: 978-1-78010-590-1 (e-book)

All Severn House titles are printed on acid-free paper.

Severn House Publishers support the Forest Stewardship Council™ [FSC™],
the leading international forest certification organisation. All our titles that
are printed on FSC certified paper carry the FSC logo.

Typeset by Palimpsest Book Production Ltd.,
Falkirk, Stirlingshire, Scotland.
Printed and bound in Great Britain by
TJ International, Padstow, Cornwall.

FOREWORD

I n the early months of 1917, the United States was teetering on the brink of a fateful decision: whether or not to enter the European war – the Great or First World War as it came to be known in the history books.

Good men on both sides of the issue pleaded their case in America. A national debate raged, for everyone knew the momentousness of such a decision: we would be entering the world stage, not simply a war. We would forever after be players in an international game, a role the United States had heretofore only partially understudied. Splendid isolationism – despite forays into Cuba and the Philippines – was still the rule of the day.

Good men on both sides of the Atlantic argued the issue, as well. The British, held in a stranglehold by a U-boat blockade and all but alone in the fight, were desperate for our help. The Germans, exhausted and ravaged by a multi-front war, saw victory at hand, and wanted at all costs to keep the US out of the fray.

Good men on both sides of no-man's-land – huddled, sodden, and shell-shocked in their trenches – considered the issue, and wanted only one thing: an end to the war. Not victory. After so many losses on both sides, there could be no winners. For these men, the soldiers of the warring nations, US entry could mean only one thing: a prolongation of the slaughter. Another half million dead before the cannons would finally cease.

And good men – and bad – on both sides plotted to either lure the Americans into war or lock them out, to somehow influence the decision-makers in Washington.

As with all things of great moment, this decision would not be left to reasoned judgment, but to the hurly-burly of good or bad luck. For, in the early months of 1917, a single scrap of paper held history in the balance; a secret message that – if delivered – would thrust the US over the precipice into war, or that – if suppressed – would steal the fire from the pro-war senators in Washington.

That scrap of paper is known as the Zimmermann Telegram.

While the events of *The German Agent* are fiction, the Zimmermann Telegram and the convoluted history of its provenance, transmission, and interception are only too real and have reverberated through the corridors of international diplomacy for the past century.

PROLOGUE

London, England
January, 1917

N ow I've gone and done it, she thought. What if that beady-eyed super, McMasterson, spotted me with me arm up to the elbow in the typing pool wastebasket? What if the other cleaning woman, Mrs Childes, saw me pocket those crumpled bits of paper?

What if? What if? To hell with them all, she thought as she got off the number nine omnibus. It's worth the risk.

Nothing much in Bess Todd's forty years had gone right. She suffered from lumbago and fallen arches. Her only child had died of diphtheria at four, and her husband had left her not long after.

She always told people that he'd died, leaving her a widow.

'Poor Mr Todd,' she would say after a gin or two, her drooping eyes filling with tears. 'Fell down an elevator shaft, he did. Left me with nothing. No insurance. Nothing but a pair of dirty britches in the laundry basket.'

Even in her lies she painted herself as a victim. Until last month.

Then Michael had come into her life.

God, how I love that man, she thought as she hurried as fast as her pudgy short legs would carry her down Whitechapel from the omnibus halt and toward her block of flats on Kentish Road.

He's my man. I love the smell of him; the touch of his smooth hands on my naked flesh.

She was hurrying because she wanted to catch her Michael still in bed; because she wanted him on top of her, inside her, covering her like a big old stallion would his mare.

She'd never known that sex could actually be pleasurable until Michael.

The early morning was so cold that white frozen plugs shot out of the tops of milk bottles on doorsteps. Gas lamps were still on; there'd be no sun today with the sky low and menacing.

She clutched her felt bag tightly to her chest; that was where she'd shoved the ball of paper she'd retrieved from the trash. But she'd been so nervous and excited after stealing it that she'd had to leave work early.

I hope Michael's newspaper will like this little bit, she thought. Maybe he'll get a rise on account of it and we can take a trip to the seashore this summer. How grand it would be to see the pier at Brighton. Maybe I'll get a new frock for the trip.

Yes, it was damn well worth the risk.

She smiled at this thought and Mr Pearson, the tobacconist, who was just opening his shop, tipped his black bowler at her, thinking the smile had been meant for him.

Bess bustled past him, giving him only a curt nod, saving all her best stuff for Michael.

But what if they do catch you?

Ah now, it was just a crumpled ball of paper I nicked from the Foreign Ministry trash. Not the bleeding crown jewels. Little enough to do for Michael after all he's done for me.

She tingled all over just thinking of his hands on her breasts, massaging them like fresh bread dough.

How lucky you are, Bess. The luck has finally found you.

They'd met in a little gin house just off Earl's Court, him a fine looking chap in his early forties with a bad ticker, he'd said, so they would not take him for a soldier. No white feathers about him. He worked for the papers, a reporter, like. And he'd sat next to her in the only available seat in the whole smoky inn and had chatted her up, actually finding her interesting.

He bought a round of gins and the next thing, you know, Bob's your uncle, they'd ended up at her bed-sit together, her moaning into her pillow while he serviced her like a man with absolutely no ticker problems at all. He'd moved in with her that very day. In between lodgings, he'd said all sheepish. She figured reporters made even less than charwomen.

Little enough to do for him, she thought, as she arrived at

her soot-blackened building and unlocked the street door with the big Chambers key that weighted the bottom of her bag like a revolver. Just nick a few papers now and again from the bucket what should go to the incinerator.

'A charwoman at the Foreign Ministry?' he'd said that first night, all surprised at learning her occupation. 'Well, you're a princess in my eyes, you are.'

He had the romantic way of talking that made Bess melt inside; actually made her wet and hot down there.

You're a sinful old girl, Bess Todd, she thought, doing a half-skip up the stairs to her third-floor bed-sit. Randy as a mare in heat.

From the landing she could see that her door was ajar. The door to the communal bath and toilet at the end of the hall was closed and a light was showing under it. She went into her cramped lodgings. Some of Michael's things were spread out on the chipped deal table, and she felt a rush of affection just seeing that he was making himself at home.

Pencil and paper; a small book open; a letter sticking half out of a torn envelope. Working. Probably writing one of his articles for the papers. She was curious about her Michael, for he would not talk of his work, would not tell her about his past or his family. Like he was hiding something from her. She dropped her bag on the table next to his papers, opened the clasp and took out her prize for him, carefully smoothing out the discarded ball of paper with the edge of her right hand like she was ironing handkerchiefs until the two pages lay flat, the lion rampant clearly visible on the letterhead of the first.

A momentary sense of guilt and shame tugged at her: when taking the job at the ministry she'd vowed never to do exactly this. Hand on Bible and all. But there wasn't really anything wrong with it, Michael had explained. The people had a right to know what their government was up to, even in time of war. And the newspaper he worked for would never print anything that would actually harm Britain, he'd said.

'We aren't traitors, just watchdogs,' he would tell her when they lay in bed together after making love, and then he'd describe what sorts of papers she should look for: heavy rag paper with the ministry letterhead; blue flimsies of cables sent or received.

She took off her hat and coat and dropped them onto a straight back chair, and then her eyes trailed to his writing on the table.

'. . . SS *Edgerton* leaving Falmouth, 0400 hours, Feb. 2, bound for New York; SS *Essex* departs Dover, 2200 hours, Feb. 3 . . .'

Strange sort of article, she thought. Like a shipping list.

Next to this was a book of tide charts. The letter half-peaking out of the envelope intrigued her. There was a Dublin postmark on it.

Is that the funny lilt I hear in his voice? she suddenly wondered. Is he a Paddy then? Is that what he's hiding from me?

She pulled the letter out of its envelope and opened it, then felt her heart skip a beat when she read the opening line:

'*Lieber Freund* . . .'

Her eye went quickly down the page. The whole bleeding thing was in German!

Bess felt a sudden shiver pass over her, like a goose crossing her grave.

'You're home early.'

She swung around at the sound of Michael's voice. He was standing barefoot in the doorway in his undershirt, pants and braces, holding a shaving mug and brush in one hand, a cut-throat razor in the other. His eyes went immediately to her hands, which still held the letter from Dublin.

'What is all this?' she said.

He shrugged, grinning. 'Nothing.'

'I was anxious to be with you. To show you my new find.'

She suddenly felt all the joy leave her, realizing she was about to become a victim once again, and this angered her.

He closed the door, walked slowly toward her, and set the shaving mug on the table. 'I can explain.'

His eyes were sorrowful looking, sincere. But she suddenly did not trust her Michael; suddenly realized she knew nothing about him whatever.

'It's from an old school chum of mine in Dublin,' he said. 'Takes himself for a marvelous linguist.'

'Is that so?' She felt the anger rising, turning red-hot in her chest. 'And these shipping lists?'

A muscle flexed in his jaw. 'Why did you have to come home early?'

'It's my bleeding home. I'll come when I want.'

'Sorry,' he said, shaking his head.

A half hour later he had dressed, cleared all traces of himself from the bed-sit and was locking the door. He looked one last time at Bess: the blood around her head had turned a dirty rust color now and was already thickening like gelatin.

He felt nothing; neither remorse nor shame at what he had done.

The pages of the purloined telegram copy were folded in his pocket, his heart still racing at its contents. Berthold will be a happy man tonight in Berlin, he thought.

Happy? Shite. Berthold's going to mess his pants over these papers.

ONE

Washington, DC
February, 1917

T he snow began at about ten that morning. With its coming, Catherine Fitzgerald decided to call it a day. She had intended to take more architectural shots for her Washington album, but with available light low and the snow dampening the lens of her new pocket Kodak camera, there was not much point in continuing. Instead she would go home and work on the enlarger in her dark room.

Thomas had dropped her off, for she had not wanted to be concerned with remembering where she had parked. She had arranged for Thomas to pick her up at one, but she was freezing and not about to wait for the old servant to come retrieve her.

The old 'servant', she thought. As if Thomas had ever been less than part of her family. He had helped to raise her; had dried her tears when a homemade kite had caught in the great elm at her father's Rhode Island estate; had risked his life scaling that tree to fetch it. He was decidedly afraid of heights, and all Catherine could remember of the incident were Thomas's eyes, large and white, peering down at her from the heights of the tree.

As she was thinking these thoughts, she left the wide avenues around the Capitol to stumble into a warren of shanties and shacks in a narrow alley. Smoke came from the chimneys of two of these structures, swirling into the falling snow. They were little more than lean-tos with corrugated metal roofing, stables by the look of them. Perhaps for the few remaining horses that pulled hansom cabs for the tourists. It took her a moment to be able to discern how many separate buildings there were. Her best count made it fifteen such miserable structures, cobbled together against back walls of brick buildings which faced onto much more congenial avenues facing the Capitol.

Then she heard the unmistakable cry of a baby from one of the shacks, the clatter and bang of cooking pans, and a woman's snarling voice: 'Shut up, will you!'

This was followed by another mournful, plaintive cry, and Catherine could not stop herself, she had to go to that crying baby. A slat-board door hung unevenly on the opening to the shed from which the sound had come, and she rapped on this.

There was no answer for a moment, then finally a woman in a greasy blouse and skirt with a baggy cardigan wrapped around her shoulders, a smudge of dirt on her cheek, and hair falling down into her face opened the door.

'What do you want?'

Catherine was taken back for a moment, wondering what indeed she did want. The harsh smell of unwashed bodies and kerosene came from the open door.

'A baby,' she finally stammered. 'I heard a baby crying.'

The woman scowled at her, filling the tiny door so that Catherine was not able to see in back of her into the shack.

'I try to keep him quiet. What's your complaint? Can't sleep in your fancy bed for all the noise of my little one?' She jerked her head toward the brick row house to which her shack was attached.

Catherine's gaze however went behind the woman, for she had now moved enough to allow a view of the interior. In an instant she was able to take in the scene: a dirt floor with here and there straw covering it; a scratched table with two rickety chairs; a simple iron bed in one corner. The baby, strapped into a sort of high chair, stopped its squalling, looking with wide hungry eyes at Catherine.

'Have you gawked long enough?' The woman slammed the door in her face.

'But I want to help you,' Catherine cried out at the closed door, a deep sense of guilt overcoming her. Here she was dressed in furs and boots, a shoulder bag stuffed with cameras and film worth enough money perhaps to rent this woman and her baby a decent lodging for a year, and all she could do was gape at them.

'Please let me help you.'

No answer came from within. She sensed eyes on her suddenly from the waxed windows of other shacks in the alley and felt quite alone and uneasy.

'They're afraid of you, Miss Catherine. They think you've come to evict them.'

Catherine swung around at the sound of the deep voice, and there stood Thomas, a fur-collared wool coat on, galoshes on his feet. He wore no hat.

'Thought I'd come looking for you early,' he said. 'Not the best day for photographing.'

She stomped through the drifting snow, full of a primal anger. 'Intolerable,' she muttered.

He tried to take her arm, but she shook his hand off, following now as he led her out of the back alley toward Pennsylvania Avenue where he had parked the Cadillac nine-seater.

'They call them alley dwellings, Miss Catherine.'

'I know what they call them. I just had never seen one before.'

Thomas chuckled softly. 'Hard to miss. I've heard it said there's over three hundred settlements like that one in Washington.'

Reaching the Cadillac, he opened the back door for her and she allowed herself to be guided in, sitting on a thick blanket Thomas had brought along for her.

He looked down at her as she huddled on the back seat. 'Right here in the nation's capital we've got probably twenty thousand people living like that,' he said, then closed the back door.

She was still fuming; these alley dwellings were a black mark on the nation. After all, this was Washington, DC, the nation's capital.

He climbed into the front seat, sitting stiffly at the wheel, and pushed the electric starter. The engine rumbled to life; she could feel it throbbing through her body.

'Why, that one was luxury itself,' Thomas said, grinning ironically at her in the rear-view mirror. 'For white folks only. Some day you ought to see where the coloreds live.'

He put the car into gear and drove jerkily out into traffic, snow falling thickly onto the front windshield. But Catherine was aware of none of it. All she could see was the little baby strapped to its chair in that shack, and its big eyes pleading with her, begging.

Twenty minutes later her anger and sense of injustice had abated somewhat as they pulled into the long driveway of Poplars on upper Massachusetts Avenue. The drive was covered in snow, as were the grounds. Thomas stopped the car at the front of the old Georgian mansion and Catherine hopped out, anxious to get into a hot bath. She entered into the main hall with its Jugendstil trappings, thought she heard voices from the music room, and quickly poked her head in there. She knew her husband would be working, Sunday or not. But she was not prepared in any way for what she saw.

Seated across from Edward in one of the club chairs by the fire was a tweedy rotund man gesticulating with a black cigar in his right hand, so intent on what he was saying that for a moment he did not notice her entry. Then their visitor flashed her a smile, his eyes twinkling and full of mischief. Catherine was immediately taken back to her youth, to her mother bending over her bed in the nursery, the yeasty smell of champagne on her breath at the goodnight kiss. The same merry eyes.

'Uncle Adrian!'

They made small talk for a time, but it was obvious the men were waiting for her to retire before they continued the discussion begun earlier.

'I have an appointment with a hot bath and my writing desk,' she said, suddenly rising. She had to prepare an announcement for the *Post* advertising the Belgian refugee relief concert to be held on Tuesday night. Recruiting the famous tenor Ganetti for the recital was part of her 'good works'.

'I leave you two to your conspiracies.'

Neither Fitzgerald nor Adrian Appleby protested over-vigorously. Her uncle watched Catherine depart and then turned to his host. 'You know, Edward, I have come to draw you lot into the war.'

Fitzgerald, a tall and patrician looking man with a shock

of prematurely white hair, was not taken back by Appleby's declaration; they had discussed this possibility before. 'That's exactly what I am attempting to do with the book I'm writing. Shake our complacent populace out of their isolationist slumber. But I'm afraid it is still an uphill fight. Out west they are none too eager to fight the "European's war", as they call it.'

Appleby made a steeple with his fingers over his ample belly. 'It may be easier now.'

The old Machiavelli does have something up his sleeve, Fitzgerald decided.

'Go on, Adrian.'

Appleby took out a Moroccan leather cigar case from the vest pocket of the thickly woven and well broken-in tweed suit he was wearing. He extracted another plump black Punch cigar as well as a cigar cutter, trimmed the end meticulously, and then used safety matches from a brass holder on the end table by his chair to light the cigar.

He's taking his good time about it, Fitzgerald thought, watching this methodical operation. Appleby puffed vigorously on the cigar, exhaling a blue cloud of smoke to wreathe around his bald head, then held the cigar out at arm's length to look at it appreciatively.

The dramatic pause, Fitzgerald thought. Adrian taught it to me himself: to unsettle the other party in negotiations. But I am not the other party: this is not a negotiation. We are on the same side in this, or are we?

'I don't have to tell you the obvious, do I, Edward. The awful rapaciousness of the Hun in tiny Belgium and now on the seas with their damnable U-boats. None of that propagandizing, moralizing cant is needed for you.'

'You would be preaching to the converted.'

'Yes.' Another puff, another appreciative glance at the cigar as if he were waiting for it to explode.

'The good war, eh? The honorable war? Well, despite whatever poppycock people spout, the fact is we are fighting for our bloody damn lives in England. The tonnage the Germans have destroyed in the past few months has been monstrous. We lost over a hundred ships in September, 180,000 tons.

300,000 tons in October. 400 in November. We've not even calculated December's or January's yet, and now they have gone hunting unrestricted once again. This is in the strictest confidence, Edward, between friends, but we will not be able to last through the summer at this rate. They will strangle us. We are rationing now; it will all be over by July if we do not get help.'

There was a profound stillness in the room after this declaration. Up to this point, Fitzgerald's pleas for American involvement had been made out of reasoned study and logical calculation. Up to now his concern had been of a somewhat academic nature, not being directly involved in the war himself. Now, however, with Adrian's presence, with Adrian's appeal, this war had become all too real. England will fall by summer if we do not help her; then it will be our turn to fight Germany – alone. It was his worst nightmare.

'Christ!' he finally said.

'Quite.' Appleby sighed once again, suddenly standing and moving toward the fireplace.

Fitzgerald remained seated, watching his old friend as he paced back and forth by the fire. He finally spoke, 'I never thought I would be saying this, Adrian. But what we need is a provocation to awaken America. We need the Germans to be bloody stupid or soon it will be too late for both our countries.'

Appleby suddenly stopped, turning to Fitzgerald. A large smile crossed his lips. 'I was hoping you would say something along those lines, Edward. Fact is, we have proof of exactly such a provocation.'

Before Fitzgerald could respond, Appleby had drawn out a piece of blue paper from the inside pocket of his tweed jacket and handed it to him. 'Read that and see if you do not agree.'

Fitzgerald looked at Appleby for a moment, but his friend nodded at the paper in his hand. It was typewritten and rather brief. Fitzgerald had a strange feeling about this message: he did not want to read it. He knew in his guts that it was Appleby's ace; England's ace, for she had been trying unsuccessfully for the past two years to bring America into the war on her side. He sensed that this would be the *casus belli* that he and other concerned Americans had so long been looking for. Yet now faced with it, he was fearful. War is a horrible thing, he knew.

But it must be. It has to be. Better to fight the Germans in Europe than in North America.

He began reading:

Berlin to Washington; 19 January, 1917

Most secret for Your Excellency's eyes only and to be handed on to the Imperial Minister in Mexico by a safe route.

We intend to begin on 1 February unrestricted submarine warfare. We shall endeavor in spite of this to keep the USA neutral. In the event of this not succeeding we make Mexico a proposal of alliance on the following terms:

Make war together.

Make peace together.

General financial support and an undertaking on our part that Mexico is to reconquer the lost territory in Texas, New Mexico and Arizona. The settlement in detail is left to you. You will inform the President of Mexico of the above most secretly and add the suggestion that he should on his own initiative invite Japan to immediate adherence and at the same time mediate between Japan and ourselves. Please call the President's attention to the fact that the unrestricted employment of our submarines now offers the prospect of compelling England in a few months to make peace. Acknowledge receipt.

Zimmermann

One phrase stuck in Fitzgerald's mind, echoing menacingly: *Make war together. Make peace together.*

The bastards, he thought. Germany's foreign minister conniving with Mexico and Japan to go to war against us. His mind raced with questions: how had London secured this telegram? How long had they had it? Was it verifiably authentic?

But all that came out of his dry lips was: 'We've got to get this to President Wilson. This means war.'

'Exactly,' Appleby said. 'I'll drink to that.'

*   *   *

Max Volkman climbed the stairs of a cold and uninviting rooming house in Washington's Foggy Bottom district whose only plus was its privacy.

'It is a sincerely bad time to visit our city,' Herr Meyer, the landlord, said as he puffed up the stairs, his ragged house slippers fraying more with each step. 'Most inclement.'

'Weather doesn't concern me,' Max said.

'Oh, really?' Floorboards creaked as Meyer continued to ascend. 'Have you business here, then?' Meyer did not look back at Max as he spoke.

Max maintained a pointed silence as he climbed, wincing now and again. Stairs bothered his left leg. The doctors had told him the leg would never be one hundred percent again, and he was self-conscious about it: a limp draws attention to a man. He wore a long voluminous blue overcoat to hide it.

'Here we are, then,' Meyer said, panting as they reached the third floor and he opened the door to a room at the top of the hall.

Max came up behind him. Five dollars a day for this, he thought: a single bed by a cracked window; a night table with a kerosene lamp; a small deal table in the middle of the bare plank floor along with one old chair; a washstand next to a wardrobe with a mottled mirror on its door.

'This will do nicely,' Max said.

Five dollars would buy me a room in one of the best hotels in Washington, he thought. But the benefit of Meyer's rooming house was that one need not register, merely pay in advance. There would be no record of one's coming or going here.

Meyer continued to stand in the doorway after Max entered, set the suitcase carefully on the bed and removed his hat. The landlord looked at the case and then at Max as if expecting a tip.

'Thank you, then,' Max said. 'I assume the facilities are . . .?'

'That way,' Meyer pointed out the door to the left. 'Water is on the first landing. The heat comes on at five.'

Only now did Max notice how bitterly cold the room was. He saw a small register on the floor between the window and wardrobe and wondered how much heat could come from that.

Meyer still stood in the doorway, and finally Max had to

ask for the key and excuse himself to use the toilet. The door closed, Meyer slumped off toward the stairs, disappointed either that he had won no tip or that he had learned nothing of his new guest; Max was not sure which. Reaching the toilet, Max discovered there was no paper, not even shredded squares of newspaper to use. He went back toward the stairs to yell to Meyer, but then saw the door to his room was open. He approached stealthily, careful not to sound any floorboard.

Meyer was in the room, bending over the suitcase, testing the latches to see if they were locked.

'Did you forget something?' Max said.

Meyer lurched at the sound of his voice, turning guiltily, but quickly covered up his discomfort.

'Only to tell you that the hot water begins at five, as well.' He gestured limply with his upraised arms as he spoke; they fanned about like seaweed.

Max approached him casually, a smile on his face. Meyer relaxed when he saw the smile. Max came nose to nose with the man, so close that he could smell beer on his breath.

'I'm glad that you had some reason to be in my room.' Max spoke very slowly and in German now. He wanted no misunderstandings about this.

Meyer smiled wanly as he tried to avoid Max's eyes.

'Otherwise,' Max said with a sudden knife edge of cruelty to his voice, 'if I thought you were snooping, I'd have to do something highly unpleasant to you.' Max's eyes flicked in back of Meyer to the cracked window letting in a chill draft. It would be a long fall to the street below. 'Do you understand me?'

Meyer's eyes squinted for a moment, giving him a porcine appearance. When the message finally sank in, fear entered his eyes in tiny black shafts showing in the pupils. He quickly nodded his head, dislodging his glasses so that they slipped down his bulbous nose.

An hour later, after having stored his meager belongings in his room at Foggy Bottom, and locking his door, Max took a green New Hampshire streetcar some twelve long blocks north, and got off at Dupont Circle, a stately and elegant acreage of trees with a huge fountain in the middle. The snow had stopped for a time, but a sudden gust of chill wind made him pull the collar up on his overcoat as he turned right off the circle down Connecticut Avenue to the corner of Connecticut and N Street, acting now like a tourist as he seemed to examine closely the facade of the Presbyterian Church of the Covenant at the corner. This gave him the opportunity to observe out the corner of his eye the three-story, mansard roofed building across the street at 1300 Connecticut Avenue. Over the entrance to this building was a bronze relief of the lion and the unicorn: the British crest.

The British Embassy was Max's only lead, and he soon found a hidden nook at the front of the church where he could take up watch without being observed by the guard at the embassy.

This was cold and unrewarding work. He watched the guard in front go off duty and be replaced by another, and wondered if his quarry were inside. Perhaps he's at a luncheon table overflowing with pot roast and potatoes fresh from the oven and bottles of red wine. Max's stomach was growling, for he had forgotten to eat this morning and now lunch had come and gone.

He knows nothing of discomfort, Max thought. Nothing of bone-chilling cold. Nor of fear that turns a man's bowels to water when the barrage starts over no-man's-land. Nor of the eternal damp and fug of life and death in the trenches where rats and fungus are one's eternal companions. He knows nothing of any of this, Max reminded himself. Yet he's blithely conspiring to send thousands of innocents to such a fate. For the sake of a diplomatic coup, he will prolong the carnage in Europe, the hideous waste of life in this war.

Max wondered if the Englishman had a family. In the photo his controller Berthold had sent from Berlin, the man looked old enough to be a grandfather. Max did not fancy killing a grandfather. Berthold had communicated – through their New York cutout, Manstein – that an incriminating telegram written by the German foreign minister, Zimmermann, had fallen into the hands of the British, one that if believed genuine by the Americans would surely bring them into the war on the side of the beleaguered British. An Irish agent working for Germany in London uncovered the fact that the British had intercepted this telegram. The same agent also discovered that the Brits were sending an emissary to hand carry the news to Washington.

'London's sending a courier with the telegram?' Max had asked Manstein, a bullish, florid man, as they gazed last week at seagulls whirling overhead. One of the gulls suddenly dove into the wake of the Staten Island Ferry, where Manstein had arranged their meet.

'Why not use normal diplomatic channels?'

'The British have a problem with credibility in Washington,' Manstein said. 'But this Englishman has the trust and respect of leaders around the world, including President Wilson. It will obviously be up to him to convince the American president that the telegram is true and not just an English ruse to bring the Americans into the war. Berthold himself feels the Englishman is capable of accomplishing such a task. Make no mistake, this English courier is the single greatest threat to Germany. He may change the course of the war. The course of history.'

Max made the simple calculation necessary: the life of one pompous English diplomat against those of all his comrades in the trenches.

'He must die,' Max had said, staring out at the densely built island of Manhattan in back of them.

Manstein nodded, smiling slightly. 'That's Berthold's opinion as well. He must die and we worry about covering the tracks when it comes to that. After all, diplomats are killed for many reasons. They make enemies all over the world. Perhaps his death will be credited to a Balkan radical, perhaps to an Irishman.'

Which means that the Englishman's death would not necessarily lend credence to the telegram he's carrying, Max thought. Logical enough. Which also means that Berthold has looked at this from all angles; that he has planned a mission.

'What are my orders?'

'No,' Manstein said, chewing now an unlit cigar. 'No orders on this one. We're looking for a volunteer, not a conscript. You see, we don't even know when the Englishman is arriving,

or if he's already here. All we know is that the newspapers
haven't carried the story, thus he must not yet have gotten to
Wilson.'

For a moment Max was back at Ypres, the smell of
gunpowder in his nostrils, the stench of rotting corpses all
about him. It was the closest thing to hell a man could
experience in life.

And the Englishman meant to prolong it by bringing
America into the war.

'I'll do it,' he had said. 'I volunteer to kill the Englishman.'

Max saw a smile form on Manstein's lips.

'But don't think I've been fooled. You're not allowing me
to volunteer for my own good, but for yours. I'm not the most
qualified agent in North America for this mission, am I? Only
the one, who, if caught, might have a plausible story. The
pacifist Volkman, representative of the World Peace League,
not the German agent Volkman.'

For that had been his cover in the United States for over
two years now.

'In case things go wrong,' Max went on, 'Germany had no
part in the assassination.'

'Excellent, Volkman. I always credit your kind with a certain
cunning. A fine sensitivity to innuendo.'

Your kind.

Max wanted to throttle the cocky Prussian there and then.
Instead he picked his mind for the rest of the ferry ride, learning
as much as he could about his quarry, and examined the
photograph of the diplomat that Manstein carried with him: a
newspaper clipping showing the British prime minister, Lloyd
George, next to a roly-poly comical looking little man with a
bald pate and an umbrella.

Brought out of this reverie by an approaching car, Max
readied himself for the deed. But it was only a delivery van
approaching the embassy, the name 'Wortham and Son' stenciled on the sides of the vehicle around the picture of a giant
bottle of port. Wine merchants come to refill his majesty's
cellar.

He focused again on his target.

Most probably the man has a country house in England,

Max thought, trying to steel himself to what he must do. An estate where he rides to the hounds with other powerful men who drink their sherry while young boys die in the trenches. All so as to keep their world of privilege afloat.

Max had seen enough of death for several lifetimes; he had done enough killing to sicken him, yet he knew that he would kill one more time.

The Englishman, Adrian Appleby will die, he promised himself.

Finally Max simply called the embassy from a phone at a nearby cafe.

A young man answered on the fourth ring. His high, nasal voice grated in Max's ear.

Max politely and with a minimum of words asked for Sir Adrian Appleby.

'Sir Adrian?' The young man repeated the name with some familiarity, and Max's hopes rose. Then there was a momentary silence.

Probably a footman, Max thought, or some under-butler who is standing in on Sundays. This could mean good luck for me: perhaps he won't know proper form.

After a brief delay the young man answered, 'Yes . . . I mean no, sir. He is in Washington, but he isn't here. I believe he arrived last night.'

Max felt his entire body tingle with excitement.

'Do you have his Washington address? It is most urgent I contact him. I'm a relation of his from South Africa.'

He hoped that would explain his accent to the young servant, and also hoped the young servant was none too bright.

'Well, we're not supposed to, sir . . .'

'Be a good chap.'

'Let me just give a look at our registry.'

Max waited for what seemed ages, his heart racing at the expectation of tracking Appleby with such ease. So he is here in Washington. And he just arrived last night. Which means that he could not have possibly gotten to Wilson yet.

I still have time to kill him.

There was crackling in the earpiece as the other line was picked up again.

'Young Jenkins tells me you wish to contact Sir Adrian Appleby.' The voice this time was older, deeper, and suspicious. 'What relation are you, sir, if I may ask?'

Max hung up, cursing the fact that the young servant had not simply looked up Appleby's residence in Washington. Had to go checking with his master, didn't he?

But he kept an even expression on his face as he paid for the call, and then left the cafe, greeted outside on the sidewalk by a blast of cold air that smelled heavily of snow. It's useless hanging about the embassy any longer, Max decided. Appleby could be anywhere in the city: staying at one of the fine hotels, probably, or with friends in some mansion. Trudging through the snow toward his lodging in Foggy Bottom, Max pulled his collar up against the wind, wondering what his 'master' in Berlin would say to this first day of work. Would Berthold be laughing if he knew I had stood outside the British Embassy for three miserable hours before having enough sense to simply call the place and ask for Appleby? Probably.

TWO

For some very few men, war is a blessing. Max Volkman was one of those.

It was in the war, in the forced intimacy of the mess and barracks, that Max finally found his home. Finally found where he belonged. Drafted into the infantry, he discovered the harsh regime suited him; he felt anonymous, absorbed in this body of men, and the men in turn trusted him. He was a natural for the military.

At Ypres in late 1914 he distinguished himself. That is what the generals said, at any rate.

What really happened was that he lost his mind for a time. A sergeant and ranking officer for his unit at the *Kindermord bei Ypern* – the Massacre of the Innocents at Ypres – Max lost twenty men one wet gray morning charging an enemy machine-gun nest.

Seeing one of those men shot to a bloody pulp just next to him, Max suddenly went beyond fear and caring. He charged on, despite a shrapnel wound to his left leg, single-handedly storming the machine-gun nest and killing the two astonished British soldiers there. Then he turned the machine gun on the other British soldiers spread out over a low and muddy slope.

By the time his own troops finally reached him, Max was calmly surveying his killing ground. The bodies of Allied soldiers lay heaped about the bloody slope. A leg jerked in a death spasm; he rattled off more rounds until the leg was no longer there.

Later, in the hospital, he learned that he had killed 123 of the enemy, badly burning his hands on the smoking barrel of the gun in the process.

They called him a hero; Max knew better.

Twenty of his own men dead; 123 of the enemy. That was six British for each of his comrades. Three left over.

An advance payment for my own death, he told himself.

Four months later, his leg still in a cast and the bandages just off his hands, Max was visited at a field hospital in western Germany by Colonel Reinhard Berthold. The Iron Cross Max had been awarded lay on the table next to his cot. Colonel Berthold, famed head of Military Intelligence and famed also for his odd recruitments, picked it up, fingering it reverently. Then he looked down at Max, who immediately despised the man's absurd dueling scar high on the left cheek, the blue eyes so light that they seemed to have no substance and no core to them, the cruel beak-like nose, and the long upper lip.

Berthold continued to turn the medal over in his fingers; Max noticed his nails were bit to the quick. Max refused to show surprise at this visit.

'They say you're not healing as fast as you should,' Berthold finally said in his high-pitched voice.

Max stared straight ahead of him, taking his eyes off the man. It was March; the first of the bluebottle flies were plaguing the hospital. A fly landed on Berthold's sleeve and he dropped the medal with a clink onto the metal night stand, calmly cupping the fly with his left hand and crushing it. The movement had been as swift as it was sure, as if the fly had been mesmerized by Berthold.

Max sympathized with the insect.

The colonel stood rigid at the side of the bed, a man forever at attention. His brown boots were polished to a fine reflective surface. From beyond their corridor, in the operating theater, came a scream that was strangled off abruptly. Berthold's eyes blinked once at the sound.

'So you lost your men. Is that what this pantomime is about? Or are you plain shit-pants scared to return to the front? Have you become a malingerer to avoid that?'

Max felt the muscle in his jaw flex involuntarily; his eyes squinted, but he remained silent.

'No, I don't suppose that's it. Not a problem of fear for you.'

Colonel Berthold now sat cautiously on the edge of the cot, holding his weight with his legs to make sure he did not tip it over.

'So you've lain here four months grieving for those men

while thousands more have followed them to the grave. Yet you don't really give a damn for those particular men. You know that, and I know that. You probably didn't even have time to learn their names. What galls you is that your heroic antics made no difference at Ypres.'

Max tried not to listen to his words, but knew that Berthold was telling him an elemental truth about himself that he would not otherwise admit to. The forward post that he had taken had been lost later that same day. The stalemate dragged on in spite of his sacrifice.

'Your great attempt at proving yourself, at fitting in, came to naught.' Berthold picked up the Iron Cross again. 'Sure, they gave you a scrap of metal to tell you how much they appreciate you, but you and I know there should have been at least oak leaves with this. There should have been stories about you in the press at home. But you don't really fit the profile of hero, now do you, Volkman? Not the bright-eyed blond Germanic youth that one expects from one's heroes.'

Max finally spoke: 'What is it you want, Colonel?'

Humor showed in Berthold's eyes. 'To use you, Volkman. You and your keen desire to prove yourself. I need a man who has nothing to lose, who has gone beyond fear. I want a man who has already lived one death. I want to make you famous, Volkman. You'll be our master spy in the US.'

Max had laughed at the idea that afternoon.

Two weeks later he was out of the hospital and in training at the army intelligence school in Marburg, learning the trade of espionage: bomb and incendiary making; English language training; secret codes; sabotaging maneuvers; self-defense and killing techniques. In another two months he had been infiltrated, via a Swedish ship, to New York to take up cover as a representative of the World Peace League, and to be fed orders vis-à-vis sabotage in the US from Manstein in New York.

Max got his first break on Monday morning. Seated in a reading room just off Dupont Circle, he was thumbing through the *Post* when suddenly he saw a familiar name in the 'Personalities' section, toward the end of the paper:

Sir Adrian Appleby, Great Britain's ambassador-at-large, is among the list of prominent sponsors of tomorrow night's Belgian Relief Concert to be held at the National Theater.

Sir Adrian, a well known and honored personality in the world of international diplomacy, will present a brief invocation and tribute to Belgium at 8 p.m., to be followed by the scheduled program: tenor Alberto Ganetti and soprano Maria Melini.

The event should prove to be one of the most spectacular evenings of the newly opened 1917 season. All proceeds go directly to the Belgian Refugee Relief Fund.

Max felt a quickening of his pulse as he read this announcement: he would take Appleby at the theater and have done with it.

If an earlier opportunity presents itself, fine, he thought, but for now I'll plan on Tuesday night for my mission. And pray that the Englishman does not get to Wilson in the meantime.

He closed the paper, got up from the comfortable corner of the warm reading room and crossed to the newspaper rack by the entrance, putting the paper he'd been reading back in its place. He nodded politely to the pleasant white-haired woman, a cameo at her throat, who acted as librarian cum hostess in the reading room, then walked out into the cold air and bustle of traffic on Dupont Circle.

His mind quickly took in the scene, freed now from worrying about Appleby's whereabouts. A woman bundled in heavy furs and a scarf hurried past him on the sidewalk, smiling at him as she passed. Her cheeks were apple red in the cold and he turned appreciatively to watch her pass.

Max suddenly felt happy simply to be alive, and realized he too was smiling. It had stopped snowing for a time, and the city was mantled in a thick crust that crunched underfoot as he walked along the sidewalk. Even the diesel from passing buses smelled good to Max. Suddenly the world was a fresh place for him, full of opportunity.

He headed southwest on Massachusetts Avenue from Dupont Circle in search of a public telephone.

I'll need to report in to Berlin as Berthold ordered, he figured.

Already the rudiments of a plan were forming in his mind, and he began composing a coded message for Manstein to relay to Berlin.

Later that morning, after phoning Manstein, Max headed back to his lodgings in Foggy Bottom to begin preparations for tomorrow night. He got off the streetcar at the intersection of New Hampshire and Virginia Avenues. The wind was raw and chill off the Potomac and the low gray sky looked as if it held more snow. He hurried along the sordid street toward the waterfront.

Once at the rooming house, Max began climbing the rickety stairs. Meyer sat reading a German newspaper in his cubbyhole office, and looked up surreptitiously to spy at Max through his window which gave off onto the stairs.

Max waved at him, but Meyer, surprised to be caught spying, acted as if he did not see him.

Up on the third floor, Max put an oversized key into the lock of his door, turned it once, then attempted to turn it a second time but could not.

He had double-locked it earlier this morning.

On his person, Max carried a .38-caliber Harrington and Richardson revolver in a leather shoulder holster. With a blue finish and a rubberized stock, the self-cocking model had been purchased from Sears, Roebuck and Co. for $5.95. There were about three million similar weapons on the streets of America; it used Smith and Wesson type ammunition available at any sporting goods store. It was not considered suspicious behavior in the US to carry such a weapon – a situation Max still found strange in a supposedly civilized nation – and that is why Max, the most cautious of operatives, felt no compunction in carrying his revolver at all times.

But the lead tube divided into two compartments by a wafer-thin copper plug: that was a different matter. Caught with that bomb casing in his possession and he could be hung as a spy, a saboteur.

Entering his room, Max could see his guidebook to Washington on the bedside table. He had left it open this morning, and open it still was. Crossing to the night table now, however, he noticed that the hair he had placed crosswise on the page was gone.

Max forced himself to control his rage and slowly bent down to the floor and reached under the bed, pulling out the suitcase he had left there. Rolls of dust accompanied it. He hoisted the suitcase atop the bed, but did not bother opening it. There was no false bottom inside for Meyer to discover. The lead tube was hidden in the handle. He closely examined this, and it appeared no one had tampered with the leather folded into the ends of the tube.

Meyer, you are a lucky man, Max thought. Perhaps you will not need to die, after all.

From his trouser pocket Max extracted a penknife. Opening the blade, he pried the puckered leather at one end of the suitcase handle open, and then pushed from the other end. The edge of a metal tube began to appear and he gripped it between thumb and forefinger, pulling it from the leather handle.

Completely free of the handle, the tube was round and made of lead eight inches long and one and a half in diameter. Max carefully examined the seam going round the tube at the middle to ensure it had not been weakened by its use as the grip for his suitcase. It was as strong as before he had concealed it there in New York, the copper plug dividing the tube apparently still securely in place.

Now he turned the bottom of the suitcase toward him and using the penknife once again, pried off two of the small metal coasters on the bottom of the bag, one from each end. These exactly fitted the ends of the lead tube.

With these components, Max had the casing for a quite deadly bomb, the type German agents had been using in the US for the past two years. He had fetched this one just last week from Dr Scheele's Hoboken factory – the German agents' arsenal in the US – and all that was missing now was the chemicals. He did not carry these with him, for if they were discovered by some fluke, they would surely condemn him. The tube might be missed – as it had been by Meyer – the end plugs as well, but the chemicals? No; they were far too dangerous to carry.

However, he knew where he could get them in Washington.

He picked up his *New Standard Guide to Washington* for 1916 and leafed through the index until he found what he was looking for. He turned to page 149 in the guide and read the description of a building on H Street between 9th and 10th Streets. Then he consulted the downtown map on page 112 to find its exact location.

He stuck the guide into one of the outside pockets of his overcoat, and then left the room, not bothering to lock it this time.

Meyer was snoring in his chair as Max went down the stairs and slipped out unnoticed.

President Woodrow Wilson stroked the ball poorly, missing the easy bank shot.

'Confound it,' he muttered, adjusting his pince-nez glasses.

'Off your game today, Governor.' It was an affectation of Colonel House's to refer to Wilson by an earlier political title, to show that he, House, was part of the old-time staff and inner circle of friends.

Thin and dapper with gray hair and full moustache, Colonel House diplomatically missed his shot, and President Wilson went on the attack once more. House looked at the coal fire smoldering in the corner of the Presidential Library. A pleasant room, he thought. Neither ostentatious nor overly clubby. Just a comfortable book-lined study with a felt-topped billiard table in the center.

Wilson missed another easy shot and stood, cue in hand, for a moment eyeing the ball as he might have a truant scholar at Princeton where he was once president of the college.

'Sorry,' Wilson said, putting the cue on the wall rack. 'I'm not much competition for you today, I'm afraid.'

'Quite all right, Governor.'

'I only wish it were, House.'

The president took his glasses off and rubbed the bridge of his nose for a long moment, sighed, and then replaced them.

'I think the newspapers have been quite supportive of your breaking off of diplomatic relations with Germany,' House said.

They continued standing for a moment, Wilson now looking between the red brocade drapes out the window to the snow falling steadily and silently. He leaned back against the billiard table.

'Yes, they would be. They will also be clambering for war soon, House. But they will not have it, not if I can help it.'

They were silent for a time again, both contemplating now the lovely white world outside. House let the silence continue without interruption. It was a fashion of thinking Wilson had; he was neither looking for support nor criticism.

Wilson finally spoke again: 'I absolutely refuse to have America dragged into the morass of war. There will be no victors in this sorry mess, I assure you. Only losers. Every reform we have won since 1912 will be lost if we go to war. None of what we have done in the way of anti-trust legislation, currency, or tax reform has had time to set as national policy yet. We go to war now and all those reforms will be distorted by the special interests. In time of war, we will be dependent on steel, oil, ships, and war materials. And they are controlled by big business.'

Wilson let out a long sigh and continued, 'Big business will be in the saddle. More than that – free speech and other rights will be endangered. War is autocratic.'

House listened to the words, ignoring their content. They had been over this ground so often before that it seemed a litany to him. The absolute evil of war; the necessity to keep the US neutral at all costs so as to form a core of a new world order after the European cataclysm had spent itself.

House was waiting for the end of the lecture before he could broach the subject of a meeting with Sir Adrian Appleby. From what Senator Lodge and Edward Fitzgerald had said, such a meeting seemed terribly urgent. Yet Colonel House knew Wilson wanted to avoid such a meeting, at least for the next few days.

It's almost as if he fears that the information Appleby is bringing might tip the scales toward war. Anything could at this time, House knew.

'It's a tightrope we're walking, House,' President Wilson said suddenly, breaking the long silence.

Colonel House was a realist: however much he might believe in the cause of the Allies, his first loyalty was to the president, and it was as if Wilson were pleading with him at this very moment not to confront him with any more bad news vis-à-vis Germany.

House looked from the window to the president. Wilson was staring intently at him, his eyes moistening in back of his glasses.

'All those dead young men. What a waste. What a terrible waste. All the pro-war fellows need is one more German blunder, House. One more provocation, and we will have the war party, Congress and Roosevelt's supporters at our throats to do battle with the Hun. Let's pray there are no more German provocations soon, no more sinkings of unarmed passenger vessels; that they for once act with tact and restraint.'

'Yes, Governor,' Colonel House said.

And then President Wilson said a curious thing, which House was later to record in the diary he so faithfully kept.

'I could do with a bit of sun, House. Warmth. Get the body out on the links for a few days. Get my mind off all this gloom and doom. It may be high time for a bit of vacation.'

'What do you mean he can't see us until Wednesday!' Appleby's face was turning beet red with anger; white flecks of spittle lodged in the corners of his mouth. 'The fellow's insane. This is a matter of life and death.'

Fitzgerald crossed to the fireplace, passing a finger over the foliage carved in relief on the mantle. 'Perhaps that's why he's putting us off. He simply doesn't want to hear any more bad news for a time. Lodge said the president won't be budged, and Wilson is definitely not one to be cajoled or bullied.'

'But this is impossible! Is there no way to get to the man?'

'We're working at it, Adrian. Cabot Lodge and I are not exactly accustomed to being on the same side of the aisle on issues, and he's still shadow boxing with me. He doesn't see the urgency. Neither should I, I must admit, if I hadn't been let in on the secret. Maybe we should tell Lodge or House the contents of the telegram? They're both pro-war men. Perhaps even Roosevelt?'

Appleby flung himself into one of the armchairs by the fire, making its springs groan loudly. 'No.' He said it with an adamancy that would not be refuted. 'No one must be told before Wilson. Most especially not that egregious fool Roosevelt. He has no sense of timing at all, and I do not want the power, the absolute shock value of Zimmermann's treachery to be the least diminished by rumor.'

Appleby's tone sounded false, but Fitzgerald said nothing.

'Wednesday,' Appleby suddenly said. 'We've got to convince him to see us earlier than that. We must.'

Again Fitzgerald said nothing; he would let Adrian fume. The man had not spent forty years in diplomacy without learning the simple secrets of the trade, such as that someone who is forced to negotiate before he is ready – as with Wilson – is a man whose ears are not open.

'We'll continue putting pressure on Colonel House for an earlier meeting,' Fitzgerald said. 'But if that fails, then we must accept the fact that a couple of days one way or the other will not affect the outcome of the war, Adrian. We could try the vice president, or Lansing at State. He's pro-war.'

'No one before Wilson.' Appleby looked like an enraged bulldog as he said this.

'Then we've got no choice,' Fitzgerald said. 'You might as well relax.'

Appleby slumped in his chair, a most uncharacteristic posture for him, Fitzgerald knew. A defeated man.

'Very well, Edward.'

Appleby soon left to prepare some notes for his speech at Catherine's benefit the following evening, and Fitzgerald sat at the refectory table in the music room. He normally loved this room with its wainscoting, leaded windows, Bechstein grand, cheery fireplace and general clubby atmosphere, but today even this space seemed oppressive to him.

He was trying to finish his article for March's *Atlantic Monthly* detailing England's losses at sea for the past six months. Hundreds of thousands of tons of food, machinery and war materiel had been sunk by German U-boats.

Words, words. Fitzgerald was sick and tired of them. Tired of writing; tired of playing politics from the sidelines. He wondered if he were too old to get a commission in the army. He was not going to play the hypocrite, propagandizing for war and then sending other men's sons off to die in France.

But even as he thought this, he knew it was a dream.

I'm too old for anything but these damned words. Too old for my wife, even.

He knew these were three a.m. doubts brought on by Appleby's telegram and his own evil premonitions about not only its provenance, but also where it would lead America.

Forget your doubts, man, he told himself. You've got your *casus belli*.

He focused his mind on Catherine at work in her dark room: wondering what prints she was developing today and whether she ever missed him as he did her. Just thinking of his wife made him begin to smile.

I love her in ways and with a depth that I can never show her, but I feel more like a father to her than a husband sometimes: the patient loving father who must give the willful child as much rein as possible. Freedom is the one great legacy we bequeath our children, he instinctively knew. It was what his own father had done for him. A shipbuilder from Massachusetts, he had never really approved of politics, but nevertheless stood behind his son one hundred percent when Edward decided that was what he wanted to do with his life. And upon the old man's death, Edward, an only child, had been left a healthy enough inheritance, unencumbered, to keep his political dreams alive.

In some ways he wanted to do that for Catherine, too.

But she is not your daughter, man, he told himself. Can't you get that into your head? Despite the difference in your ages, she is your wife; your lover. Hold her to you tightly. She is no doll. She won't break.

Yet he was still awed by her, still amazed by her beauty and wit.

It had been that way since first meeting her fifteen years ago. He could remember that first meeting clearly. It was the fall season of 1902 and Edward Fitzgerald had been a freshman senator. His outspoken opposition to US imperialism in the Philippines and elsewhere abroad, coupled with his raw good looks had made him something of a scandalous sensation in Washington. With the uncommon logic of the upper classes, such notoriety made him for a season or two a distinguished and eccentric guest to have at soirées and fashionable dinner parties. His wealth did no damage in this regard, either.

Fitzgerald was never comfortable at such affairs, but took them as an extension of his elected responsibilities. He was a representative of the people of his state; perhaps their welfare could be served by his attendance at such affairs. So he attended them with a certain cold professional distance, as a painter might view the *Mona Lisa* for its mastery of technique rather than for its passion.

He'd had no great expectations for Mrs Bradley Wells's dinner party at Newport. He was not unfamiliar with the antics of the New York-Newport set, still he was completely surprised, shocked even, at the extravagance which awaited him upon arrival.

Upon reaching the estate in Newport, his carriage passed under a high, specially built arch: 'Welcome to Showtime' three-foot high white lettering proclaimed on it. Mrs Wells was, he only then remembered, recently enamored of Broadway. The main drive to her mansion had been transformed into a brilliantly lit midway with shooting galleries, Negro dancers, singing groups, fire-eaters, all the accoutrements of a carnival, and he gaped out his carriage window, amazed, at all this extravagance laid on just for a dinner party.

He had not seen anything yet.

Reaching the main house he saw that a special amphitheater had been constructed onto the front of the rambling old façade. Descending his carriage, he began milling about in the crowds of other finely dressed guests: men in white tie and tails, women glittering with diamond tiaras and necklaces, wearing elegant brocade evening gowns with their hair piled fashionably on top of their heads.

'Five days they say it took them,' one dapper little man holding a glass of champagne was saying. 'A crew of fifty carpenters at it day and night. Our Maggie has outdone herself tonight.'

Maggie was Mrs Bradley Wells, Fitzgerald remembered, née Margaret Bateman of the Cincinnati Batemans.

Liveried servants carried hors d'oeuvres and champagne on silver trays through the crowd until the theater opened. The guests were then entertained by the entire company of *Dream Song*, the current musical rage on Broadway. Mrs Bradley Wells had bought the entire house out in New York and shipped the show down to Rhode Island for the night, cast, set and orchestra, to present the first act.

Properly entertained before dinner, Fitzgerald along with the other two hundred plus guests were then ushered into Mrs Bradley Wells's Gobelin draped dining hall, seated at an oak table one hundred feet long fitted out with golden plates, and served what seemed to Fitzgerald an agonizing dinner of ten courses, beginning with oysters, soup, hors d'oeuvres, soft clams, and progressing to saddle and rack of lamb, terrapin, and duck, to be topped off with cake, cheese and grapes. All of this was washed down with successive showers of Rhine wine, Château Lafite '78, champagne and cognac.

The only saving grace to the entire ridiculously extravagant evening, was the young black-haired beauty seated to Fitzgerald's right, who seemed to be the loneliest and saddest young woman he had ever seen. Never a shy man around women, Fitzgerald was nonetheless made near speechless by this one. In between the terrapin and duck, the only thing Fitzgerald could find to say, while his wine glass was being filled for the fourth time by a white-gloved servant, was the truth. He blustered out exactly how he felt to this lovely young woman and felt miserable for doing so immediately afterward.

'Don't you find all this just a bit much?' he said as she sat in front of another unfinished course. 'Ten courses served on gold plate while much of America and the world struggle to make a living wage. It's gauche. Damned gauche.'

She reddened at this comment and he apologized for his forwardness and set to work on the duck, trying to avoid eye contact with her for the rest of the evening. But somehow he felt she agreed. As they rose to leave the table, their eyes met, and he thought he detected a kindred soul.

Still he felt like a bull in the china closet for being so forthright with her. Before departing that night, he learned from another of the guests the name of the lovely young lady: Catherine Devereaux.

Fitzgerald spent two sleepless nights thinking of the woman. He had never even given this much consideration to a vote in the Senate. He tried to put Catherine Devereaux out of his mind. She is just another pretty little rich girl without a thought in her head, he told himself.

The second day he was summoned to the White House by Roosevelt. There was an open ambassadorship in London. Perhaps he would like to be considered for the position?

Fitzgerald only later put more Machiavellian interpretations to this offer: Roosevelt's desire to remove voices critical to his international policies from Washington. But at that initial meeting, seated in the elegant Blue Room across from the grinning Rough Rider, all Fitzgerald could say was: 'Yes. Most definitely, Mr President.'

'Fine. That's arranged then. By the way, Fitzgerald,' Roosevelt added, 'you're not married, are you? Doesn't do for an ambassador to be without a wife. Single, you'll be spending most of your time in London fending off the advances of long-toothed dowagers with chinless but eligible daughters. Why don't you see what you can do about that before leaving for the new posting this summer?'

The massive gold clock on the marble mantle – a gift of Napoleon I to Lafayette, as Roosevelt never tired of telling guests – ticked loudly in the ensuing silence. Fitzgerald gazed around the elliptically shaped apartment with its heavy corded blue silk covering the walls. They sat opposite each other in white and gold chairs upholstered in blue and gold, and suddenly Fitzgerald knew for the first time the awe of power.

Yet Roosevelt would continue speaking of marriage and of choosing an eligible partner as if it were a horse auction, Fitzgerald thought.

'I'll give it some thought, Mr President,' he said, rising as Roosevelt did, signaling the end of the interview.

'Do that, Fitzgerald. A little domestic regularity does a man good, if you take my meaning.'

A wink from the pug-faced man let Fitzgerald know what sort of regularity he was alluding to. Fitzgerald was happy for that last remark; it completely dissolved any awe he had begun to experience of the man.

It's absurd, he thought as he left the White House grounds, the elms and beeches in full greenery now. I'm not the marrying kind. Not just yet, at any rate.

After another sleepless night, however, he looked up the Devereaux address in *Who's Who*, sent a telegram begging an interview of Mr Charles Devereaux, and not waiting for a reply, set off that very morning for Rhode Island.

The interview with the father took a quarter of an hour, just long enough for the elder Devereaux to ascertain Fitzgerald's financial status, and then young Catherine was called down to be introduced to her suitor.

God! What a beginning, Fitzgerald now thought, sitting in front of the unfinished article.

A recipe for disaster straight out of the Middle Ages, yet their marriage had seemed to work. In many ways Fitzgerald felt he did not know his wife at all, especially in the bedroom. He was fearful of showing his full passion for her; she seemed not very demonstrative in that respect, either.

He now heard her footsteps in the hall, and his heart soared, but he returned his attention to the article: it wouldn't do to show her how much I love her, he thought.

The first ingredient for the bomb was relatively easy to come by. Once downtown again, Max stopped in a Liggett's Drugstore on F Street and asked the clerk for a packet of potassium chlorate.

The man smiled knowledgeably at him, an owl-eyed fellow in a white coat. Max had practiced the speech over and over until he hoped he had lost any trace of accent.

But still there was the solicitous smile as the druggist went in back and weighed out a measure of the whitish powder. Bringing it back to the counter and setting it in front of Max he said, 'I bet I know what you're up to.'

Max tensed. 'How much, please?' he said trying to control himself.

'Fifty cents,' the man said still smiling infuriatingly at Max.

Max dug out a palm full of change from his right front pocket and placed two quarters on the counter.

'Yes,' the clerk said, picking up the change. 'I know about these things.'

At this point Max most definitely wanted to run, but instead forced himself to return a wan smile at the clerk. 'What am I up to?' he said.

'Photography, of course. You're doing your own developing. There's been a run on this stuff in the last few years. Am I right?'

Max beamed, his body relaxing. 'Absolutely.' He wanted suddenly to hug the silly clerk, but instead put the packet of potassium chloride in his vest pocket and turned to leave.

'And remember,' the druggist called after him, his owl eyes gleaming with superior knowledge. 'You want only the slightest pinch of the potassium chloride in the bleach bath. Too much and you'll ruin the prints.'

Max nodded and left.

The next and final ingredient was the hard part. No drugstore this time. At four o'clock, just as his guidebook advised him to do, he lined up for a tour of the laboratory building of the Medical Department of Georgetown University on the south side of H Street. He was alone on the tour which a long-limbed intern from the south of the country conducted. Max loved the sing-song of the youth's accent, but could not place it exactly. Nor did he want to: he was otherwise busy, recording entrances, exits, windows, fire escapes, locking procedures. His particular interest was roused at a door marked 'No Admittance' on the third floor, the far west corridor.

'Is that where you keep the corpses?' Max joked, nodding at this door.

The kid was flustered for a moment, taking Max seriously. Then seeing the grin on Max's face, he said, 'No, sir. That's the chemical pantry. Acids and poisons and that sort of thing. I don't think you'd find it very interesting.'

But Max did, and he moved to a nearby window for a moment as if to take in the view of an alley below before following the intern on the rest of the tour.

That evening he ate in town, waiting for nightfall. After

dinner he went to a movie, *Birth of a Nation,* which he had
seen three times before, but he so loved the scope of it and
the beauty of the camera work that he never failed to become
completely absorbed in the moving images, as if they were
his own life unfolding before him. Also, he liked the feeling
of being close to all these strangers in the dark, as if he were
truly one of them.

By eleven that night he had scouted the lab building and
saw only one old guard on duty at the rear, sitting in a tiny
cubicle. There would be no trouble from that quarter: the man
looked old enough to be a grandfather and was nodding off
with a newspaper in his lap.

On the west side of the building, in an alley across from a
windowless side of another brick building, the fire escape stairs
hung ten feet above ground level. Max pulled a disused crate
under the stairs, stood on it and by jumping up was able to
grab hold of and bring the stairs down to ground level. He
looked out toward the street: there were no passersby.

It took him only five minutes to climb the stairs, find the
window he had left unlatched earlier in the day during the
tour, climb into the lab building, jimmy the lock to the door
of the chemical pantry, light a match and track down a small
bottle marked H_2SO_4 among the plethora of other chemicals.
This he wrapped in a lab towel and put in the coat pocket
opposite the lead tube.

In another three minutes he had closed the door, climbed
out the window and closed it after him, and then climbed down
the fire escape to street level.

They'll discover the jimmied door, he knew, but there was
nothing to trace him to it. Not unless the intern remembers
me, he thought, and he might. But I gave him no name. And
will they even miss one tiny bottle of sulfuric acid?

He jumped down the last couple of feet to the snow-covered
alley, feeling happy with himself.

My bomb is now complete.

Before turning to the street, he straightened his overcoat. A
hand clamped on his shoulder, swinging him around.

'Hey now. What's going on, fella?'

It was the old guard looking rheumy eyed but wary. Max

quickly took in the situation: if I don't act swiftly the old man is sure to raise an alarm, if he hasn't done so already. He's armed, but his revolver is still holstered. Max could see its butt just showing under the tunic of his watchman's uniform.

'What the hell you doing up there?' the man said, his voice louder this time.

God or whomever forgive me, Max thought. He has seen me now; there will be a description. I cannot risk a description; not now. Not with Appleby in my hands.

'I'm sorry,' Max began, then threw a punch to the old man's face, landing precisely on the bridge of his nose.

The blow sent the man reeling, and he grunted, blood spurting from his nose. Max simultaneously grabbed the back of the man's head with his left hand and brought his right knee sharply upward, jamming the guard's face on it and sending cartilage and broken bone into the old man's brain. His body crumpled to the ground.

Max looked out to the street: a car went by, then another, but no pedestrians.

He looked down at the old man's lifeless body, at the pitiful strip of white shin showing where his pant leg had rucked up. Dark splotches in the snow next to his face would be blood, Max knew.

Tears built up at the back of his eyes. 'You stupid old man,' he said out loud. 'Why did you have to come along? Why couldn't you just stay in your office and sleep?'

He stepped over the body and began leaving the alley, forcing himself not to hurry, not to draw attention to himself. As he got closer to the street lights on H Street, he could see bloodstains on his right knee, and he wrapped the coat tightly around him to hide them.

A couple fresh from the theater, by the look of the man's top hat and the woman's fur, passed him laughing and smiling at each other. They did not glance down the alley. Max pulled the brim of his hat down and walked away from them to the streetcar stop, a hollow feeling in his stomach.

THREE

Until the delivery van pulled up at 8:30 on Tuesday morning, Fitzgerald had completely forgotten about the fountain that he and Catherine had purchased several months ago from Paul Davidson, the well known Maine sculptor. It seemed quite inconsequential in light of recent events.

Eight workmen, dressed in dungarees and tweed jackets with wool caps pulled down over their faces, hauled the crated fountain on two timbers: two men in front, two in back, and two on each side. Their rough h: ids were turning white with the strain. The morning was gray and raw; snow was still frozen underfoot at spots; a cutting wind blew off the river.

The men trudged down the snowy slope to the lower garden, skirting the limestone wall hung with ivy which separated the two levels, and avoiding use of the icy stairs leading down to the lower level. He watched the men gently set the crate down and begin rubbing blood back into their hands.

At that very moment, Appleby, dressed in Norfolk jacket and breeches, a gray worsted coat draped over his shoulders, made his way down the path and Fitzgerald waved at him.

'That should do it, Mr Fitzgerald,' the foreman of the crew said. 'Shall we be unpacking it then?'

'Not just now,' Fitzgerald said. 'It's a bit cold for that.'

The man nodded. 'Good enough. We'll be on our way, then.'

'You'll let yourself out,' Fitzgerald said as he went to meet Appleby whose face was smiling but ashen and drawn.

'You're up awfully early, Adrian.'

'I just received a cable from London,' Appleby said, reaching into his coat pocket and retrieving a flimsy yellow piece of paper with no watermarks, no engraved address. Its top edge was ruffled where it had been torn from a pad.

Fitzgerald took the message and read it slowly:

London–

Intercepted message this p.m. via German Trade Legation New York. Contents herewith decoded: 'British target found in Washington STOP Will eliminate him Tuesday evening STOP M.'

Said message routed MI Berlin, Colonel Berthold. Advise personal discretion in matter.

Balfour

Fitzgerald had to read it a second time before he got the full impact of it. Suddenly he felt his stomach churn.

'Someone means to kill you! Some German agent!'

It was something that happened in thrillers and detective novels, not in real life, Fitzgerald thought. There was a certain absurdity to the situation, yet looking at Appleby, Fitzgerald knew he found nothing absurd in the proposition.

'That about sums it up, yes,' Appleby said with forced sang-froid. 'I do not think I am being immodest if I say that I am the most likely "British target" to be found in Washington. It looks as though this M chappie means to have a go at me tonight at the Belgian do. It was announced in the *Post.*'

Fitzgerald felt the enormity of what he had read finally sink in: not only that Appleby was a target for a German assassin, but that London had somehow become aware of the fact.

'Lord knows how he got on to me,' Appleby was saying, almost to himself. 'Loose lips in Whitehall. How many ministers know of my mission, I have no idea.'

Things were beginning to come into focus for Fitzgerald: the evil premonition he'd had about the telegram and its provenance.

'You want to give me the full story now, Adrian?'

Appleby looked at him quizzically for a moment, then gave it up as Fitzgerald continued to fix him with an icy glance.

'You mean about this intercept?'

Fitzgerald nodded.

A clump of snow fell from a branch of a noble fir in back of them, making a splatting sound as it hit the ground. Appleby visibly jumped at the sound. All around them the world was white and gray. A black crow cawed angrily overhead.

Appleby sighed. 'Well, Balfour himself advises personal discretion. And you were not deceived with the Mexico City rigmarole.' For it had been Appleby's story that the Zimmermann telegram had, in fact, been intercepted by one of their agents in Mexico.

Fitzgerald said nothing, fixing Appleby with a hard stare.

Appleby went on blithely: 'Well, now I suppose there is no need for subterfuge vis-à-vis that. You see, old boy, we've broken the German code. Our Navy Intelligence fellows have this top-secret code-breaking section. Room 40, they call it, under the direction of Admiral Hall. It is all very hush-hush, cloak and dagger stuff. That is how we got *this* message.'

He took the yellow slip of paper back from Fitzgerald, holding it up to the light as if looking for marks of forgery. Then he looked back at Fitzgerald expectantly.

'And that's how you got the Zimmermann telegram, as well?' Fitzgerald asked.

Appleby nodded.

'And you withheld that vital bit of information from me.'

Another nod from Appleby. 'Had to, old boy. We could not risk compromising the code.'

Fitzgerald felt his face going red at the implication of Appleby's last remark. 'You don't actually think I would—'

Appleby cut him off: 'Let me explain, Edward. Room 40 is only part of the problem. There is also the origin of the Zimmermann telegram to consider. In point of fact, it was sent from your embassy in Berlin to your State Department in Washington.'

Fitzgerald could not disguise his surprise. 'What!'

'True, I'm afraid. We cut Germany's undersea cables early in the war, but Wilson and his aides appear to have allowed Germany the use of your own diplomatic cables to help conduct peace negotiations with the Kaiser. Encoded messages to boot.'

'The fools!'

'Yes,' Appleby said.

A further level of understanding was granted Fitzgerald now, like peeling away successive layers of an onion.

'And you've been eavesdropping on our State Department cables, haven't you? That's the other difficulty.'

Appleby, to his credit, did not blush. 'We can hardly go to President Wilson with Zimmermann's telegram and tell him it came from his very own State Department cable service. Such an admission could very well rankle his sense of decency. Perhaps even give him an excuse to discount the onerous nature of the proposed German alliance with Mexico. In that case, we would not only lose the U.S. as an ally, but also risk compromising the fact of our having broken the German code. And it is absolutely vital to protect the code, Edward. Granted, we have lost thousands upon thousands of tons of shipping already, but we have also saved uncountable tons. Were the Germans to suspect that we are listening in on them at will and thus alter their code, why the effect could be devastating. Devastating.'

The black crow overhead continued circling in the bruised sky, calling out occasionally as the two men looked at each other, saying nothing.

Fitzgerald had suspected chicanery on Appleby's part. Now that it was exposed, other fears about Appleby's reliability arose: is the telegram itself authentic? Is this German agent just one more invention to get me and other influential Americans lined up on Adrian's side?

Fitzgerald now understood why Appleby had not used normal diplomatic channels for the delivery of the telegram: Wilson cannot be allowed to wonder too deeply about the provenance or authenticity of this cable. Yet at the same time, Fitzgerald knew none of this mattered. What did matter was that America get into the war before it was too late. His feelings on that score had not altered in the least: the Zimmermann telegram still had to be gotten to the president.

He broke the silence finally. 'I don't envy you your mission, Adrian.'

'Oh, all in a day's work,' Appleby joked rather lamely. 'And really, were our German friend to succeed, that would eliminate the problem of proof, would it not?' His voice was heavy with irony as he continued, 'After all, my assassination would be proof positive to Wilson of the authenticity of the Zimmermann telegram.'

He was joking, Fitzgerald knew, but there was a grain of truth in the quip.

'Don't rely on it, Adrian,' Fitzgerald quickly replied. 'Dead men are notoriously poor negotiators. Your only value is in remaining alive and vocal.'

'It looks like I'll have to cancel my appearance tonight, Edward. We'll have to make some excuse for Catherine.'

Fitzgerald was not listening to Appleby. His mind instead was calculating, planning, and putting pieces together. Suddenly the solution to their problem was so clear to him, so simple. A bold plan, it came to him all in one piece, entire and rather lovely in its simplicity.

'I think you're partially correct about the German assassination plot being your proof. In fact, the Germans are handing you a solution to the problem of protecting the secrecy of Room 40 on a platter. This M has let you know both his mission and his venue. What we have to do is catch him red-handed before he can kill you.'

'That would be nice,' Adrian said.

'And catch him alive, as proof to the president of just how important it is to Germany to stop your mission. Wilson will have to listen to reason then, and without being over-curious as to the origin of the Zimmermann telegram.'

The blood was slowly coming back into Appleby's cheeks as he considered this. 'It may work, Edward.'

Fitzgerald had to smile at the typical understated nature of his friend. 'Yes, Adrian. You might be able to both win an ally and keep your life.' He clapped him on the back.

'Come on, then,' he said. 'We have some planning to do. We can hardly call the police in on this. They'd want to know how we found out about the assassination plot, which would bring us right back to square one at your Room 40. I think we may have to bring in some Pinkerton agents to lay this little trap.'

With that, Fitzgerald took the slippery steps two at a time back to the house; Appleby followed behind him more cautiously.

The first few strokes of the oars came with difficulty. Catherine had not worked out in several days and it was always the same after a period of inactivity, she knew. The body was reluctant; it took time to warm up. She stuck with it and soon her muscles began to loosen, to feel the rhythm, and sweat began to form on her upper lip. She was dressed in a heavy white linen gym suit: tunic, pantaloons and canvas rubber-soled shoes. Even with the room unheated as she demanded it be, she was warm from the exertion. One thing she did not have to be concerned with was her hair: she had cut her long tresses several months before so to keep them out of her face while exercising. It had made her feel boyish at first and had brought stares from people in the street, but now many other women were beginning to 'bob' their hair, as the salons called the cut.

Suddenly the image of the poor woman in the alley dwelling came back into her mind; the pitiful cries of the big-eyed baby rang in her ears.

After another twenty minutes of exercise, Catherine's heart was pounding and sweat was dripping off the tip of her nose. She felt clean and vital and ready to get on with the day.

Yesterday she had gone to Brentano's bookshop, and with the help of a friendly shop assistant had purchased a bag full of books in an attempt to understand what she had seen. There were books by Upton Sinclair and Sinclair Lewis, and of special interest were two photographic books: one by Jacob Riis and the other by Lewis Hine, both clearly men with heart and vision who portrayed the poor and the dispossessed of America in a way that Catherine had never before experienced. Their photographs made you feel the squalor, the hunger, the thwarted ambition without turning the people depicted into either objects of pity or disgust. The child at work on the loom, the immigrants sleeping ten to a room caught in the phosphorescent glare of Riis's flash still had their dignity, their humanity.

These were angry photographs, a call to action. And seeing them, Catherine knew at once her vocation. She would photograph the poor of Washington; she would capture the injustice of such poverty in the very shadows of the White House and the Capitol; she would raise a clarion call for change and reform.

While at Brentano's she had also come across a lovely blank book bound in green Moroccan leather with Italian endpapers.

In it she had begun to keep a journal of her photography: the lens setting used at various times of the day and the locations photographed. She also reserved a back section of the journal for jotting down her thoughts, something she had not done in far too long. Personal and private thoughts about everything from her life with Edward to impingements of the bigger world, as with the visit of her Uncle Adrian and what it might mean for the United States.

It seemed suddenly ridiculous to her that there should be all this rubbish of talk about the US going to war to save Europe while thousands of its own citizens lived worse than the most oppressed people in the world.

Catherine left her exercise room and went down the hall to her bath, appointed with modern built-in enameled tub and brightly colored tiles from Italy. Edward's bathroom next door was like some hospital room by comparison: all sterile white tiles and a monstrous tub that sat on paws.

She let the water fill her tub before sliding into the warmth. This was a sensuous pay-off to her exercise routine.

How far apart Edward and I have grown, Catherine thought as she allowed the heat to steal into her body. But whose fault is that? There was a time when we truly were together, when we felt like becoming partners.

Wasn't there the initial enthusiasm of the honeymoon months? The love-making deep into the night; the one lovely time Edward and I even made love in a bathtub in Venice and were bruised for days afterward. She felt a tingling in her loins from this remembrance.

And it was still good those first years together in London, she remembered. Exciting and new. It was only when we returned to America, when Edward's political career floundered, that the marriage began to flounder, as well. It can't be easy for him, she suddenly realized. He writes his books and articles, his voice is influential and powerful, but his loss of office when Wilson came to the White House must still hurt him. She felt sudden pangs of guilt at having grown so far apart from her husband.

She scrubbed her back and legs vigorously with the boar bristle brush as a sort of penance and got out of the bath, her fair skin pink from the heat and the rubbing, and wiped herself dry with a large soft ivory-colored bath towel.

Catherine was suddenly filled with the same sense of purpose toward Edward that she was about photographing the Washington slums. There is still time, she thought: time to make our marriage work, time perhaps even for children. I know Edward would love an heir, and a daughter to raise for me could be a fulfillment. What things I could share with her!

She threw on a bathrobe and went quickly to her room, dressing in a simple mauve-colored woolen skirt and long matching cardigan top. She did not bother with any make-up, merely combed her short hair out in the mirror.

Perhaps I'll let it grow out again; Edward loved it when it was long.

White stockings and brown half-boots completed her outfit, and then she went downstairs to the music room where she knew Edward and Uncle Adrian would be ensconced.

As she entered the room, her husband was just finishing a phone conversation, his back turned toward her so that he did not see her enter. Adrian was seated, rather white-faced, in one of the armchairs by the fire.

'Yes,' Fitzgerald was saying into the mouthpiece. 'We'll need perhaps twenty men, fully armed . . . No, not over the phone. We'll gather here and I'll explain the situation. Fine. Two o'clock then.'

He hung up, turned and saw her. She stared at him, unable to grasp why they would need twenty armed men here this afternoon.

'What is it, Edward? What's wrong?'

Fitzgerald looked from his wife to Appleby as if trying to make up his mind how much to tell.

'You two can't go on prevaricating forever, Edward. What's happening? Tell me.'

Appleby spoke for him. 'My dear, it seems some fanatic is after me. Means to kill me, in point of fact.'

She rushed to Appleby's side, kneeling beside his chair. 'But that's awful, Uncle Adrian.'

'It's Adrian's mission,' Fitzgerald said, coming to join them by the fire. 'Someone does not want Adrian talking to President Wilson.'

She knew they would keep her out of the full truth, but suddenly that did not matter. It was Uncle Adrian who mattered.

'What are we going to do about it?' she demanded of her husband.

'We have evidence to show that he means to attack tonight at the benefit performance at the New National Theater,' he said.

'Then we'll cancel it,' she said, standing now and facing her husband.

He smiled at her; she knew the meaning of it. His resolute persona.

'Just the opposite, dear. We will go on with it as if no one is the wiser, and when our man attempts to get to Adrian, we'll spring a handful of Pinkerton agents onto him. What is important is that the performance goes ahead as scheduled with no fuss so that our man is not scared off. It's the best and safest way to protect Adrian's life in the long run.'

She looked into her husband's eyes for a moment, liking the strength and resolve she saw there. For an instant she felt like a heroine in one of the cheap romance novels she occasionally indulged in, swept away by the power of her man. And it was a good plan, it seemed to her after giving it a moment's thought. Better to lay a trap for someone stalking you than to be forever looking over your shoulder. She kept her curiosity at bay about the who and why of the killer. This was not a time for questions, but for action.

'That's settled, then,' she said. 'We'll all go together, as arranged.'

Fitzgerald made to argue with her, but she simply held up a hand to him. 'You said it yourself: nothing should happen before the performance to scare off this man. I shall accompany you as planned. Now . . .' She rubbed her hands briskly together. 'How about some coffee? It looks like being a long and busy day.'

FOUR

Max stood outside the New National Theater in the freezing cold. He thought he had figured out everything; the lead tube, one end filled with potassium chlorate, was tucked in his coat pocket, a vial of sulfuric acid in the other pocket. He had cleaned and loaded his revolver and had taken the precaution of leaving his lodgings and the overly-curious Herr Meyer at Foggy Bottom, dumping the old suitcase and the rest of his clothing in the Potomac when no pedestrians had been within sight. The suitcase had served the purpose in disguising the pieces of his cigar; he no longer needed it. What he wore on his back and in his pockets were all that would be needed now.

Max would be traveling light after tonight.

Departure had also been arranged for. After Appleby's death the trains and river steamers out of Washington were sure to be watched. He would lay low at the German Embassy for a few days and then leave disguised along with the remainder of the staff when they closed up the embassy permanently at the end of the week.

All so carefully planned, he thought, as he stumped up and down the sidewalk to stay warm. He had even joined a tour group going through the theater this morning to survey the interior and determine the position of the boxes, in one of which Appleby would be sitting, to figure out the best place to plant the bomb. He'd decided upon the foyer of the third-floor gallery where the acoustics were perfect for his purposes. He had also laid out the escape route, one possible avenue being the fire escape on the west side of the building, and a second being via the back stage door taking advantage of shock and surprise. The alley in back of the theater led off in both directions into a warren of turnings and access routes to major thoroughfares in the heart of the city.

But all of this careful planning was for nothing, he thought again, clamping his arms about his chest for warmth. All because I forgot one piece to the plan: a ticket.

Max had planned simply to purchase a ticket at the door for the top balcony. Any ticket would do; he was not intending to watch the performance. But upon arrival at the theater there was, in addition to the colorful placards striped in American and Belgian flags advertising the gala event, a new card in the ticket window: 'Sold Out'.

He had asked the buxom older woman at the ticket window if there was not even standing room left.

She had looked at him severely, at his old coat and battered fedora.

'No.' Said flatly; end of conversation.

'But I need to purchase a ticket. Any ticket.'

He noticed a magazine in her lap, *The Police Gazette*. She looked up from it in a huff.

'There are no tickets,' she said loudly, noticing his accent now. 'You understand, or do you want an interpreter?'

At which he had given up on that approach, fearful of causing a scene.

Now a long black limousine arrived at curbside in front of the theater and an elderly couple in evening finery got out, illuminated by the weak electric lights along E Street. Max knew it was not Appleby. He had arrived a good half hour ago in a solid looking Cadillac accompanied by a very tall man and a woman. View of them had been blocked to Max by a sizeable crowd gathered at curbside in front of the five-story brick theater. Max had known it was Appleby only because the reporters gathered outside had said so, shouted so actually, as they jockeyed for position to get a photograph for their morning editions.

At that point, knowing he could not get into the theater, Max had thought of simply shooting Appleby as he arrived and taking his chances with the crowd. Somehow he would escape. But that course had not been possible, either. The crowd of men at the curb had crushed in the British diplomat and his companions, and Max could neither get a clear view nor shot at the man. The only one he had been able to see was the man accompanying the British emissary, tall enough to stand a head taller than the crush of people all around him. Max had automatically taken in the man's features: fine nose, high cheekbones, a strong rather than handsome face, pure white hair under the top hat; prematurely grayed. All in all it was a very American face, full of optimism and self-confidence.

And then they had gone inside the theater, much of the crowd along with them. Odd, he had thought at the time, so much of a crowd surrounding them. And another chance missed.

The older couple bustled into the theater now, the last to come and not wanting to be late.

Max knew the performance would start in a few minutes. The colored doorman in red livery had closed the doors under the awning after the elderly couple, and was now busy digging at his left ear with his little finger, his back to Max. The buxom lady at the ticket window had her head bent to her magazine, her lips moving as she read.

Now or never, he thought.

He ducked under the ticket window and got to the front doors without the woman seeing him. The doorman was still cleaning his ear as Max slipped through the door farthest from him. The lobby was large and grand with red carpets, red plush on the walls, crystal chandeliers overhead, and gilt scroll work on the ceiling trim. The warm air inside greeted him like an embrace. He quickly took off his hat and coat and began walking slowly, deliberately toward the wide flight of stairs.

A deep voice sounded in back of him. 'Hello, sir.'

Max turned smiling.

The colored doorman was coming toward him.

'Your ticket, sir,' the man said, his long-fingered hand outstretched to Max as he approached.

'No,' Max said brightly. 'The press doesn't need tickets.'

The doorman stopped, looking confused. 'You with the press? You're late. Got a pass?'

'It was last minute,' Max said. 'Our regular man got sick. Call my editor. He'll tell you.'

'Your editor?' The colored man looked skeptical now.

'Yes. The *Evening News*.' Max had seen a newsboy hawking

the paper outside the theater earlier. It was the first name to come to mind.

'Just call him,' Max urged. 'I'll wait here.'

The doorman shrugged. 'OK. Sorry, sir, but I got my orders.'

'Certainly.' Max smiled at him. 'It's Samuels at the paper. Just tell him Per Walloon is calling. You see, I'm Belgian. Still improving my English; I write better than I speak.'

The doorman wasn't concerned with the explanation, Max figured, for he moved off toward a door leading to a tiny office without really attending to this last bit.

Max waited for the fellow to enter the tiny cubicle, then gave a twenty count. Sure enough, the man peeked back around the door to make sure he was still waiting there. Max smiled broadly, and the man ducked back into his office reassured, but still leaving the door open. From where he was at the phone, however, he could no longer see the stairs.

Instantly and stealthily Max dashed up the stairs toward the gallery foyer on the third floor.

I've got five minutes, he figured, maybe ten before the doorman and ticket lady get together and realize I've gatecrashed.

And what if I have? he thought, taking the stairs two at a time and ignoring the subsequent pain in his left thigh. They're not going to stop the performance for one gatecrasher, for one culture lover who sneaks into the National Theater.

Reaching the second landing he saw that the audience was just taking their seats, the halls were emptying. He slowed his pace, not wanting to call attention to himself.

Bells rang once: the performance was about to begin.

Max had to work quickly now; his schedule had been thrown off by the ticket fiasco. He circled the fan-shaped corridor going past the second-floor boxes, searching for telltale clues to where Appleby was sitting. He had to be very quick about this, for the milling people were filing into their boxes in all their evening finery: flashes of diamonds; cigars butted out in tall brass urns; feathers atop women's heads wafting as they walked; the silk of evening gowns whispering with movement; the creak of patent leather shoes. Dressed in his blue serge suit, Max would stand out too distinctly from the rest once the crowd dispersed.

If there are any watchers here, he thought, they'll see quite clearly that I don't belong.

No panicking now, he told himself. No quick movements that might draw attention to yourself. He felt the knot of anticipation in his stomach that had built up over the past few days begin to loosen. He was in action now, and that was the important thing. He had a discernible goal, a mission, and he was underway. No more waiting and planning.

He noticed other men dressed in daytime suits with stiff collars stationed at strategic points along the corridor, but they had not seemed to notice him yet, caught as he was in the flood of audience filling the auditorium.

The bells rang twice now.

Max looked at these men as he passed by: heavy men for the most part; men whose necks looked almost as big as Max's thighs. Stolid, purposeful, dumbly diligent. Max knew them instantly for what they were: plain-clothes policemen. Yet there was no going back now.

They are a good sign, he told himself, as he passed the final arc in the semicircular corridor. They mean that I'm getting closer to my quarry, to Appleby.

And he was, for around the far side of the semicircular corridor he caught sight for an instant of the tall white-haired fellow who had accompanied Appleby into the theater. He was conferring with another one of the thickset plain-clothes policemen in the hall, tapping the man's forearm for emphasis as he spoke to him.

Max knew the type the tall man represented: money, power, influence. It was written all over him. He took an instant dislike to the man, wondering what connection he had to Appleby. Was he American at all? He seemed now to hold himself with the upright easy confidence of the British upper classes.

Max put these thoughts out of his mind as the man finished his conversation with the jowly plain-clothes policeman and re-entered his box, closing the door in back of him. The door closed away from Max, giving him a fleeting glance at its brass number plate: 23.

Right, then, he thought, turning on his heels and passing as calmly as possible back to the stairway leading to the third floor. The crush into the auditorium still shielded him from the notice of the watchers along this corridor.

I know where Appleby is, he thought; the rest will be easy. Even with the beefy watchers protecting him.

As Max reached the third floor the bells rang three times, the auditorium doors began closing, and the house lights dimmed. Max heard an announcement being made from inside: 'Ladies and gentlemen, welcome!' a deep male voice boomed out. 'This evening's program has been slightly altered. We regret that our distinguished English visitor, Sir Adrian Appleby, will not be speaking tonight due to a case of laryngitis. He is, however, in attendance . . .'

At this point the third-floor usher closed the auditorium door nearest Max and the rest of the announcement was muffled followed by polite applause.

Warning signals sounded in Max's brain: I don't like this. Too many damned watchers here; too much difficulty getting in. And now Appleby's not giving his address to start the program off as the newspaper promised.

But Max had no time to attend to these signals, nor did he actually want to. There was no more time to waste; he was in action, he wanted only to continue, to finish this job. He could hear Berthold in Berlin if he missed this opportunity: the high piercing tone of his voice as he would curse and rail at the incompetence of certain races.

'We always knew you were not cut out of quite the right cloth . . . not meant for the life of action. Your kind never is.'

A muscle flexed in Max's jaw at this imaginary upbraiding; he would not give Berthold that pleasure.

So it's the old game again, is it? his ironical voice said to him. You have to prove yourself as good or better than them.

'Yes,' Max whispered aloud. 'Yes, I do.'

'Beg pardon?'

Max had not noticed the man until now, so intent had he been on Berthold's possible criticism, on avoiding failure at all costs. He was still staring at the auditorium door and the man, clearly another watcher, had approached without his being aware, and was now standing next to him so close that Max could smell cigarettes on his fetid breath. Max did not know if he had muttered the words to himself in German or English. A momentary panic gripped him and he forced it down, willing himself to remain calm.

He wiped his brow, looking at the man dressed in a brown wool three-piece, a button missing from the vest.

'Sorry,' Max said. 'I'm not feeling at all well.'

The man looked at him closely.

It's my accent, Max knew.

The man's eyes squinted; his thick lips pursed. There was a tiny patch of toilet paper under his left ear where he had probably nicked himself shaving. Max wanted desperately for the man to go away, but he continued standing there.

'Can I help you?' he said finally, reaching out as if to hold Max's arm.

'No . . . thank you. I need to find the men's room.'

More squinting. Max recognized the danger signals.

'It's over there.' The man indicated with a bent thumb a door in the corridor wall behind them.

From inside the auditorium came the sound of an orchestra, the bell-clear tones of a tenor. Something from Puccini, Max registered automatically. He nodded at the big man and moved off to the bathroom.

And what if he calls for help? Max thought. I can't allow that.

He faked a stumble, holding onto the wall for support, and the man came to his side.

'I just need some water,' Max said, almost in a whisper.

Again the man's eyes narrowed, but more now with self-doubt than suspicion, Max hoped.

The watcher pushed the swinging door open revealing a white-tiled well lit space with stalls to one side, tall porcelain sinks with brass fittings to the other below a line of mirrors.

Max waited for the door to close.

'Water's over here.' The man began helping Max to the sinks.

No attendant on duty inside, Max saw. A quick glance under the stall doors: no feet there. They were alone. Max let his coat and hat trail to the floor, careful to cushion the vial of acid in his coat pocket as he did so.

The rest happened too quickly for the watcher to react. With the man still hovering behind him, Max thrust his elbow into the fellow's solar plexus. A rush of wind came out of the man as he doubled over from the unexpected blow; Max used the man's own momentum to propel his head into the edge of the sink with a sickening plonking sound. After the blow, the watcher still stood, doubled over, gasping for breath, his stocky legs trembling. Max grabbed the back of his thick woolen jacket and rammed him head first again into the sink and then a third time. A crimson streak showed on the side of the white porcelain, garish in the harsh electric light of the bathroom. Still the man stood like a stubborn mule, vomiting now, and Max wanted only for this to be over. He pulled out his pistol from his shoulder holster.

I have no argument with this man, he thought. I have no vendetta against the police, public or private. I want only for this animal to lie down and be quiet. But he's seen your face, he thought. He was inches from you. He knows you.

Max held onto the woolen jacket as the man twisted spasmodically, half unconscious already.

It doesn't matter now, Max thought. Let him see my face. Any description will come too late to help Appleby. My work in the US will be at an end after Appleby, anyway. It's Germany for me and the trenches again. Berthold cannot risk keeping me in America after I kill Appleby.

All this debate was the matter of a few instants in Max's mind, and he felt a kind of relief after making his decision. He reversed the pistol, holding it by its barrel and brought the butt down onto the back of the man's head. This did the job, for the man crumpled at Max's feet, his mouth wide open. Max holstered his pistol, dragged the unconscious man to the stalls, pushed him in and closed the door. A spray of the man's vomit was on the toe of Max's shoe, and he opened the stall door again, ripped off a piece of toilet paper, cleaned the shoe, threw the soiled paper into the toilet bowl, and closed the door again.

Suddenly he felt the exhilaration of battle; the challenge, the life and death gamble of it. And it buoyed him.

I'm going to bring it off, he told himself. Against all odds, I'll do it. Me against all of them.

He quickly picked up both his hat and coat and put them on. Out of the coat pocket he took the lead tube and placed it on the back of the sink. One end of it was plugged already with a lead stopper from the bottom of his suitcase. He pulled out the other lead stopper from his pocket and set it next to the tube.

From the other coat pocket he brought out the vial of sulfuric acid. He took a long breath, calming himself, then opened the glass stopper and picked up the lead tube in the other hand.

Let's hope Dr Scheele in his Hoboken laboratory got the thickness of the copper divider correct, Max thought as he brought the tip of the vial to the lip of the empty half of the tube, ready to pour.

'It is so simple,' Max remembered Dr Scheele saying as the tiny man pushed wireframe glasses up the bridge of his nose.

'A child's experiment, really. You put potassium chlorate in one end of a lead tube, stopped off by a lead plug at the end and by a copper disk from the other compartment of the tube. Into this second compartment you put sulfuric acid, plug it with lead, and the acid eats its way through the copper. Once it reaches the potassium chlorate – poof! – you have a nice little explosion. Big enough to kill a man or set off munitions in a ship's hold at sea. The copper disk functions as the fuse, you see. The thinner it is, the shorter the time it takes the acid to eat through it.'

Pray that strange little chemist got this copper fuse right, Max thought as he tipped the vial toward the lead tube. He had lost two of his agents in New York over the past year because of faulty copper fuses – the bombs had blown up in their hands as they had poured the acid.

Behind him the unconscious watcher in the stall made thick snoring sounds, reminding Max that there was more than one fuse to worry about. Soon the doorman might raise an alarm. With this many watchers about, surely something is amiss. Some warning may even have reached Appleby.

But again, he had no time to think of this, for the clear

liquid from the vial began to dribble into the lead tube and Max held his breath. What if the disk had not been inserted properly? What if there were a leak between compartments?

Nothing happened. The acid poured into the compartment and stayed. He breathed more easily and continued pouring, feeling sweat at his lower back, and finally filled the lead tube. It began to feel warm in his hand.

'The acid would like to eat the lead,' Scheele had instructed, speaking to him like a primary school teacher to a first grader. 'But it can't. The lead also works to impact the explosion. You must plug both ends securely after adding the sulfuric acid so to build pressure for the explosion.'

Max filled half of the tube with the acid, then set the vial down and inserted the lead plug tightly.

He now had a quite lethal and loud bomb in hand, and the fuse, the copper disk, was burning. He had only a matter of minutes.

Out in the corridor once again, he placed the bomb under the counter of the cloakroom. The attendant had gone in with the audience and would not be injured by the blast, but the counter would provide an echo effect to the blast as well as shield any accidental passerby from the direct effect of it.

I'm not out to kill any innocent people, he told himself, moving slowly away from the cloakroom. I'm not like Appleby, trying to bring innocents into the carnage of war. I'm above that. It's that which separates me from them.

The old guard last night at the medical laboratory: that was different. He had to die. He could have set the police on me before I had a chance to get to Appleby. It's the luck of bad timing that cost the old man his life. I had no choice; he gave me no choice.

Max took the stairs slowly down to the second floor. There was still the matter of watchers to deal with there, and once again he began to wonder about all the protection for Appleby. There was no way the authorities could be on to his plan, he knew. Perhaps it's only my imagination. Was the man upstairs plain-clothes at all? Perhaps he was just another innocent caught up in the maelstrom.

You are going soft in the head, he told himself. Of course

he's a watcher. And the others, as well. Now shut your mind down; finish with this stupid moralizing, and concentrate on one thing: killing the Englishman.

He reached the bottom of the stairs and heard the muffled sound of applause from inside the auditorium. Two men were walking up and down the hallway with that absolute look of boredom about them that Max knew so well.

Watchers on duty.

He kept himself concealed at the bottom of the stairs to the second floor behind a massive plaster of Paris Corinthian-style column, and began counting. He reached three hundred and began to worry. By four hundred he knew that Scheele had messed up. The damn copper fuse was not working. He could not wait all night.

Soon enough one of the watchers will discover me, or the colored doorman will come looking for me, or my friend in the lavatory will wake up with a headache and vengeance on his mind. All of whom have seen me, can describe me minutely.

The blast when it came surprised Max as much as the watchers patrolling the second floor. A rumbling concussion trembled the column he was hiding behind and a rush of air warmed the back of his neck.

He was instantly in action, though, dashing out into the corridor and shouting: 'Fire! Fire!'

Bulging-eyed watchers moved past him toward the sound of the blast. From inside the auditorium came the sounds of women screaming and of startled cries for the lights to be put on. Max raced along the corridor as doors to the boxes opened. He gave no more thought to appearing calm; no one in the entire National Theater at this moment was acting calmly. People were dashing out of their boxes in a panic. He had to get to Appleby's box before the fellow left; had to catch him at close range.

The door to 23 was still closed, he saw, as he turned the top arc of the half-circle corridor. And outside stood the same bulky guard as before, not moving.

'Fire! Fire!' Max shouted as he ran, and now more women were screaming, hands to their mouths. The guard, however, did not budge and turned to Max as he kept running toward him.

Max was unsure what to do at this point. The simplest would be to shoot the man as he ran toward him, but that would warn those inside box 23.

Why doesn't the fool go toward the blast like the rest of his colleagues? But Max knew: orders. The man only knows his orders. In his mind Max could see the tall white-haired fellow earlier tapping his forearm for emphasis: 'You are not to move from here, no matter what.'

The man's orders were apparently to stay with Appleby.

A sudden inspiration struck Max. Orders.

'They want you upstairs, officer,' Max said as he ran up to the man. 'A bomb has gone off. They need you there.' His voice blended into the general pandemonium in the corridor so that Max was sure they would not hear him inside the box.

The watcher chewed on his lower lip, looking from the door to Max.

'Now!' Max ordered, using his best military voice.

The man heard the tone and obeyed, loping off along the corridor to the stairs.

Max waited for him to get out of sight, for the corridor to be flooded with screaming women and bustling men, then pulled his hat low over his eyes, drew the pistol out, and flicked off its safety. From inside the box he heard muffled voices, but could make nothing intelligible out. They're still in there, he thought. As if waiting for me.

He took a deep breath, turned the door handle, and suddenly threw the door open.

FIVE

Max could see three of them seated in the box. Appleby was between the white-haired man and a woman with short black hair, their backs to him. He aimed the revolver at the back of Appleby's head just as the other two were turning around.

'What is it?' the man began saying, peering into the shadows. 'Have they caught the fellow . . .?' Then his voice trailed off as he saw the gun.

Max took in the woman's features all at once, just as she began screaming. He saw the wide-flared nose, the high cheeks, the hint of bosom at the top of her cornflower blue evening gown. The absolute look of horror on her face made him hesitate.

At the sound of the scream, the figure of Appleby suddenly crumpled to the floor; Max had no clear shot now. He was vaguely aware of movement from his left, from the white-haired man. Shifting his attention in that direction, Max saw that he had drawn an abnormally large pistol from inside his evening coat and Max jumped backward just as the boom of its discharge reverberated in his eardrums, just as a bullet thudded into the door jamb in back of him, splintering wood.

More screams came from the corridor at the sound of the shot, and Max bolted from the box, stumbling into the crowd of theatergoers, knocking down a buxom matron in his panic, her long necklace breaking and pearls scattering across the floor.

He jumped over the fallen woman, landed on some of the pearls strewn across the ground and stumbled for a moment, then righted himself and continued running through the crowd. He looked over his shoulder as he rushed along the corridor, and the white-haired man was still following him, trying to take aim once more, but the crowd prevented him from shooting.

'Stop him!' the man shouted from in back. 'He's an assassin!'

The word galvanized the crowd, Max noticed. Men and women stared with frightened eyes as he lunged past them, seeing the gun in his hand and making way for him. No one laid a hand on him as he reached the stairs and leaped two steps at a time to the ground floor foyer. His left leg almost gave way under him as he took the last step, and he grimaced with pain.

The audience here was in the same sort of panic as those upstairs. Max added to it by yelling, 'Fire! Fire!' as he raced toward the front doors.

A trap. They have laid a trap for me, he thought. He looked left and right as he neared the front doors. Would there be more men waiting for me out here? But he had no time to worry about this, for he was swept along in a flood of people rushing from the theater for their lives. Others had taken up his chant: 'Fire! Open the doors!'

In back of him, towering above the others coming down the stairs, the white-haired man was still in pursuit.

Max held his pistol under his coat as the crowd pushed through the street doors and onto the sidewalk under the marquee. He caught a glimpse of the old colored doorman and the fellow seemed to recognize him, but then Max began running east down E Street, and then out onto Pennsylvania Avenue. He looked back once, and the man following him had got bottlenecked at the street door to the theater. Max ran one block, the night-time strollers looking at him suspiciously; then glancing back and seeing no one following him, he deftly holstered his pistol and slowed his pace. A streetcar passed, jangling its bell, and halted at a stop half a block away. He raced to it, jumping on the back platform just as it was pulling away from the stop.

Looking out the back window, Max saw the white-haired man and three other burly fellows turn the corner onto Pennsylvania Avenue. They looked up and down the busy street once, twice, then shrugged resignedly, turning to go back to the theater. All except the white-haired man who continued staring, it seemed to Max, straight at the streetcar carrying him, but then he too finally turned and headed back to the theater.

Max breathed deeply. His depth of focus suddenly shifted so that he was now looking at his own reflection in the window of the streetcar.

Smiling, he thought. I'm damn well smiling. I've made a botch up of the Appleby job, nearly got myself killed or at least captured, and I'm smiling.

But he kept his mind off that one for a bit longer, closely inspecting the busy avenue outside of the streetcar for any signs of being followed. The streetcar lurched along the rails; gaslights mingled with newer electric streetlights; commoners and moneyed members of the American aristocracy rubbed shoulders, as well. Oyster shops and elegant restaurants, light spilling onto the sidewalk from their windows, were side by side; horse-drawn cabs and honking Model T Fords shared the road. But no sign of anyone following him. Yet.

The conductor, a small man in a blue uniform and cap came up to him, and Max almost jumped at the sight of the uniform, then calmed himself, taking his hand off the butt of the pistol in his shoulder holster, and fetching his change purse instead.

Got to figure this out, he thought as the conductor left him, a censorious look on his face for the unorthodox manner in which Max had caught the streetcar. The watchers, the dummy in the box where Appleby should have been – for it was now clear to Max that the figure of Adrian Appleby had been a mannequin, which explained why it toppled over the way it did. And the question the white-haired man asked when he thought Max was the guard: 'Have they caught the fellow?'

All of this made it obvious. They expected me, Max thought.

Had Appleby been at the theater at all? I saw him come, pull up in the Cadillac, get out amid the crowd of reporters, and bustle into the theater.

Correction: I saw some short round man with a top hat rushing into the theater. Had it been Appleby at all? he now wondered.

But in the final analysis it's not important whether Appleby actually arrived or not. What is important is the fact of the dummy in the box. That means they knew of my plan beforehand. Which means that they – I don't even know who they are – have somehow tumbled to my mission and that it will be much more difficult to get to Appleby now.

He had no doubt that he could still get to the Englishman; gave no thought to calling off his mission. He knew only that the job would be more difficult now.

Damage assessment: Appleby knows that he's being hunted and will be on his guard now. There may be a description of me as a result of this fiasco. May be, he thought ironically as the streetcar slowed to another stop. Hell, the pork-faced watcher I left breathing spit bubbles in the men's toilet will damn well remember me. The doorman also got a fine look at my face. I might just as well have posed at a photographer's studio.

He thought for one bad moment of the old night watchman at the medical building whom he had killed to prevent just such an eventuality.

One saving grace, he thought, is that when attempting to make the kill I had my hat pulled down low over my eyes and my coat on. The white-haired one won't have gotten a good look at me, nor did the others in the box.

Several people got off at the next stop, two more got on; older men in evening dress chattering about a musical evening they had just been to.

Not like the one I attended, he thought, edging farther away from the new arrivals, continuing to stare out into the night as the streetcar started up again with a lurch.

I'll alter my appearance, he thought. Shave my beard for one. That should be simple enough. I need to get rid of this fedora; substitute it for a cap. And again the thought came up: how did they get on to me? Max was certain it had something to do with Manstein in New York. Either the fool had been talking to the wrong people, or else the message to Berthold had been intercepted. Whichever, it meant that Max had to go it alone from here on out. No more communicating with Manstein or Berthold.

That decision made, Max began to almost relax. The rest fit together easily after that: first a lodging needed to be found for the night. Some cheap accommodation, and he knew the spot for that: in the area between the Capitol and Union Station, the very direction in which the streetcar was now headed. A place where no one would be overly concerned that he had no luggage; he could say he left it at the station.

He got off the streetcar at 1st Street and felt suddenly quite chill. He took off his hat and rolled it up, stuffing it into his pocket, then continued down Pennsylvania Avenue toward the Capitol, looming white and almost iridescent with the snow all about it. Tour busses were parked in front of hotels along this part of the avenue; local restaurants were Chinese and Italian. Only then did he remember that he had not eaten since breakfast, and he suddenly felt ravenous. He went into Wu Lee's Chop House, had chop suey and fried rice with a steaming pot of aromatic tea, and felt much better. After paying, he went back onto the street and turned left, going north, on New Jersey Avenue. The first hotel he came to, the Central, he went into. He paid $1.75 in advance for one night, using the name Adrian Lee, the first to pop into his head: Lee for the Chinese food he'd just eaten, and Adrian for the man he would kill. He gave his address as 2321 Wood Avenue, Brooklyn, having no idea if there even was a Wood Avenue in Brooklyn, and if there were, whether or not it went into the two thousands. But the clerk, a sallow faced middle-aged man, did not care; so long as he had the money in hand and some name and address to put in the book.

His room was on the second floor, bath down the hall, an iron bedstead painted white, pictures of Washington, DC on the walls, a frayed rug on the wooden floor. Exhaustion overcame him now. He needed sleep. In the morning he would go out and buy a razor and shave; then he would make further plans. He locked the door and lay down fully clothed on the lumpy bed, the aged springs creaking loudly.

He was asleep in two minutes, a skill he had learned in the trenches.

Fitzgerald felt like a damn fool. Firstly, that the German had been able to gain entrance to the theater at all without raising suspicion. But the Pinkerton men had concentrated on patrolling the second floor once the street doors had been closed and had not expected their man to enter late. The theater staff was not looking for anyone suspicious: they had not been apprised of the situation for fear that the theater management would simply cancel the performance were they to learn of an assassin stalking the corridors. And then Fitzgerald himself, along with the Pinkerton agents he had hired, had been completely taken in by the firebomb the German had set as a decoy. Their attention had been diverted so that the fellow had actually been able to walk right up to the door of their box seats unmolested, brazenly open it and take aim at where Appleby would have been sitting had he come to the theater at all.

They were now back at Poplars and Catherine, fortified by two glasses of brandy, had gone to bed.

Brave girl, Fitzgerald thought. And I let her in for possible bodily harm by my carelessness. She could have been injured, even killed by that German madman. The thought sent a chill through his body as he stood by the fire in the music room. He could not imagine life without Catherine.

Yet she had seemed to bear up bravely. After the small fire had been put out in the third-floor corridor, and after the panic was over and he had returned from chasing the German, he found her still sitting in the box. The dummy made up to resemble Appleby was propped up once again in the chair next to her. The Pinkerton agent who had posed as Appleby for the arrival at the theater had switched places once inside the theater.

'There you are,' she had said brightly as he came running back to her, out of breath, fearful that she might have been injured in the crush of people. 'This is the most entertaining evening of theater the National has ever seen, I am sure.'

But he could tell, once he took her arm, that this was bravado on her part; the cheeky Devereaux side of her at work to cover up a case of nerves. He could feel her trembling as he walked her out of the theater.

Now Appleby was sitting silently in one of the armchairs in the music room, his face ashen, forehead creased in thought. He had remained at the Poplars under Pinkerton guard while the fiasco unfolded at the theater.

In the other armchair, a snifter of brandy in his hand and damn the regulations, sat Chief Inspector Lewis of the Washington Metropolitan Police. A big man, easily 6'3" and well over 200 pounds, he looked uncomfortable in any enclosed space, and his legs stretched out drastically as he sat in the chair. He was one of those men of Scots ancestry who seemed to have hair growing in the most unlikely places: swirling out of his ears and nose, swooping horn-like up from his eyebrows. He wore a moustache clipped short in military fashion and salt-and-pepper hair combed from front to back. No uniform; a worn and baggy gray suit instead.

He had arrived not long before and was still looking rather flummoxed. Fitzgerald was considering his last question; Appleby looked up at Fitzgerald and shook his head.

'I'm afraid we cannot divulge that, Inspector Lewis.'

Fitzgerald added, 'Let's just leave it at "informed sources".'

Lewis nodded; the entire chair seemed to rock with the motion. He set the snifter down on the leather-covered table next to his chair, fixing first Fitzgerald and then Appleby with a determined look.

'So let me get this straight. These informed sources of yours tell you that there is someone gunning for Sir Adrian. That he means to do his work, in point of fact, at the benefit affair. And instead of calling the whole thing off, or at least calling the police, you two go ahead and set a trap to catch the fellow. You bring those incompetent Pinkertons into it and almost burn down the New National Theater as a result.' He paused for a moment. 'Am I being too severe, Mr Fitzgerald? Am I stating it perhaps too baldly?'

'No, inspector,' Fitzgerald said. 'I'm afraid you have it only too right.'

'You'll pardon me for saying so, sir, but amateurs should not meddle in these affairs. I do not attempt to advise the Congress on matters of diplomacy, if you take my meaning.'

Fitzgerald nodded. 'I do.' He felt like a damned ass, as a matter of fact.

Appleby, however, was not prepared for contrition. 'We are not schoolboys, inspector. We had a plan, we engaged professionals for the task. Were we to have come to you with our bit of information, uncorroborated, what would you have told us? Fairy tales? Paranoia? If in doubt, cancel the event. None of which would have caught our man.'

'And neither did your scheme get your man.'

Lewis stood now, an imposing figure, quite manfully built. Fitzgerald, tall enough in his own right, felt rather diminutive next to him.

'What you managed to do, Sir Adrian, was to risk the lives of several hundred innocent people at that theater. What if our fellow was truly a madman? What if it did not matter to him how many he killed in the process of killing you? Why, that bomb he set as a diversion could just as easily have been a much larger one, or a series of incendiaries that could have burned down the entire theater, killing many of those inside, and you wouldn't even have been there.'

'You sound disappointed at that prospect, inspector,' Appleby quipped.

Lewis ignored the remark, pausing dramatically and staring at Appleby, who sucked in air angrily. A moment of strained silence followed; the fire in the hearth crackled.

Finally: 'Point taken, inspector,' Appleby said.

'So tell me,' Inspector Lewis said almost jovially now that he was shown a degree of respect. 'Who wants to kill you and why?'

Fitzgerald watched closely as again Appleby sought his eyes, a question on his face. Fitzgerald raised his eyebrows at him noncommittally. Let Adrian decide how much he tells the inspector, he thought.

The exchange did not go unnoticed by Lewis.

'We know next to nothing about the assassin,' Appleby began. 'He is German and he means to kill me before I have an opportunity to confer with President Wilson.'

The inspector raised his bushy gray eyebrows at this revelation. 'War business?'

'Something like,' Appleby replied vaguely. 'A message of the greatest moment and secrecy.'

'So why haven't you talked with the president already?'

Lewis, Fitzgerald noted, was as naive of diplomatic affairs as he, Fitzgerald was, of police matters.

'It's not quite that easy, Chief Inspector,' Fitzgerald said.

'We're scheduled to have a meeting tomorrow.'

The one positive side effect of the fiasco at the theater was that it might help convince Wilson of the authenticity of Adrian's Zimmermann telegram, Fitzgerald thought.

'I'm sure nothing in Washington is simple, Mr Fitzgerald. But it appears that from this point what we must do is clear-cut.' Lewis turned suddenly to Appleby. 'We've got to keep you alive until you see President Wilson.'

'Well,' Appleby drawled, 'I was rather hoping there might be life thereafter, as well.'

Lewis chuckled slightly at this.

'The worst of it is,' Appleby sighed, 'I was hoping to feast on your lovely shellfish at an oyster bar downtown. To see the latest Chaplin film. Now I am beginning to feel rather like a shut-in.'

'And that is exactly how you will remain until we get you to the president or until we catch this German.'

'Do you really hold out much hope for the latter?' Fitzgerald asked the policeman.

'Well, we have a description of him now.'

'I am afraid as eyewitnesses, I and my wife will not be able to provide much information. I told you, he had his hat pulled down low over his brow; I could barely see his eyes. He did have a beard. Reddish-brown. And he appeared to be slightly built, though it was difficult to tell under the bulky overcoat he wore.'

Lewis pulled out a leather notepad from the breast pocket of his coat, flipping through the pages until he found what he was looking for, and then began reading out to them.

'Subject is approximately five feet ten inches, one hundred and fifty pounds. Bearded, with reddish-brown hair worn medium length, parted high on the right. Goes by the name of Per Walloon, posing as a Belgian.' He looked up from the pad. 'At least tonight he did.' Then he continued reading: 'Walks with a slight limp, according to one witness.'

He closed the pad and stuffed it back into his breast pocket.

'I noticed no limp,' Fitzgerald said.

'You wouldn't then, would you? Not if he were wearing an ankle length overcoat.'

Fitzgerald thought about this for a moment. The man had moved strangely, now he came to think of it. He had not remarked on it before because they had both been jostled through the crowded theater as Fitzgerald had chased the man.

'The doorman gave us a pretty thorough description,' Lewis said. 'This Walloon, or whatever his real name is, came in late claiming to be with the press. Had a quite noticeable accent. It was the doorman who noticed the limp. One of your Pinkerton hires is the other witness. He saw our man up close, before he got his head nearly bashed in, that is. The fellow was feigning sickness, so the Pinkerton fellow is not too sure about the limp. He's only sure about his own headache. I should say he's lucky to be alive at all.' Lewis paused and scowled suddenly. 'Isn't it about time we cut the bull?'

'What do you mean, inspector?' Fitzgerald tried his best to sound taken aback, but he knew he was not fooling Lewis, and he also knew suddenly why the big man was a chief inspector.

'Look, this is not just any German, is it? This is an agent, probably a damn clever one at that. We found traces of the bomb: bits of lead tubing. That is a signature with the Germans, these tube bombs. So he's a professional, not just a vengeful maniac. He's a man with a mission. And we know he's clever enough to figure out your Pinkerton set-up and to set a diversion of his own that allowed him to get past all the men protecting the dummy. And I am not referring to you, Sir Adrian, but to your stand-in. So please, let us talk like mature men. How much do you know about the assassin?'

He glowered first at Appleby, then at Fitzgerald.

Finally Appleby replied, 'Truly not much more than I have already told you, inspector. He signs himself as "M". That is his only name thus far. And he communicates personally with Berlin Military Intelligence.'

At this, Lewis let out a whistle. 'Big enough.'

'Yes,' Appleby said. 'Big enough.'

'I suppose I should not ask how it is you came to know about the Berlin communication.'

Fitzgerald knew they were in good hands now with Lewis; he put things together quite rapidly.

'No, you should not,' Appleby said.

'Is that why you hesitated to call in the police to begin with?'

'Perhaps,' Appleby replied.

A knock came at the door and Thomas poked his head in.

'Another policeman to see you, Mr Edward.'

Fitzgerald glanced at Lewis who shrugged in answer to the silent question.

'Did my men send him?' Lewis asked the butler.

Thomas nodded, plainly irritated. 'The man's with the police.'

Only then did the enormity of the situation strike Fitzgerald: Lewis had asked the seemingly obvious because he thought it possible that M, the German, might have tracked Adrian to Poplars and might be capable of posing as a detective to gain entrance. An assassin here in our house. It's part of what this telegram has brought into our lives.

Lewis seemed satisfied at Thomas's answer, nodding at Fitzgerald.

'Show him in, Thomas,' Fitzgerald said.

He was already doing so, unbidden.

A short sparkling man was ushered in, hardly the typical looking policeman, Fitzgerald thought, wearing a loud checked suit cut in the jazzy fashion of a couple years ago: a wide shouldered jacket that hung down well past the waist, and pants tapered to cuffs ending a good inch above the man's spats. A tiepin that looked to be diamond was affixed in the middle of his green tie, and a yellow vest completed the ensemble. His bright red hair was brilliantined back flat off his forehead.

'Oh, Jesus,' Lewis muttered as the fellow sauntered into the room. Then louder: 'Hello Niel. I didn't think this was a Bureau case.'

The short man came right up to the inspector and shook hands energetically with him. Fitzgerald now saw that this man's jaw was working, chewing quite avidly on gum.

'Inspector Lewis,' he said, continuing to pump the large man's hand. 'Good to see you on the job so late at night.'

'The Metropolitan Police never sleeps, Niel. Haven't you heard?'

Fitzgerald could see that there was no love lost between the two. The mention of 'Bureau' by Lewis let him know why: Niel was obviously an agent for the fledgling Bureau of Investigation at the Justice Department. The Bureau did not sit well with most of Washington, for it had been rammed down the throats of lawmakers by presidential decree during a Congressional recess.

Niel snapped his gum and turned from Lewis. 'You'll be Fitzgerald, then, I suppose.'

Fitzgerald shook the tiny proffered hand with its cool palm. The man continued chewing gum at a furious rate.

'Sorry to be so long in getting here,' he said holding onto Fitzgerald's hand and seeking out his eye. 'Agent Niel's my name.' He pulled out an engraved card with a phone number under his name. 'You may need to contact me. Anytime night or day.'

Fitzgerald pocketed the card; he found the little man quite ridiculous.

'Sir Adrian Appleby,' Agent Niel said turning to Appleby. 'Am I right?'

Appleby grunted assent. Fitzgerald could see he did not much care for Agent Niel's appearance; to Adrian he will appear an uppity Irishman, Fitzgerald thought.

'I understand someone tried to kill you tonight.'

Lewis finally spoke up, 'Really, Niel. I believe we have this investigation under control. There's no question of interstate violations here.'

Agent Niel ignored Inspector Lewis's statement. 'It must have been a bit of a fright for you, sir,' Niel said to Appleby.

'Not really.'

'Well now,' Niel began in an effusive vein, 'I've heard of the cold blood of the blue bloods, but I would think if a man tries to take a shot at you, it would put your hair up.'

Fitzgerald could see that Adrian was not amused by Niel's forced folksy approach.

'Very little hair to get up, I'm afraid,' he said, swiping a hand over his glistening pate.

'Say, that's good. I like that. You've got guts, and a sense of humor.'

'Nothing to do with "guts", as you so quaintly put it. I was simply not in attendance at the theater. One with more scintillating verbal skills took my place.'

Niel's face made a wide-eyed expression of revelation. 'Oh, I get it. Laying a trap, eh?' He suddenly reached in a vest pocket and drew out a small green paper covered packet, pulled out a thin stick of gum and offered it to Appleby.

'Here. Have one. Does wonders for the digestion.' He patted a nonexistent paunch. 'The pepsin in it, see. Helps break the food down wonderfully. Medicinal stuff, chewing gum.'

Appleby took the gum and stuffed it into a pocket of the silk smoking jacket he was wearing. Fitzgerald only now noticed the felt slippers Appleby had on: monogrammed on the toes with AA.

'Thank you. I'll save it for after my next meal.' Deadpan.

'Well,' Lewis said. 'Now that introductions have been made, I assume you'll be going. We really do have things under control here.'

Niel shot him a look of contempt. 'I'm sure you do, inspector. The Metropolitan Police have been doing wonders with foreign agents and saboteurs, I'm told. Quite a success record.'

For the first time, Fitzgerald began to suspect that Niel was more than just a loudly clad gum-chewing would-be policeman. There were obviously intelligent processes going on behind his beady little eyes. He took a quick look at Niel's face as Lewis and he glowered at each other. The nose looked to have broken more than once; his brow was high, not just because of his hair style. On this second glance, Fitzgerald saw not a faux dandy, but a fighter, a street brawler whom he had underestimated. And there was cunning in his eyes as he fixed Chief Inspector Lewis with his squint.

'I'll let you gentlemen get on with your discussion,' Niel said as he suddenly turned from Lewis to Fitzgerald, half-bowed and then went to the door. 'Remember the number,' he nodded to Fitzgerald's pocket where he had placed the agent's calling card. 'You can get me any time. Leave a message. We'll be seeing each other again, I'm sure.'

Then to Appleby as he opened the door: 'And I would stay

indoors until returning to England if I were you, sir. Pesky cold out it is. Bad for the health. Try the gum, won't you? I'll let myself out.'

And he was gone.

'Stupid little man,' Lewis muttered. 'Ought to stick with his prostitutes and interstate bookies.'

'Word seems to travel fast in Washington,' Appleby said. 'Perhaps this Bureau can be of help.'

'Believe me, Sir Adrian, those fellows are not the ones you want on your side. They couldn't detect a flea on a dog. All flash and no substance. It's all about climbing, getting their precious Bureau more prominence. It may seem unprofessional for me to mention it, but it needs to be said.'

Agent Niel had left a bad feeling in the room; Fitzgerald understood now just how silly had been their grand scheme at the National Theater, how spurious their thoughts of handling the affair quietly.

Inspector Lewis dispelled the atmosphere somewhat by becoming quite practical: arrangements were made for an all night watch to be set up at Poplars. Five men would be on duty outside, five inside.

'We'll see Wilson in the morning,' Fitzgerald said. 'We're scheduled for eleven. Then this whole thing will be over.'

Lewis nodded. 'No going out, Sir Adrian. Not without a couple of my men at your side. Understood?'

Appleby nodded glumly, ready for a refill of his cognac.

'I'll be here first thing in the morning,' Lewis went on. 'We'll arrange for a safe route to the White House. And home safe after that.'

Catherine wanted to put the events of tonight out of her mind; wanted to forget that evil looking figure at the door who made her feel so vulnerable. There would be no sleep for a long time, she knew, her body was full of adrenaline, her heart still pounding violently in her chest.

What a world, she thought. A terrible world we're tolerating, where families are enslaved in tenements, where wild men roam the streets hunting down loveable old men like Uncle Adrian.

She began to feel a helplessness overcoming her and set her jaw against it. Tomorrow I'll work; I'll photograph the slums and thus begin my own Jacob Riis documentation of Washington. In my own way, I'll battle against the darkness overcoming the world.

She felt better after making this decision; she would take control of her life once again. She got up from bed, wrapped a dressing gown around her shoulders, turned the small lamp on at her writing table by the window, and recorded some of the events of the day in her green, leather-covered journal. The mere act of writing soothed her nerves. Finished, she climbed back into bed.

Soon afterward Edward came into the room, quietly changing into his pajamas, considerately leaving the lights off as he did so. This simple gesture touched her profoundly. He slipped under the covers on his side of the massive four-poster, and reached out to pat her shoulder as he did every night when he thought she was sleeping. A tender gesture as she lay there night after night feigning the regular deep breaths of sleep so as to avoid physical intimacy.

But tonight she took his hand in hers, surprising him, pulling him to her.

'Hold me,' she whispered as he slid expectantly over to her side under the covers. 'Hold me tight.'

SIX

Next morning, Max went out at first light and found both a neighborhood drugstore and haberdasher's open; bought a razor and scissors in the one and some clothes in the other. On his way back to the hotel, he purchased a morning paper from a boy in a red-checked mackinaw who'd just appeared on the icy street.

Back in his room, standing in front of the cracked mirror, Max worked for fifteen minutes, carefully trimming and shaving, until tufts of reddish brown hair lay curled around his boots.

Looking at himself in the mirror now, he was startled at the transformation. The face that grinned at him in the reflection was no longer the gaunt wounded soldier he had grown accustomed to. Instead, with his face clean-shaven and his hair close-cropped, Max looked much younger, vital.

He then changed into the clothes he had purchased at the haberdasher's: baggy green corduroys, new and stiff; a blue roll-top sweater; brown leather jacket; and a tweed cap.

Only now did he allow himself to sit down on the bed and look through the morning paper. The front page was covered with war news and a story about Wilson's new hard line vis-à-vis Germany. Max flipped through the pages hurriedly until he found a small article on page seven: 'Violence at the National' was the headline. He read the article eagerly.

Prominent politician and diplomat Edward Fitzgerald was apparently the target of a lone assassin at last night's Belgian Relief Concert at the New National Theater.

Fitzgerald, accompanied by his wife Catherine, née Devereaux, was set upon in his private box during the performance by a man with a revolver who had earlier set a small bomb in the third-floor corridor.

The assailant, described as a Caucasian male, forty, is

about five feet ten inches in height and of normal body
build, with brown hair and reddish-brown beard. When
last seen, he was wearing a blue overcoat and fedora.
The Metropolitan Police would appreciate the help of the
public in tracing anyone fitting this description. An artist's
rendering will be available for later editions . . .

Max went quickly through the rest of the article, concentrating
on particulars about Fitzgerald. He must be the tall white-
haired one, Max thought. And the screaming woman from last
night was clearly his wife.

There's no mention of Appleby, Max noted. Nor of the
nationality of the assassin; no conjecture that I'm German.
Which means they're playing that part down for some reason.
Maybe they don't want the public to know that they risked
innocent lives laying a trap for me. And failed.

But whatever the reason, Max finally decided, it means I
still have a chance to kill Appleby before he gets to Wilson.
He did not question his good luck, but immediately set about
making plans for a new attempt.

Cleaning up his hair from the floor, he wrapped it in the
newspaper and stuffed this in the wastebasket. He left his old
clothes hanging in the closet.

I'll be long gone by the time the police trace me to this
hotel, he thought. There's nothing they can learn from my
clothes: no incriminating labels or laundry slips. He took
off the sweater momentarily, strapped on the shoulder
holster, and then put the sweater back on over it as well as
the new jacket. He picked up the tweed cap and bent the
bill, working it into a peak the way workingmen wore their
caps in America, then pulled it low over his eyes and left
the room.

Downstairs he waited five minutes, concealed on the bottom
step, for the clerk to leave the desk, then quickly made his
way out of the hotel unseen. They may trace me to the hotel,
he thought as he walked past a Negro throwing gravel from
a bucket onto the icy sidewalk like a farmer sewing seed. But
they won't know what I looked like when I left.

*   *   *

The train hurtled through the Virginia countryside. Woods to both sides were bare of leaves and carpeted in snow. Crows circled overhead, dropping occasionally to peck through the snow-crusted landscape for food.

Such an inelegant bird, Mrs Woodrow Wilson, née Edith Bolling Galt, thought to herself as she sat in the train as it sped through the countryside.

She did not know that there were those in Washington who might use the same expression, the same species, to describe her. The 'big-breasted wood thrush' was one nickname bandied about by the wags in Congress. The 'protective mother hen' another.

Mrs Woodrow Wilson was benignly unaware of such soubriquets: she knew only that, as the president's wife, it was her duty, not only to their union but also to the country, to look after Woody.

Nobody outside our immediate circle knows how really vulnerable he is, she thought, as she took her gaze from the white and brown landscape rushing by outside the train and fixed it on her husband, napping in the window seat of the presidential car, his jaw slack, lightly snoring as he rested his head against the red plush headrest. His hands were clasped across his vest and watch chain. Before napping he had taken his glasses off, laying them on the pile of papers he had been working his way through all morning.

Without the spectacles he looks strangely naked, Mrs Wilson thought. So vulnerable. So easily hurt by critics.

And Washington is full of those these days, she thought. Full of would-be presidents second-guessing Woody. Men like Roosevelt, Cabot Lodge, and Edward Fitzgerald whose jibes in the press sting him, cause him sleepless nights. Men who know better, yet who persist in accusing the president of being disingenuous; who claim he is playing a calculated political game with his anti-war stand; accuse him of jockeying for votes under the guise of his 'too proud to fight' stance.

And Washington is also full of press people and caricaturists who do not flinch from portraying Woody as a bandy-legged intellectual, a naïf as world politician who is leading his country to ruin by his refusal to enter the war. They root out the tiniest scrap of information around which to fabricate one of their lurid stories. Why, they even implied impropriety at our marriage in 1915, less than a year after his first wife's death, she remembered.

There will come a time, she thought with great disgust, finally laying down James's *Portrait of a Lady*, which she could not get into, when public figures will not be safe from the grossest calumny about their personal lives. When the politics of the bedroom will take precedence with the silly public over the politics of statecraft; when the term 'foreign affairs' will automatically imply sex rather than diplomacy.

It's good to be out of Washington, if even for a few days. Colonel House said it's in the seventies in St Petersburg, Florida. That will be lovely, especially after the harsh winter conditions we've been having for the past few days. We can golf daily, she thought. That will be good for Woody considering the Washington links are under several feet of snow.

The president stirred in his sleep, mumbled something incoherent, and then went back into deep slumber.

Yes, she thought, again looking out to the snowy countryside under a low gray sky. We shall have a real vacation in Florida; quite incommunicado. No newspapers, no visitors, no telephone. Only Colonel House and a handful of Secret Service agents know our destination. We shall get right away from the world for a time. It's not a luxury, but a necessity.

Only I know how troubled Woody really is over this war issue, how it tears him apart inside to think of young American boys being sent overseas to kill and be killed in a foreign land. And for what? For national honor? It's too cruel, she thought. Stupid, really.

The world will still be there when we return to Washington on Monday, she thought; with all of its problems and all of its critics. And as Woody says, the capital could stand a period of cooling down its war fervor. The next days will be ones of absolute rest and relaxation, and no one shall disturb that.

She picked up a leather-covered appointment calendar from the seat next to Wilson, opened it to today's date, and using her husband's fountain pen, carefully put a line through the eleven o'clock slot: Fitzgerald and Appleby.

No one shall spoil Woody's rest, she thought, closing the book.

The train suddenly whistled through a small station; faces on the platform blurred past the windows, eyes wide, seeking a glimpse of the president in his special car. He awoke with a jerk at the sound of the whistle, rubbed his eyes, and yawned. He was disorientated at first, then he found his glasses, put them on, and smiled at his wife.

'That was a lovely nap, dear. I was a million miles away. So quiet. So peaceful.'

'There's nothing for it then, but to wait,' Fitzgerald finally said, breaking the silence caused by news of Wilson's departure.

'Confound the man!' Appleby spluttered.

Fitzgerald did not know if he were referring to the assassin or the president.

'You'll just have to stay indoors, Uncle Adrian,' Catherine said. 'Pretend you have a cold. It'll be good for you, you'll see. We'll play whist together like the old days.'

But Appleby would not be cheered up.

We could go to other men in the government, Fitzgerald thought. To the secretary of state, Lansing, or to the vice president, perhaps. But in the end, that's no good. We could talk until we are blue in the face, but without the president speaking directly to Adrian it will be a no go. Wilson as commander-in-chief is the only man who can rally the people at this point, who can make the Congress awaken to the German threat.

Thomas opened the door to the music room. 'Chief Inspector Lewis,' he announced, and the police inspector entered the room, crossing immediately to the fire to warm his hands.

'This is about the coldest February I can remember,' Lewis said. 'The streets are like ice.' He looked at the other three, only now noticing their dampened spirits. 'We've arranged the transport to the White House all safe and secure.'

'That won't be necessary, Chief Inspector,' Fitzgerald said, and quickly explained about the president's unscheduled vacation; the need to wait five more days at least.

'Right, then,' Lewis clapped his beefy hands together, all business.

His manner buoyed Fitzgerald. What's needed now is practicality, he knew, not remorse.

'Let's look at what we have here,' Lewis said. 'There are the usual feelers out for our man. The description is being routed to hotel and innkeepers throughout the district. After all, he's got to be staying somewhere. We've doubled the watch at the German Embassy. Most of their fellows left a week ago Monday after we broke off diplomatic relations, but there's still a skeleton crew there. They should be out by the end of this week. But if this M is among them, we'll bag him. He won't be coming in and out of that building without our knowing it. We're also on to New York, liaising with the bomb squad there. From the description we have at the theater, our fellow's got a healthy accent. Probably not a homegrown boy, then, and he had to come from somewhere. We've had no trace on anyone fitting his description at work in the district before. Maybe New York can give us a lead on him. Not much to go on with the fragments of the bomb, I'm afraid. Our lab fellows have examined the bits of lead tubing, but they're too small to get any ID on. Could be adapted from commercial piping, or they could be produced here special for tube bombs.'

'You mean the Germans actually have bomb factories here in the US?' Catherine asked.

'We suspect so, Mrs Fitzgerald. The number of these devices we discover before detonation would indicate as much. Anthrax culturing laboratories, as well.'

'To kill civilians?' Catherine said, appalled.

'The horses, ma'am. We suspect they get some man inside government stables to infect horses scheduled for shipment to England. Kills the whole lot of them on board the ships.'

'Bloody Huns,' Appleby added.

'I guess they would say that war is war,' Lewis said philosophically.

'Not as gentlemen fight it,' Appleby said with great contempt.

'Gentlemen or no,' Lewis went on, 'our boy's a professional. And he may have more of these bombs at his disposal. Most probably does, in fact. Under the circumstances, it may be best if we removed Sir Adrian to another location. One both unknown and shall we say, more defensible.'

He looked at Fitzgerald now. 'After all, your name was mentioned in the news articles this morning. This M may put two and two together and come poking around here to find Sir Adrian. And the perimeter is just too large here. Until I can requisition more men, I need to narrow the field of play. One well-placed bomb . . .'

Lewis did not finish the statement, but the suggestion was enough to send shivers down Fitzgerald's spine. It was unconscionable that they put Catherine in this sort of danger.

'Yes,' he said. 'I see your point, and I wholeheartedly agree. Do you have any place in mind?'

'As a matter of fact, I do,' Lewis said.

'Make sure there is room service,' Appleby joked.

'Oh, I think this place will suit your tastes, Sir Adrian.'

After lunch Edward went back into conference with Uncle Adrian and Lewis, so Catherine retired to her room for a time, further writing in her journal. Then, ten minutes later, she did not bother the men with adieus. At the hall closet she put on her Persian lamb coat and matching hat she'd purchased in St Petersburg, and selected a pair of kid gloves. They would not be so warm as the lined ones, but she needed mobility to manipulate her lenses.

A policeman on duty at the front door looked rather startled to see her come out, but finally tipped his hat at her when she greeted him. The day was bitterly cold and the sun had long ago retreated behind clouds.

There's still enough light for photography, she thought. Diffuse, but adequate. She did not, in fact, like high full sunlight that washed all modeling out of the pictures.

Guilty feelings arose in her because she was leaving her uncle in the state he was in. But I cannot simply stay here holding Uncle Adrian's hand, she told herself. That would be of no help to him or me.

She had decided on public transport today; there was a streetcar stop not far from Poplars on Massachusetts Avenue. She had no desire to drive on the snowy streets, nor did she want to enlist Thomas as chauffeur, for she had a desperate need to get off on her own for a time.

A half hour later the green Massachusetts Avenue streetcar line deposited her near the Treasury on Pennsylvania Avenue, where she transferred to another car for the Capitol. She felt good being out in the rush and bustle of humanity again; the atmosphere at Poplars was stultifying at times. Out here in the city, at the heart of the political life of the entire country, Catherine felt part of something much bigger than herself. Here were diplomats, congressmen, bureaucrats, workers, shopkeepers, school children, nannies, wives – a cross-section of the world, and this human tapestry never failed to take her outside of herself.

It was after two by the time she had finally taken up position at the alley dwellings where she had been on Monday. Workmen unearthing water lines at the mouth of the alley had built a fire of old timbers and were roasting pork chops on their shovels over the flames. She stopped momentarily to snap three quick candid shots before the men became aware of her and began posing artificially. The smell of roasting pork permeated the air as she entered the alley, leaving behind the busy thoroughfare.

The snow had gone unploughed here and stood in great filthy clumps all about. An occasional pathway had been cut to one of the shacks, but in other places there were only footsteps in the snow to mark the path.

She found the dwelling she was looking for immediately. No path had been cut to it, but there were footprints in the snow. Following the impressions in the snow awkwardly, for the steps were long, she reached the door more or less dry.

Once at the door, however, she did not know how to proceed. It had been her intention to ask the woman if she might photograph her. Catherine had brought money along, as well, in case it took that to convince her. But now on the scene, Catherine felt suddenly cheap. She could not simply pay the woman to photograph her misery, and then run off with her prize photos to develop. She would need to establish trust somehow; to share, however fleetingly, in the life of this woman and her baby.

Then there was the question of available light. Catherine saw now that she had not properly considered that. Surely she would need flash equipment to photograph inside the shack. Even with the door open she doubted there would be enough, for the afternoon light was blocked here by the front buildings.

I'll come back in the morning, she told herself, beginning to back away from the door.

At that very moment it opened, a huge man in shirt sleeves with stubbly face and brown teeth gaping at her.

'What do you want?' he demanded.

'Oh, I'm sorry. I must have the wrong place. I was looking for a woman, and a little child.'

She felt so foolish standing there in her expensive fur coat, trying to catch a glimpse of the woman in back of the man. She heard no baby.

'They're gone.' He looked at her shoulder bag, saw the cameras inside.

'What you doing here? Slumming?'

His manner frightened Catherine, but also challenged her. She was suddenly tired of placating men, of feeling guilty for her actions, of being frightened by male bluster.

'I came to photograph her, if you must know. For a book.'

'A book, is it?' The man laughed. 'You've come to see how the poor live, have you?'

She realized too late that she had underestimated the man: his menace was real, not merely vocal. He grabbed her wrist before she could move away and literally lifted her over the threshold and into his arms. Her hat fell off in back of her.

'Well, I'll show you how we live, miss rich lady,' he hissed in her face as he tried to kiss her. 'I'll even let you photograph me . . . afterwards.'

She was paralyzed by fear for a moment and went limp in his arms, but was finally awakened by his lips on hers, his hands groping her breasts.

'No!' she screamed and bit his lip.

He yelped with pain and threw her onto the sawdust-covered dirt floor, closing the door behind him. A kerosene lamp illuminated the small room and she watched him put the back of his hands to his lips and look at the blood there.

'Why, you bitch! You little bitch. You want to play rough, do you? Is that how you like it?'

Before she could move or think he threw himself on top of her, his legs between hers, his right hand tearing at her stockings, his left holding her down. She struggled under him, screaming for him to stop, but this only seemed to excite him more. Now his hand found her underwear, a finger was digging underneath, touching her skin, and his fetid breath was in her face.

Oh God, this can't be happening, she kept thinking. Not to me. She began to sob and hated herself for such weakness.

The man laughed at her. His eyes were wild and his mouth open as he entered her suddenly with a finger and probed her. He began biting her neck and she cried helplessly.

'No, please.'

Suddenly the man's weight was lifted from her; she vaguely saw another figure over her and heard a hollow plonking sound, and then the big man fell to the floor next to her, blood at his head.

She could not see for her tears; sobs kept coming uncontrollably; she felt she would burst from shame and fear. Another man's face loomed over her. She blinked several times, clearing her eyes.

'It's all right, ma'am,' a voice was saying to her. 'All right.'

She looked up into his eyes and saw a kindness and caring written there, and then, for a moment, fainted.

SEVEN

Catherine had no idea how much time had elapsed. When she came back to her senses he was still there, looking down at her with those seeking, penetrating eyes of his.

She heard regular breathing to her right; looking about quickly she took in the miserable conditions of the shack at one glance. The pig who had tried to violate her was the source of the breathing: he lay unconscious on the earthen floor where he had fallen.

And it all came back to her, the fear and pain. The man's finger entering her. She avoided the eyes of the man who had saved her; her hands went to her skirt front, but it had already been pulled down and straightened.

'Better?' he said.

She nodded.

'Can you walk? We should leave here.'

'I think so.' She sat up, felt dizzy, and allowed herself to be helped up by the man.

'Come,' he said with a smile. 'This is your hat, I believe.'

She put it on and he led her out of the shack, carrying her bag full of cameras. They walked through the snow and back past the workmen to the main thoroughfare. They did not speak as they stepped through the snow; she glanced at him occasionally.

'Thank you,' she finally said.

But he shook her words away. 'The man was a swine.'

'I need to find a taxi. I have to get home.'

He put a guiding hand on her elbow. 'What you really need is a hot cup of something. You've had a nasty shock.'

She was about to counter this, but then just gave in. He seemed a pleasant man and she did still feel lightheaded.

He led her into a warm teashop on Pennsylvania Avenue, neither chic nor rundown, and to a marble-topped table and two bentwood chairs by the condensation-fogged window facing the street. White-globed lamps in the brass chandeliers were turned on against the midday gloom. Catherine unbuttoned her lamb's wool coat once seated and looked at the backward stenciled lettering on the window in front of her, finally deciphering its meaning: 'Murphy's Tea Room'.

Neither spoke for several moments. When the silence was finally broken, it was by Catherine. 'Thank you again for helping me.' She could not bring herself to say 'save'. But in fact he had saved her. She did not want to think about how close she had come to harm.

He still carried her shoulder bag full of cameras and film in his hand; he slung it onto the table now, peering inside it.

'Is this a hobby, or do you sell photographic equipment door to door?'

She laughed at this. The laughter felt good, dispelling the sense of fear her attacker had left her with. 'A bit more than a hobby, I hope,' she said. And then: 'It really was the most wonderful luck, your happening along when you did.'

He laughed low and mirthlessly. 'Actually, it was hardly a matter of luck. I saw you get off the tram on Pennsylvania Avenue and could hardly take my eyes off of you. I was following you into that alley, if you would like to know the truth. Hoping you would drop something so that I could retrieve it and make your acquaintance.'

She pinched her eyebrows at this, and he hurriedly explained, 'Do not worry, miss. I am not that sort of person. Never before have I done such a thing. Neither in my native Johannesburg, nor in any of my travels. I do not know how to explain it, but it was as if I had known you before in a previous time, a previous life . . . Forgive me. I am making no sense.'

This admission gave her a small thrill, but at the same time sent a shiver of fear through her.

The waitress finally came, a rather greasy-haired young brunette in a gray muslin dress and white apron who reminded Catherine of a nurse's helper. He placed the order: two black teas with lemon slices.

'Is that all right with you?' he asked after the girl had left.

'Yes, please.' She felt a bit of a fool, took a deep breath, and tried to calm herself. 'Johannesburg,' she said, deciding for the safety of polite conversation. 'You're South African?'

He cast a wan smile. 'I imagine you hear it in my voice, no?'

'But I am forgetting my manners,' she said, putting a hand across the table to him. 'Fitzgerald is my name. Catherine Fitzgerald.'

He took her hand in his and shook it firmly. 'Voetner,' he replied. 'Maximillian Voetner.' It was always best to keep such basics as one's name as close to the original as possible.

'Are you in business, Mr Voetner?' she asked. 'It sounds as if you travel.'

'Business of a sort,' he said. 'The anti-war sort of business. I'm with the World Peace League. The representative of South Africa to the United States. I've been here for over a year.'

The waitress now delivered the tea on a little silver tray. She made to pour the water in the pot.

'I'll take care of that,' Max said, nodding at the pot. 'Thank you.'

The waitress shrugged. 'As you like.'

Then she left them in peace once again. Catherine looked out the steamy windows at the traffic, both foot and vehicular, for a moment.

'Not here in Washington, that is. New York actually,' Max said while pouring the water slowly into the pot. 'But there's a meeting I need to attend here in Washington.'

He passed a cup to her. 'Will you call the police?' he said.

'Why ever for?'

'The man who attacked you.'

'No. He's a poor ignorant soul. He's already been punished enough by the system.'

'I see you have a social conscience.'

'I try.' And then she sipped from her tea.

They talked for another fifteen minutes, and Catherine was amazed at how free she felt in this stranger's presence. He listened to her, took her opinion as valid, not discounting it out of hand as Edward so often did. It was with a sort of reluctance that she finally decided to leave.

'I am grateful to you for helping me, but I really should be going now. Edward will be worried.'

She stood, and he did, as well.

'Will I see you again?' he asked. 'I know it is terribly forward of me. But perhaps for a cup of tea sometime.'

'I don't think that would be a good idea.'

He said nothing, giving only a bow of the head as if to say, 'As you wish'.

She held out a hand to him; he took it softly in his for a moment.

'Thank you again for the rescue. It was nice meeting you. I wish you all the best.'

She turned and walked out of the tearoom as quickly as her trembling legs would carry her. Outside, a Pennsylvania Avenue streetcar clanged its bell angrily at a horse cart plodding along the tracks. The cold stung her cheeks. She kept walking west on Pennsylvania Avenue toward the streetcar stop, in a vague way hoping that Mr Voetner would follow her, would press an invitation to tea.

She turned abruptly, but he was not following her. A large florid-faced man in a brown overcoat and a bowler hat almost walked into her as she turned; she ignored his apologies.

Max watched her from a doorway down the street. He understood what her turning around meant: she was hoping I would follow.

Good. He might be able to put that emotion to use. For now he settled with perusing the green leather notebook he had taken from Mrs Fitzgerald's bag while she lay unconscious in the miserable alley shack.

Several pages were full of notations about what appeared to be shutter speeds and lens openings, calculations for photography. But flipping through the pages, he came across a section that appeared to be more private thoughts. He quickly skimmed these, finding allusions to the events last night at the National Theater. The last entry, made today, proved most interesting.

Poor Uncle Adrian. They are moving him today to a safer location than the Poplars. A hotel of all places. I am sure he will tax the room service staff.

So the old fool is not at the Fitzgerald house any longer. A valuable piece of information. One that made his machinations this morning worthwhile.

After leaving the hotel this morning, Max had gone to the nearby City Post Office next to Union Station – joined to it actually by a covered and elevated breezeway for mail transport – and looked up Fitzgerald's number and address in the telephone room. Then he had taken up position at Catherine's home. Police were everywhere; not a chance of gaining entrance even if he had known for sure that Appleby was in there.

At a little after twelve he had seen a fur-coated form appear at the bottom of the drive to the grounds surrounding Fitzgerald's estate. He had been playing tourist again, attempting to keep watch on the house without attracting police attention, and had just about come to the end of that ruse. He had been grateful to see the figure appear, recognizing the woman immediately as the screaming face from the theater the previous night. He had followed her, taking the second wagon of her streetcar when she had gotten on, transferring as she did, and getting off finally near the Capitol. He was not sure exactly what he would do. Kidnap her and propose to trade her for her uncle? Far too melodramatic. But perhaps he could use her somehow, he thought.

He had continued to follow at a discrete distance as she had ventured into the alley dwelling; had heard muffled screams after the fellow closed the door. He hesitated for a moment, unsure what to do. But at the sound of a second scream, he burst through the door and tore the animal off the woman, bashing his head as he did so with a skillet from the primitive stove.

Max watched now as Catherine Fitzgerald climbed aboard a streetcar down the street. Odd. When that man was attacking her, Max had felt a wild frenzy of jealousy, of protectiveness. Emotions he had not experienced for many years. Not since the death of his lover, Erika, before the war. The senseless death – shot by a madman in the course of a robbery – that had sent Max wandering for years, leaving Munich and his painting behind, blindly searching for forgetfulness.

What are you searching for, my Max? the woman in Paris had asked him. *Is it something you will find by moving?* The woman in Arles had told him he had a sensual mouth. Another in Tangiers said there was a lost-boy look to his face that made her want to tuck him under her ample arm and protect him. Which he'd allowed her to do for several months, until setting off on his travels once more.

It always surprised him that women would be attracted to him; he felt in no way attractive. But he took their kindnesses, accepted the small gifts of their bodies and hospitality. For a while.

Perhaps I can use this woman, he thought. She has already supplied invaluable information: that her uncle is in hiding in a Washington hotel and that he has not yet met with Wilson. Indeed, cannot meet with the president until Monday.

Luck is with me, he thought. It should be easy enough to trace the hotel: simply follow the white-haired Fitzgerald to and from his home.

Max stepped out of the shadows of the doorway as Catherine's streetcar pulled away.

At 30th and N Street in Georgetown the cab pulled to a stop. Max paid and got out. His address was two blocks from here, but he was being cautious, alert. With Wilson gone, he had time to make plans; he would also need new lodgings.

It was the sort of neighborhood that Max liked. With its tumbledown houses, mixture of taverns and shops on every street, and the bustle of students from the nearby university, the area reminded Max of Schwabing in Munich; of his own student days.

He felt suddenly as if he had come full circle in his life.

The World Peace League house was mid-block between O and P Street on 31st Street, a three-story stucco structure from the Federal period. Here and there the stucco was chipped away, revealing lovely warm red bricks beneath, the original facade. There was a half-basement and dormer windows on the attic space, a fine Georgian door – its white paint flecking – surmounted by a fanlight, and windows three abreast on the first two floors whose green shutters were badly in need of paint.

A tall bare linden tree grew out of the patterned brick walk in front of the house, reaching almost to the peak of one of the dormers, providing a natural fire escape. Most likely there would be an enormous garden in back, he thought; tumble-down and overgrown, judging by the condition of the front facade.

As Max mounted the eight concrete steps to the front door, he began planning what he would say. His cover as a repre-sentative of the league would come in handy here. He knew that the Washington chapter ran this rooming house in addition to club rooms and lending library, and that its proprietor, one Annie McBride, was a woman known for her outspokenness and lack of curiosity about guests.

He knocked at the door and waited patiently. No answer came, but he could hear voices within, and finally he let himself in.

The entrance hall was empty; beyond an arched partition the stairs led up to rooms on the second floor. He heard voices coming from the room to his right and saw a large woman of almost sixty dressed in a baggy shawl-collared cardigan and long wool skirt seated there at a table. Her gray hair was worn in a bun bristling with two pencils, and her cheeks were red and venous. She was talking to a passionate young Russian, obviously a recent émigré, about the possibility of revolution in his home country.

'If it happens, I shall return,' he was saying as Max entered the room.

The lady looked the young fellow up and down with an appraising eye and said, 'You should be there making it happen, is what I think.'

She winked at Max when she noticed him. 'What do you say? You think Sergei belongs in Petersburg or here?'

Max shrugged. 'Long ago I gave up such advice. Only Sergei can know that. What will happen will happen.'

'A fatalist,' she said merrily, rubbing her hands together.

Meanwhile Sergei beat a hasty retreat to a corner chair where he took up reading an English edition of Marx's *Das Kapital*.

'Lots of textbook revolutionaries about,' she said. 'Maybe

you're right. Maybe what is intended to happen will happen with or without our intervention.'

The library, the former dining room of the house, was a small chilly room with a bay window.

'I'm Annie McBride,' she said, getting up and shaking Max's hand with a firm grip.

'Voetner,' he said. 'Maximillian Voetner, representative of the Union of South Africa to the league. I need a room for a few days.'

'You're welcome here, Mr Voetner. Even if you are a fatalist.'

Max could see his breath as he spoke. 'Such a philosophy does not rule out direct action. Neither does it prescribe it.'

She sighed. 'If my John had thought that way, he might be with us today.'

She sat again, a sadness coming over her. 'My son, you see. Died ten years ago this very day. He was a union organizer, a Wobbly, in the Virginia coalfields. There was an accident, they said. A cave-in while John was on an inspection tour. A handy accident for the company, as it turned out. It broke the union, did John's death. Ten years ago today.'

She looked up at Max again quite suddenly, a film of moisture in her eyes. 'It's a bit of a coincidence you coming here today, Mr Voetner. You see, you're a dead ringer for John. That is, if you had twenty more pounds and a few more inches of hair. John was very particular about his hair. Brushed it fifty strokes each night. His one bit of vanity. I used to tease him about it.'

She looked down at the table, cutting her eyes from Max. The young Russian left, giving them both a curt nod of his head. Mrs McBride did not even notice his departure. They were now alone in the chill precincts of the tiny library.

So I remind her of her son, he thought. That makes things easier.

She looked him up and down a moment, her sadness turning to sudden shrewdness as she sat up straight in her chair.

'You know, Mr Voetner, you seem a pleasant fellow. And there is something about you that reminds me of my son, that's true. But you really should wear a bulkier jacket if you are going to carry a weapon. It bulges unseemly like under your left arm.

And I ask myself, what does a fellow who says he is representing the Union of South Africa at the World Peace League need a gun for? And, being a British dominion still, I wonder also why the Union of South Africa would be sending a Boer – by the sound of your accent – instead of a good Oxford-educated boyo. And I decide that maybe he is not being altogether straight-forward with me. I decide that maybe he is in Washington for some entirely different reason than meeting other Peace League members or doing research in the Library of Congress. Am I right?'

'You may be,' he said, beginning now to think that he had grossly misjudged the cunning of Mrs McBride, feeling the sweat break out on the back of his neck. *Will I need to kill her? Is she a threat? What will I do with the body?*

She paused for a moment, searching his face. Finally: 'I am a great believer in faces, Mr Voetner, or whatever your name is. And I like yours: I see a kind of purity in it, as well as pain. Not for you the happy, easy life, I think. And that's like my John, too. None of the simple pleasures of hearth and home for men like you. Are you out to do mischief, Mr Voetner?'

'No.' He said it simply, honestly. There was no need for subterfuge with this question. 'I'm out to prevent mischief on a grand scale.'

He did not want to kill her, but knew he would if he had to. There were many things he did not want to do, but would in order to complete this mission.

'But then –' he spread his hands in a shrug – 'I can't expect you to believe that.'

'Oh, yes you can. And I do. Provisionally.'

Max thanked her. He was, with one part of his mind, quite unable to believe his good luck; with the other, suspicious of her still. Yet there are times when you have to play the odds, he told himself; when you have to gamble on a person. This is one such time. He felt his body begin to relax.

'And I think I might have one of John's old jackets for you, as well,' she said. 'Something a wee bit bulkier. He had need of the extra roominess, like you.'

*   *   *

They sat at dinner in formal attire, the eight-foot expanse of
the rosewood dining table separating them. Sèvres china and
Lobmeyr crystal delimited their place settings; off-white
candles burning in the silver candelabras.

Mrs Greer, the cook, had excelled herself, Fitzgerald
thought. She'd prepared a delicious consommé. Thomas, in
white gloves, was taking the soup tureen away and glanced
reprovingly at Catherine for not eating hers.

Catherine's eyes went to the candelabra on the table,
following the candles' flames as they danced in the draft of
air created by Thomas's departure.

'You seem particularly introspective tonight, dear,' Fitzgerald
said, now they were alone again. 'Any reason?'

She looked up at him with a gaze clearly distant. 'I'm sorry.
What were you saying?'

'Introspective. Speculating upon something. You're being
awfully secretive about your photo session today. Whatever
are you working on? Portraits of Washington's monuments?'

Her mouth formed a sardonic grin as she answered, 'Yes,
Edward. Washington's monuments. It should be an interesting
series.'

Her expression bore the same sort of ironic grin that Bateson,
his history master at Groton used to wear when he, Fitzgerald,
would ask a particularly naive or thick question vis-à-vis global
politics and political motivation. She's hiding something from
me, he knew. It's unlike Catherine to play this sort of game;
ergo it must be important. It must be something she needs to
keep to herself. She'll share it with me when and if she's
ready. 'In the fullness of time,' as Bateson was so fond of
saying, rubbing the bridge of his nose where his glasses rested,
as he did so. Fitzgerald inwardly shrugged at the memory.

'Actually,' she went on, smiling at him now, 'I was thinking
of poor Uncle Adrian.'

Fitzgerald nodded. This is as difficult on Catherine as it is
on us all, he thought, putting on a jovial air. 'Poor Uncle
Adrian, my foot. The man's in the lap of luxury. A suite of
rooms on the top floor of one of Washington's finest hostelries;
handmaids, in the guise of police detectives, at his beck and
call round the clock; caviar upon request. Why, the old boy's

got it made. When I left him, he was already impressing one of the detectives with tall tales of his mission to Baghdad in '88.'

'He must be frightened beyond belief.'

'Yes,' Fitzgerald said, putting aside the merry facade. 'He is that, as well. But Adrian's a resourceful fellow. And he's been in worse situations than this, I can assure you.'

'He has? Why haven't I ever heard of them?'

'Well, government business, you know. He cannot very well go spreading it about.'

'Telling his niece would hardly be considered spreading it about, would it?'

'I'm sorry. I didn't mean to imply—'

Thomas entered with the saddle of lamb and mint sauce, catching the last words as he did so. Then they had to sit through Thomas's slow and laborious cutting of the lamb and serving it, and all the while Fitzgerald was trying to determine what was bothering Catherine. It seemed much more than simple concern for her uncle. Like a child, he felt her concern: when Catherine was sad, so was he.

I take so many of my moods from her, he suddenly realized.

It seemed to Fitzgerald that Thomas was deliberately taking longer than required, but when finally he had served the meat and departed Fitzgerald went back to the matter at hand.

'What is it, Catherine? Please tell me.'

She lay down her silver and faced him with a determined chin across the length of the table.

She looks damned lovely in candle light, Fitzgerald thought.

'All right,' she said emphatically. 'I'll tell you what's bothering me. Why is it you haven't told me what this is all about? Why is it I have no idea what Uncle Adrian wants to talk to President Wilson about? Why is it I can be trusted to risk my life for him, yet not trusted enough to be told for what purpose?'

Fitzgerald looked at her with infinite fondness and compassion. She's right, he thought. Absolutely right. 'I apologize, dear. Truly I do. There is no excuse, other than that we were trying to protect you.'

'Protect me!'

Thomas poked his head in the door. 'Did you call, Miss?'

'No, Thomas,' Fitzgerald answered angrily.

Thomas's eyes went to Catherine and she nodded for him to be off.

'Yes,' Fitzgerald continued, 'a rather outmoded idea in the twentieth century, I'm sure. But neither of us wanted you to be overly concerned. You must forgive us; both Adrian and I are products of another century, I'm afraid. Of a time when ladies were hothouse species, to be kept in blissful ignorance of such male domains as politics and finance. This is not an excuse, but an explanation.'

'But you don't want an orchid sitting across from you at dinner, do you, Edward? Nor in bed next to you?'

The last comment took them both aback momentarily; Catherine flushed after the words escaped her mouth, as if she had not intended them.

'No, I do not,' Fitzgerald said finally, feeling that they were on the threshold of real honesty with one another for the first time in their marriage. The thought both thrilled and frightened him.

'Well, then, why don't we begin by you telling me exactly what Uncle Adrian is up to? I promise I won't swoon.'

And so he did; he told her about the Zimmermann telegram and the desperate need to mobilize the country for war against Germany before she conquered the Allies and was able to encircle America.

Catherine listened patiently, not interrupting, and when finally she asked a question, it went right to the heart of the matter, Fitzgerald noticed.

'Is it for real? The telegram, I mean?'

'I'm not so sure that matters, actually. The important thing is that Wilson receives it from Adrian, one Englishman whom he trusts. That will give it cachet enough. That will seal the fate of the anti-war parties.'

'But my God, Edward. If the telegram isn't genuine, then it would all be a lie, a mere pretext.'

He began to wonder about his decision for forthrightness. I should have foreseen such a reaction, he thought: that of someone unaccustomed to the uglier side of politics. He began to back off on his statement.

'It's genuine. Of that I'm sure.' Though he was not at all.

'But how did they ever get their hands on it?'

'I'm afraid I can't tell you that, Catherine. If it were simply on my head, I would. But Adrian has strictly forbidden me to discuss that with anyone, even you.'

She sat rigidly in her chair. 'Fine. So much for trust, then.'

'I am sorry.'

'You needn't be. I'm such a delicate little creature, such an ant brain, that such things would go right over my head, anyway. It must be my female inadequacy that makes the whole affair seem tawdry and deceitful. Uncle Adrian has come to America to scare the president into going to war with Germany because of some ridiculous telegram that the German foreign minister purportedly sent to Mexico, enlisting that country's aid against the US in case of war. We're supposed to believe that it's genuine in spite of not knowing how the British got their hands on such a compromising bit of diplomacy. And moreover, on the strength of this mythical scrap of paper, we're to send thousands of American boys over to France and Belgium to die in the mud.'

'I had no idea you felt so strongly, Catherine. No one likes war, but there may be no way to avoid this one. We may be able to put it off for a few years, but not avoid it.'

'Is that what the diplomats say? But then diplomats never fight in wars, do they?'

The comment stung him, being a former diplomat.

'I'm sorry, Edward. I know you're not being cavalier about this. I've watched you deliberate and agonize over this for almost three years. You honestly believe that war is inevitable. And so did I, for a time. I even thought it was a glorious event at first. A nineteenth century cavalry charge, sabers drawn. I'm not so sure, anymore. This is the age of mechanized war; of tanks not horses. There's nothing glorious about war, nothing romantic.'

He had never heard her speak so eloquently before; had not, more is the pity, realized her capable of it. Though she disagreed with him, he was proud of her; proud as a father might be of a precocious child announcing its independence in matters of the intellect.

'I could not agree with you more,' he said. 'And perhaps, by fighting this hideous war, the entire world will come to its senses. Perhaps we shall all see the futility of war, now that it's stripped of any vestige of romance. The trenches are the metaphor for this war, not crimson trousers and black plumes blowing in the morning breeze.'

'Yet meanwhile you're willing to enlist America into this global insanity.'

'For our country's ultimate good, yes. What is right and just cannot always be defended by logic or reason.'

'Well, I thank you for at least telling me about this telegram. I understand now why an assassin would be out to kill Adrian. He might very well be the most important target in the world at this moment.'

They ate for a time in silence; the lamb had long since cooled off. Neither of them had much of an appetite.

We were so close to another kind of honesty with each other, Fitzgerald thought regretfully as they got up to leave the dining room for brandy in the music room. Catherine's comment about him not wanting a hothouse plant in bed had hit home; it had opened doors, however, that were immediately closed when the conversation returned to things political. Damn politics, he thought.

Try as he might, there was no retrieving the intimacy so close to being established over dinner. It seemed their comments had driven them further apart rather than closer together.

Catherine took up reading an article in the latest *Scribner's* magazine, and Edward worked on the page proofs for his book, so that he did not have time to worry about Adrian and the assassin, nor about Catherine and her new-found independence and distance from him.

They retired early that night; Catherine was asleep by the time Fitzgerald came to bed.

EIGHT

By eight a.m. on Thursday Max had set up watch at Poplars, having borrowed Mrs McBride's electric car to enable him to follow anybody leaving the house. Keeping an eye on the Fitzgerald house was an easier affair now that the police had gone. No reason for them at Poplars any longer, he thought.

At eleven thirty Fitzgerald came out the drive at the wheel of a long Cadillac. Max followed, keeping a half block behind him as Fitzgerald drove east on Massachusetts Avenue; there was no problem keeping up with the big car in town, especially with the snowy condition of the roads.

If he goes out of town with it I'm lost, he knew. There's no way I can keep up with his twelve-cylinders on the open roads; not in this electric car.

But Max's luck held. Fitzgerald went through Lafayette Square and past the Treasury Building onto Pennsylvania Avenue and then pulled to a stop at the corner of Fourteenth Street and Pennsylvania Avenue. Max parked a half block away and stayed in the car, watching Fitzgerald through his rear-view mirror as he got out of his car and crossed the street to enter a tall corner building.

'New Willard Hotel', the sign said over the pillared entrance.

A little more than an hour later, Fitzgerald re-emerged from the hotel, crossed the street once more to his car, started it and then drove off, checking over his shoulder as he did so. The Cadillac passed Max's parked car, shifting into second.

Max got out of his car, a smile on his face. He surveyed the tall building down the street from him: twelve stories, he counted, newish in construction, though it aped French Renaissance in style, with a row of two-story Doric columns in front, and a cupola along with mansard roofs on the top floor. It was a massive structure, he saw as he walked toward it. Quite the largest building around, filling the entire block

along 14th Street to F Street, and fronting half a block of
Pennsylvania Avenue, as well. There was a steady stream
of people going in and out of the place, and two liveried
doormen stood at the front entrance.

Max stayed on the south side of the avenue, across from
the entrance, as he strolled idly along, looking in store windows
and examining the hotel across the street in their reflection.

Ten minutes of such surreptitious watching told him the place
was bristling with police: two at each corner of the building
on Pennsylvania Avenue, another pair at the door itself.
Plainclothes, all of them, but unmistakably police. How many
more inside? This was confirmation and challenge, all in one.
Police presence means it's fairly certain that Appleby is here,
he knew. But it also means that it will be extremely difficult
to get to him.

Max knew that this would take time. He had agreed to get
Mrs McBride's car back to her this afternoon. It seemed absurd,
he knew, in light of what he was planning that he should be
concerned with this triviality. Yet he had no desire to implicate
the woman in this, and if he were caught in her car, she would
be. The car had served its purpose, anyway. It could not go
fast enough to be a getaway vehicle. So he returned it to
Georgetown, taking a streetcar back to his watch post later
that afternoon.

He kept watch on the front of the hotel for a couple of
hours, careful not to draw attention to himself as he did so.
He was looking for patterns, schedules, something to give him
a framework upon which to build a plan of action. The police
in front never budged; there were no relief officers during this
time; no regular patrolling of the block. Just sitting tight, they
were.

I would, too, if it were my job to protect Appleby. No sense
in advertising your presence; no need for displays of strength:
all the cards are in their hands.

He looked up to the ornate top floor of the hotel. Suites are
up there, he figured. That's where they'll be keeping Appleby:
top floor, officers in the corridor and inside his rooms. They'll
sit there and wait me out; sit there until President Wilson
returns.

I'll torch the place, he thought. Set fires throughout the building, wait for Appleby to come scurrying out in his night-shirt, and then shoot him down.

Max finally rejected the idea of arson simply because it was too difficult to accomplish; to light such an enormous structure successfully would demand that he had access to the entire building. If I can gain access to the building, I don't need to set it on fire. I'll simply go to Appleby's room and kill him. And that is what gave him the idea of watching the employee entrance to the back of the building on F Street.

The day was already drawing in by the time he changed his watch post to the north side of F Street, opposite the back entrance to the New Willard. Max only saw one man back here who looked to be police, and he was at the corner, back-up for the other men at the main entrance. He wasn't needed, for the hotel had its own security man at the employee entrance, he soon discovered.

A metal awning covered the stairs going down to a half-basement at the northwest corner of the rear of the building. After watching the building for a time, he crossed the street to the hotel side to examine these stairs more closely, and then he saw the hotel guard seated at a desk just inside the door to the half-basement. Over the door was a sign: 'Employees Only'.

Max crossed back to the other side of the street and went into a cafe facing the hotel. It was a simple, bare bones sort of place with a counter and wooden stools, and separate tables scattered about on a wooden plank floor. There was the smell of chili in the place and Max ordered a large bowl, taking a table by the window. It was well after lunch and too early for dinner: no other diners were in the place. The cook was drinking a cup of coffee at the counter, his white apron front smeared with cooking stains. Max ate the chili without tasting it; a plan was taking shape in his mind. He was beginning to see how he might get to Sir Adrian Appleby right under the noses of the men who were guarding him. The rest of the afternoon he spent drinking cup after cup of coffee, and keeping watch on the rear of the hotel from his window seat.

At five thirty several young men emerged up the steps from

the employee entrance, playfully throwing punches at one another and laughing loudly as men fresh off work would. Max quickly left coins on the table for the chili, coffee, and tip, then began following one of the young men, roughly his own size, who happened to be heading west, away from the officer at the corner.

Max caught up to him a block away from the New Willard.

'Excuse me,' he said coming alongside the young man. He was barely more than a boy, Max now saw. 'I saw you come from the hotel back there.'

The kid was chewing gum and his breath smelled of mint as he looked smugly at Max. 'What's it to you?'

'My cousin, you see. He works there. Do you work at the hotel?'

'Yeah.' Suspicion manifested itself on the kid's face with wrinkled brows, pinched eyes.

Reassure him quickly or you'll lose him, Max told himself. 'I am so sorry, but I am new to America, from Switzerland. My cousin works in the kitchen at the hotel. He tells me to meet him at the employee entrance at five. I wait, but he does not come.'

'Well, that's too bad, Fritz. But I don't work in no kitchen, see. I'm a bellhop. No chopping onions for me.'

Max tried to look impressed. 'You are a bellhop? But where is your uniform?'

'We leave them in our lockers.' He looked suddenly peeved with himself that he had answered the question so automatically.

The kid was about to move off, but Max blustered on. 'This is quite the coincidence,' he said brightly. 'I, too was a *portier* in one of the finest hotels in Zurich. But we had the necessity of wearing our uniforms to and from work.'

'Well, this ain't Zurich, pal. This is America and they give us our very own lockers in a changing room.' He said this with haughty pride.

'Imagine,' Max said reverently, 'one's own locker. America surely is the land of opportunity.'

The kid warmed to him at this comment. 'That's right. Opportunity. I only been at the Willard two months and already

I'm assistant to the head bellhop. Hell, in no time at all, I'll
be a head myself. Look, I gotta be going.'

'Imagine, only two months and they give you your very
own locker.'

'No,' the kid said impatiently. He was eager to leave, but
also eager to set this silly foreigner straight. 'They give you
the locker straight out, see? Me, they must've heard of my
special talents, 'cause I get number sixty-nine.'

The kid nudged Max in the ribs. 'Get it? Sixty-nine.'

Max smiled dumbly, playing the ignorant foreigner to the
hilt. 'It is an honor, this sixty-nine?'

'Ah, Christ. I give up. See you later, Fritz. I gotta run. Say,
what's the name of that cousin of yours? I'll look him up
some day. A buddy in the kitchen is a good buddy to have.'

'Max,' he told the kid. 'My cousin's name is Max. An
assistant chef.'

'OK. I'll remember that. Maybe he had to work overtime
today, huh? There's a crowd of people at the hotel today:
twelfth floor is completely booked out.'

'I shall wait,' Max said.

'Yeah,' the kid said, hurrying off. 'You do that, Fritz.'

Max waited for the kid to turn off of F Street out of sight,
and then he went back toward the hotel.

Now to get past the hotel guard, he thought. That should
be the easiest part of the plan.

Two hours later, however, frozen to the bone, he was not
so sure. He pulled the lapels up on the tweed jacket Mrs
McBride had given him, and eyed the back of the hotel. He
had taken up watch from a front porch across the street from
the hotel, elevated enough so that he had an angle of view
down into the half-basement entrance, hidden enough so that
the policeman on the corner of F and Fourteenth did not see
him, and deserted enough – it was a law office and the tenants
had gone home at five – so as not to attract attention to himself.
Yet for all the advantages of his watch post, it did him no
good in getting the guard to leave his post for a moment.

The man's inhuman, Max thought as he watched the hotel
guard sit there like a statue, unmoving, eyes fixed on the

entrance. At one point he thought that perhaps, like Appleby at the theater the other night – as he had learned from Catherine Fitzgerald's journal – this guard too was a mannequin, a plaster of Paris model. Then the man suddenly scratched his head, giving Max a start.

Max examined his options: I could simply go around to the front entrance. There is a steady stream of foot traffic in and out of the main foyer there. He remembered something in the guidebook he'd purchased, in fact, about the main hall of the New Willard being called the 'Peacock Way' for all the internationals who promenaded about, using it like a piazza in an Italian village. I should have no trouble simply getting into the building that way, though my clothes leave something to be desired in elegance. Yet there would still be the difficulty of finding my way to the employees' changing rooms.

Alternately, I could simply go up to this automaton-like guard, stick my gun in his face and tie him up somewhere. This option, however, would be sure to cause problems for me when his absence is noted.

Or . . .

At this very moment the guard arose, stretching, and hitching up his pants with his elbows. He turned and disappeared down the hall, and Max just as rapidly headed down the steps from the stoop where he was hidden and crossed the street directly to the entrance. The policeman on the corner had his back turned away from him, so Max had a clear path to the entrance. As he reached the awning over the steps leading down, he could see the guard was still gone. He hurried down the steps, careful to keep his shoes from clicking on the cement, opened the glass door at the bottom of the steps, and entered the warm hallway. No one was about; he heard water running behind a door just to the left of the guard's desk and hurried down the hall past it, hoping the changing room the kid had mentioned was down here close to the entrance as he had expected, otherwise he was going to be stuck out in the hall when the guard returned, and then option two, tying up the guard, would take over. He felt for his gun: it was under the jacket and sweater, not the most easily accessible weapon. From behind him he heard the sound of a flushing toilet, and he hurried on down the hall, finally coming to a door on his right marked 'Changing Room'. He ducked into this just as the lavatory door opened down the hall in back of him.

Inside were rows and rows of lockers with wooden benches in front of them, a concrete floor and walls, and electric lights hanging from exposed girders. He saw no one about; it was between shifts. He soon found locker sixty-nine and swore out loud. There was a padlock on it.

Max looked quickly about the room for something to force the lock with; there was a broom cupboard in one corner of the room and he opened its metal door and was looking at the arsenal of cleaning supplies within, when the door to the changing room opened and a young bellhop stopped abruptly at the door.

'Jesus, you scared me there for a minute,' the bellhop said, coming in and closing the door in back of him. 'I wasn't expecting anybody down here between shifts. I guess you gotta clean when you can, huh?'

Max had said nothing, his mind busy calculating what he should do. The young bellhop had done the thinking for him, he realized, placing him as a janitor because he was at the broom closet. Max picked out a three-foot-wide push broom and closed the door, saying nothing. He began sweeping, keeping his head to the floor.

'Had to have a smoke,' the kid was saying as he rolled a cigarette deftly with one hand. 'Bastards won't let you smoke up there.' He jerked his head toward the ceiling. 'Say, you're a talkative guy, aren't you? You new here?'

What Max had seen in the broom closet had given him a new plan, and he continued sweeping until the kid took his attention away from him, and then Max swept his dust into a far corner, his back turned to the bellboy for a moment, a hand maneuvering in his clothes. He then began sweeping back toward the bellhop, who was now luxuriating on a bench under a swirling blue veil of smoke. When Max reached him, he dropped the broom and held his gun to the bellhop's head.

'No sound. I don't want to have to kill you.'

The young man's eyes bulged in terror at the gun; the cigarette had reached the end and now burned his fingers, but he dropped it without a yelp, looking sideways with eyes only at the gun.

'I got no money, mister.'

'I don't want money. I want your clothes.'

The bellhop's eyes narrowed.

Max prodded his temple with the barrel.

'Quickly. Off with them. Now!'

Max's eyes darted to the entrance; this will have to be fast, he thought. If someone else comes in now, this will turn into a real fiesta.

The young man stood and Max pushed him toward the broom closet where he reluctantly took off his clothes, leaving them in a heap at his feet.

He's at least a size bigger than me, Max thought, but I'll have to live with that. Just suck up your chest, he told himself. He realized he was enjoying this; he felt a shiver of exhilaration pass through him. From the closet he took the coiled bit of rope he had earlier seen and quickly trussed the bellhop up like a prize bird, then stuffed his handkerchief in his mouth and bound that as well. He helped the young man hop into the closet, and before closing the door he rested the barrel of the gun against his nose.

'I'm going to be right outside this door while my friend upstairs goes about his work in the rooms. I hear one peep out of you, and I come back in here and kill you. Understand? One move, one jiggle at this door and you are a dead bellhop.'

The young man's eyes broadened like a horse's before the jump, and Max knew he was terrified enough to believe anything, even the robbery story Max had alluded to. He would stay put quietly for a good long time.

Long enough for me to do what I need to do, at any rate, he thought.

Max shut the door to the closet, propping the broom against the latch to lock him in, and then quickly shed his own clothes and put on the bellhop's uniform.

A good thing he is a size larger, Max thought, looking at himself in a mirror at one end of the room. The bulk hides the gun under my jacket.

He took his things out of his own clothes and stuck them

into the pockets of the uniform: money, leather notepad, extra bullets, and pocket watch. His own clothes he bundled and tossed on top of a row of lockers against the wall, planning to gather them again after killing Appleby.

He pulled the rimless bellhop hat down low over his forehead and left the changing room. The guard looked his way as he came into the hallway.

'Coming down for a smoke again, Bill?' he called out.

Max waved at him, turning his face away quickly, and made for the service stairs at the end of the corridor. These took him up a flight to the kitchens where black-suited waiters and cooks in tall white hats were scurrying about, steam and rich aromas filled the air, and silver serving dishes were hoisted onto wide shoulders and carried through swinging doors to the dining room. Max heard the chatter of voices and clinking of silverware in a sort of Doppler effect as the doors swung open and closed.

He left the kitchen precincts by another door to the main hall. It was promenade hour out here, it seemed: elegantly dressed ladies and men strolled about casually; two Italian men upon meeting one another embraced; a plumed lady seated on a divan was having her hand kissed by an officer in dress khakis; a small white-haired gentleman smoked an enormous cigar as he spoke with two other men, punching the air emphatically with the Havana as he emphasized some point he was making.

Part of the staff, Max blended perfectly.

'Boy! Oh, boy!'

It took Max a moment to realize the little white-haired man with the cigar was calling him. Max held his chin to his chest in the best military fashion as he walked over to the group.

'I need an ashtray. Would you be good enough?'

The man's cigar ash was a good inch long. Max retreated with a nod of the head, found a cut crystal ashtray on a low table by a seating arrangement of plush chairs and a potted palm, and brought it back to the man. He was handed a nickel by one of the cronies gathered around the tiny man, and he put it in his pocket with a smile.

The main desk was unoccupied except for a clerk dressed

in a tuxedo, looking very self-important. Max gazed around
the foyer, avoiding eye contact with any of the guests who
might decide they needed his services. Located to the right of
the entrance was a small closet-like room, with a half window:
a phone room. He walked busily toward it, ignoring at one
point a shouted 'Boy!'

'Well, I never,' the person's voice trailed off in back of him
as he passed by.

The small phone room was unoccupied and he went in,
looking in the district directory for the Willard's number. He
found it quickly: Main 3100. Then he picked up the receiver,
got an outside line, and gave the number to the operator,
watching the clerk at the main desk through the window as
the number rang. The clerk looked at the phone to his left
with pique, for he was busy serving a customer now.

The clerk picked up the phone on the fifth ring. 'Good
evening, New Willard Hotel. May I help you?'

Make it brief, Max told himself. Give him no chance to
affirm or deny Appleby's presence. 'A message for Sir Adrian
Appleby—'

'Let me check the register, sir.'

Max went on as the man looked into the ledger-sized book
of guests. 'It's most urgent that he receive this immediately.
President Wilson will see him on Monday evening. Have you
got that?' He watched the man now scramble for pencil and
paper.

He doesn't even hear my accent, Max thought. Not once
the word president was uttered.

The man wrote quickly; Max could hear the scratch of
pencil to paper over the phone.

'Yes,' the clerk said. 'Is that all?'

Max hung up, watching the clerk mouth more words into
the speaking horn. Finally the desk clerk hung the earpiece
up, saying some fawning words to the guest who was waiting
impatiently, turned and placed the message in a pigeonhole
behind him to the far right of the matrix of boxes.

One of the last room numbers in the hotel, Max calculated.
So the kid on the street was right: the large party that took
over the entire twelfth floor will be Appleby and friends.

He left the phone room and walked to the desk. The clerk spotted him and waved him over to the desk, then turned from the guest once again to fetch the message out of its pigeonhole and hand it to him. All the while he never looked at Max's face, only his uniform.

'Take this at once to room 1220. The presidential suite. No loitering about, mind you. It's urgent.'

Then turning back to the customer who was beginning to fume, he said, 'So sorry. Matters of state, you know.'

So easy, Max thought as he headed toward the elevator. Like a duck shoot. So much for security.

Near the elevators he spotted two more policemen, but they too only looked at his uniform; looked past it really. He was not the bearded assassin they were looking for.

As he waited for an elevator to arrive, he noticed a newly installed fire alarm next to the elevator buttons. It was a glass cage with a tiny hammer on top; you broke the glass with the hammer and pulled down the lever inside to activate the electric alarm. He had been hoping there would be such a device.

Once on the upper floors I'll search out another such alarm, activate it, wait for Appleby and his entourage to rush out of their hiding places like rats, and then shoot him down. There will be a crush of people; if I'm lucky, the confusion will be my shield. It worked once before, at the theater. No reason it won't work again. And this time I'm certain that Appleby is here.

The descending elevator finally arrived, and its door opened slowly, revealing the occupants inside, one of whom was Edward Fitzgerald.

Fitzgerald brushed past the bellhop, who looked rather shocked, with mouth agape. Fitzgerald was to meet Catherine for dinner at Rausher's, and he was late already.

Poor old Adrian, Fitzgerald thought as he moved on through the main hall. He would insist on further consultations about his telegram at this late date. Something was bothering Fitzgerald, however, apart from the lateness of his departure from the hotel.

After all, Catherine will be all right at Rausher's for a few moments: the Ashbys will be there as well, eager to discuss the Art League raffle next month, the ostensible reason for the dinner. No, it's not that.

He looked back at the elevators: the bellhop was only now entering, along with several other passengers. Strange, Fitzgerald thought. Fellow must be forty if he is a day. You'd think the Willard could afford a bit of a younger sort to lug suitcases about.

He was out the front doors of the hotel and the chill of the evening hit him. He pulled the lapels of the camel hair coat more tightly around his tuxedo. People hurried by to catch taxis or streetcars; no one loitered about the cold streets, save for a couple of plainclothesmen Fitzgerald recognized and nodded to.

As he looked about for a taxi, he felt a tapping at his arm. 'Nice to see you here, sir.'

He looked to his left and there was Agent Niel, hatless, his mouth working on a wad of gum.

'Hello,' Fitzgerald said. 'I didn't realize you people were involved in this watch.'

Niel grinned impishly. 'Giving an extra hand. It never hurts.'

'No. I'm sure it doesn't. And I'm sure Chief Inspector Lewis would appreciate your help, if he knew of it.'

At which Niel had the good grace to laugh. 'The inspector's a bit rough with his tongue, if you know what I mean. He's a good policeman, just a little territorial. He doesn't have to be. There are more than enough criminals to go around . . . And how is Sir Appleby?'

'Sir Adrian is fine, Mr Niel. Worried, but in good health.'

'The president will be back by Monday, I understand. This isn't such a bad spot to spend a few days.'

'How did you know about that?'

Niel tapped his nose. 'Not much I don't know about in this town.'

Fitzgerald wanted to be away, but still there were no taxis to be seen.

'Like the police, aren't they?' Niel said, following Fitzgerald's searching eyes.

'What's that?' Fitzgerald said.

'Taxis. Always there when you don't need them; never there when you do.'

He laughed at his little joke; Fitzgerald smiled wanly at him. 'To be sure.'

'I just thought it might be a good idea if I took up watch here, as well. Training, you see. The Bureau believes in training, not like the Metropolitan Police where they hire you on if you're over six foot and like sports. I know what to look for, know the ruses a fellow like ours might attempt.'

Fitzgerald debated walking to Rausher's, but that would take a good half hour.

'These fellows,' Niel nodded toward the two plainclothesmen as examples of all the regular police. 'I bet they're still looking for a bearded man in a heavy coat. But that's not our man, is it? By now he's shaven the beard, if it were actually real in the first place, and gotten rid of the blue coat. He'll be dressed in workingman's clothes, most likely. Maybe even a stolen uniform. Who knows? But it takes training to figure out those sort of tricks.'

Suddenly Fitzgerald's attention was diverted from his search for a taxi. 'What did you say just then?'

'Training,' Niel said, looking at Fitzgerald strangely, popping the gum as he did so.

'No. About the assassin.'

'He'll be clean-shaven by now. And in some disguise, most likely. Somebody you'd never look twice at.'

'Oh my God!' Fitzgerald suddenly realized what had been bothering him since leaving the hotel. The bellhop. The one waiting for the elevator. The way he looked; the surprise and almost fright in his eyes as I walked out of the elevator. And then turning to watch me even as he entered the elevator.

'He had a limp,' Fitzgerald said out loud.

'Who?'

'The bellhop I passed in the lobby. I think it was him. The right size, the right frame. Clean-shaven and too old for a junior bellhop.'

But Niel was no longer listening. He was running to the entrance.

NINE

I t didn't work. Hell, he thought. He pulled the lever again inside the broken glass. Nothing.

Some fool neglected to wire the fire alarms properly, Max thought. Or maybe they're simply cosmetic. Maybe they're meant to give the residents a good night's sleep, but don't work at all.

Max had no time to try and figure it out, however. The bellhop in the basement cannot be expected to keep quiet all night. As soon as he's discovered, the game is up.

Max was on the eleventh floor; he looked quickly up and down the hall. He saw what he was looking for midway down the hall, to the left. A tray with a champagne bucket on it, and an obviously empty bottle of champagne in it, sat on the floor outside a room, waiting to be picked up by the maid service. Max moved quickly down the hall, retrieved the tray and folded a white serviette from the tray over the bottle to hide the fact that it had been opened. He pulled out the gun from his shoulder holster now, making sure that no one was in the hall to see, and hid it under the serviette as well. The ice was still somewhat fresh in the bucket.

He took the service stairs up to the twelfth floor. Arriving there, Max found a guard was on duty just outside the door to the stairs, his arms folded and all but asleep as he stood, resting against the wall. He gave a jump when Max came out of the door to the stairs, and reached into his coat for a gun.

Max smiled at him, showing him the tray, and the man relaxed, felt through the napkin for the chill of the ice bucket, and then let Max pass.

'I could do with a drop of that myself,' the policeman said as Max went to the door of 1220.

Max smiled again at him over his shoulder, saying nothing; not wanting to risk having his accent heard. At the door he squared his shoulder, balancing the tray in his left hand.

He knocked with two sharp raps, then put his right hand under the serviette, gripping the gun. He heard steps coming toward the door.

Fitzgerald watched the arrow going round the semicircle of floor levels inside the elevator. It seemed like they would never get there. Eight, nine, ten.

Niel pulled out his gun, double-checking the chambers to make sure they were full of ammunition. Dressed in evening clothes, Fitzgerald had not bothered to take his gun along.

Eleven.

Come on. Come on, he thought. Maybe I was wrong. I hope so. Maybe this is all a farce.

Twelve.

The doors hesitated for a moment; Niel grabbed them and began pulling them apart, and finally they released.

Maybe I'm simply being paranoid, Fitzgerald was thinking. Then he saw the bellhop down the hall at Appleby's room.

'Stop him!' he shouted, running toward the man.

The bellhop turned at the shout, saw Fitzgerald running toward him, and the door to Appleby's suite opened at that very moment. The bellhop had drawn a gun from under a napkin, Fitzgerald now saw, but he continued running for the man, heedless of the danger to himself.

Chief Inspector Lewis stood in the doorway, looking from the bellhop to Fitzgerald racing down the hall, confused for one fraction of a moment.

In back of Fitzgerald, Niel had taken up a shooting position, the pistol held in a triangle from his body.

'Get down, Fitzgerald,' he yelled. 'I've got him in my sights.'

The guard by the service stairs had finally reacted and was drawing his gun. Suddenly the bellhop dropped the tray and put his gun to Lewis's head, pulling the burly policeman from the doorway.

'One move from any of you and I shoot him,' he said.

He put Lewis in front of him, his own back to the wall now. Fitzgerald stopped dead in his tracks. He had no doubt the man meant business.

'He's no good to you dead,' Fitzgerald said, looking the

assassin straight in the eye. 'Let him go. There's no way out for you.'

The assassin jabbed the barrel into Lewis's temple. 'You don't want to die, do you?' he said into Lewis's ear.

Fitzgerald could hear the accent and his entire body began trembling, but he would not show his fear.

'Tell them you don't want to die,' he said with a snarl.

'I think he'll kill me if you boys make a move,' Lewis finally said.

The assassin began inching along the wall with Lewis still in front of him. 'You,' he hissed at the guard by the door to the service stairs. 'Get over here with the others. Away from the door.'

The policeman stood his ground for a moment and the assassin cocked the pistol.

'Do as he says,' Lewis said, sweat breaking out on his forehead now.

Fitzgerald was closest to the man; he was thinking desperately of how he could get to him without risking Lewis's life.

'No heroics,' the assassin said, as if reading Fitzgerald's mind. 'He will live if you all act sensibly. Anybody follows me down the stairs, and this one will be the first to die.'

He had been inching along the wall all the time he spoke and now was at the door to the service stairs.

At least we kept him from Adrian, Fitzgerald was telling himself. This time.

The assassin fixed Fitzgerald with a steely gaze for a moment, one hand in back of him to open the door.

'I could have killed you now,' the man said to Fitzgerald. 'Remember that. I allow you to live for the time being.'

With that, he pulled Lewis through the door with him, slammed it shut and was gone.

They all stood transfixed for a moment. Niel by the elevator was the first to react.

'Get on the phone to the front desk,' he commanded as he raced toward the door to the stairs. 'Tell them to bar the front exit. We've got the bastard.'

He reached the door and the policeman on duty grabbed his arm.

'He said he'd shoot the chief if you follow.'

Niel put his gun to the man's forehead. 'And I'll shoot you right now if you don't do as I say. Get on the phone, tell them to stop him at the front doors. Move, man!'

The policeman did as he was told and Fitzgerald followed Niel as he made to open the door. It was blocked by something, and they both put their shoulders to it and opened it slowly.

Chief Inspector Lewis lay unconscious, blocking the door. Niel jumped over him, on the chase, but Fitzgerald paused momentarily to make sure Lewis was still alive. There was a nasty bruise on his head where the German had obviously struck him with his pistol, but his breathing and pulse were regular. Fitzgerald then searched in Lewis's coat for his police revolver and took it with him as he raced down the stairs, following the sound of clattering feet on the stairs beneath him.

Max left the service stairs at the ninth floor, knowing that there would be a greeting party waiting for him at the bottom. He closed the door to the stairs securely in back of him.

They won't find which floor I've gone out onto for a time, he thought. I'll have enough of a lead by then to lose them. Let's just hope that my memory of the outside of the building is accurate; let's just hope that the fire escape is on this end of the building and that it begins on the ninth floor.

The rooms he was looking for were on the west side of the building. Any would do, he knew. He picked 913 and rapped on the door, looking over his shoulder all the while at the door to the stairs. They could be coming at any moment, he knew. Answer the door, damn you. Whoever you are.

No sounds came from inside, so he quickly went to the next door, 915, and knocked.

A sleepy voice sounded from inside. 'Who is it?' A woman.

'Service, madam. A telegram for you. They say it's an emergency.' Come on. Hurry, will you.

'Oh,' came the startled and worried voice from inside. 'Just a moment.'

He thought he heard footsteps on the stairs. Finally the door opened in front of him, and a woman in a white linen robe stood in the doorway, her hair piled on top of her head in a bun.

'Is it from Howard?' Anxiety played on her lined middle-aged face.

Max immediately pushed her inside, putting his hand to her mouth, letting her see the gun in his hand.

'Say nothing, and I won't harm you.'

He heard a door open, then slam shut in the corridor; voices called to one another: 'Did you see which way he went?'

'Not a sign.'

'I'm sure he came out on this floor.'

The voices died away as the steps went to the other end of the floor.

The lady was trembling against him; his hand over her mouth was wet from tears. He realized how terrified she was, wanted to solace her, and took his hand from her mouth for a moment.

'Please don't hurt me,' she whimpered.

'I won't. I promise,' he said. 'You must only remain quiet.'

'What do you want with me? Why have you come in here with a gun?'

She was working herself into hysterics, but before he could either soothe her or cover her mouth again, she screamed as loudly as she could, a cry that would wake the entire floor.

Max dashed to the window, flung it open, and started crawling out onto the fire escape leading from it, his left hand on the sill for balance. A sudden searing pain shot through this hand and up his arm: the woman had stabbed him to the windowsill with a letter opener and then ran to her door screaming for help.

Max pulled the blade out of the back of his hand. Blood flowed freely from the wound and it began throbbing imme-diately. He had no time to worry about that at the moment, but took off down the fire escape, moving as fast as his game leg would allow.

He heard voices from above him, and then felt the thud of weight applied to the metal ladder and knew that they were just behind him. He looked up once as he neared the fifth floor and saw two forms in the darkness above him, a couple of floors away.

Keep your body inside the metal framework of the fire

escape, he ordered himself. Don't give them a clear shot at you.

His lungs felt as if they were bursting and the wound to his hand was still bleeding, sapping his strength. It sounded as if the heavy pounding of steps above was gaining on him; he could not be sure.

Ridiculous, he thought. Here I go again: the assassin being pursued, and I have not yet even seen Appleby after two attempts on his life.

How could this attempt have gone wrong? But he knew. It was that damn Fitzgerald spotting me at the elevators. Yet how did he know it was me? My beard is gone and I'm in disguise. I should have killed Fitzgerald back there in the hallway. I had the opportunity. But I couldn't; not in cold blood and him unarmed. I should kill him now, though. If he is one of those chasing me, I should lay a trap and finish him.

He felt tired of running like some coward or failed villain, but he knew that he could not waste time on personal vendettas: if he were going to escape, he had to keep moving; stay one step ahead of the pursuers; give them no chance to cordon off the entire block.

He got lucky at the third floor, finding an open window and diving into it, and then discovering that the room was unoccupied.

He made for the door automatically, then thought a moment. He glanced at the window, its curtain fluttering in the breeze. I should at least close the window; put them off my trail.

Then he had a better plan. He threw the door to the room open, then went to the wardrobe and got into it, closing its door firmly in back of him. A strong smell of mothballs hit his nostrils, making him nauseous. Soon came the sounds of his pursuers on the fire escape.

'An open window,' a voice called out. 'He's gone inside again.'

Max could hear the men climb through the window and jump onto the floor. They were only feet away from him now. He gripped his gun tightly in his right hand and tried to still his breath to a shallow intake.

'Quickly,' the same voice said. 'Out in the hall! He'll be making for the stairs again.'

Max waited tensely as he heard one of them move off into the hall, but he thought that the second was still there. A creak of a floorboard sounded near the wardrobe where he was hiding.

He suspects I'm in here, Max thought. He's going to open the door now. Bathed in sweat, he could hear his heart pounding so loudly in his chest that he was sure the man in the room could hear it, as well.

'Come on, will you,' a voice cried out from the hall. 'They're after him on the service stairs.'

The man next to the wardrobe now raced out of the room and Max let out a long sigh, closing his eyes reverently in thanks as he did so. He waited a thirty count before opening the wardrobe door and climbing out into the room. There was no sound of his pursuers in the corridor. He got back out onto the fire escape and resumed his downward journey, checking over the side to see no one was waiting for him below.

Only now did he examine his hand, as he continued to take the metal stairs as quickly as possible. It was covered in blood; the brown pants of the bellhop uniform were stained down the side. He quickly thrust the injured hand into the jacket pocket to hide the blood. His whole arm throbbed painfully; he felt light-headed, out of breath.

At the bottom of the fire escape he tucked his gun into his waist to avoid drawing attention to himself, jumped down the few feet to the alley and then made his way cautiously out to the street.

Obviously the police had had no time to cordon off the entire hotel, Max discovered once he stuck his head around the corner at the mouth of the alley. There was only the lone policeman at the corner of F and 14th Street as before, and he did not seem particularly agitated.

Thank God for small favors, he thought as he waited for the man to turn his back to him before going out onto the sidewalk. At first he made himself walk slowly, jauntily almost. It took a giant will to manage this, for his one instinct now was to run. There were no shouts for him to stop; no steps chasing behind him, yet he feared there would be at any moment. He continued walking naturally for a full block, reaching the Treasury, and only then did he allow himself to look back over his shoulder.

The policeman at the corner was not pursuing him, only staring quizzically after him.

As Max turned north at the Treasury he began running for all he was worth, racing like a track star, his lungs near bursting. He did not let up his crazy pace until he had gone past Lafayette Square. Just beyond there he caught a Georgetown line streetcar, out of breath and about ready to pass out, but free.

They were gathered in Appleby's suite of rooms, somber as guests at a teetotaler's wake. Fitzgerald stood at the tall windows, looking out at Pennsylvania Avenue far below. Normally he would be cheered by such a bird's-eye view of the capital's premier street: tonight it depressed him to see the people, cars, and streetcars so small looking, so insignificant. It made him feel helpless.

I could be dead right now, Fitzgerald thought. Running blindly toward the killer as I did; it's a wonder he did not simply shoot me.

Fitzgerald looked back in at the sitting room: Adrian was sprawled out on the divan like a swooning diva, a bag of ice to his head. Anyone would think he was the one to get bashed over the head, Fitzgerald thought. But Lewis had won that dubious honor, and sat meditatively in an armchair, a white bandage wrapped around his head. Moments before, the house doctor had warned ominously of concussion, and Lewis had chased him off with a bear growl and a threat to concuss certain parts of said doctor's anatomy if he did not leave that instant.

Niel stood by the door, a fresh stick of gum in his mouth, grinning at all and sundry.

A baseball pitcher, Fitzgerald thought. That is what the fellow reminds me of, with his gum and interminable grin.

'A complete fiasco, Edward,' Appleby sighed. 'That's what this is. Twice the fellow has been within our grips, and twice he has escaped.'

'I'm sure Scotland Yard would do better, Sir Adrian,' Lewis said.

Fitzgerald looked at him with surprise: he had not known irony was among Lewis's repertoire.

A police sergeant knocked and entered the room out of breath. 'Sorry to interrupt, sir,' he said. 'But Philips says to tell you that our man posted around back got a look at the suspect fleeing the premises.'

'What?' Lewis was on his feet, but had to grip the back of the chair to steady himself. 'How do you mean "got a look"? Didn't he give pursuit?'

The sergeant shrugged. 'That's what Philips says, sir. I guess no one expected a bellboy. He said the fellow walked away from the hotel calm as you please, right up to the Treasury building. Turned north on Pennsylvania, but that's the last we saw of him.'

'Brilliant,' Appleby said from his divan. 'Bloody brilliant.'

Again the feeling of helplessness swept over Fitzgerald. Here we are in an elegant Regency suite in the finest hotel in Washington with armed police littering the premises, and the German is able to breach our defenses with impunity.

'If I might intrude?' Agent Niel said from the door.

'Niel, I'm in no mood for this, understand?' Lewis growled at him. 'None of these inter-agency rivalries tonight. This is my turf; I'll take care of it.'

'Sorry,' Niel said with a bright smile. 'But it looks like it may be Bureau turf now, as well. You see we've been doing a fair bit of digging on our own with our meager resources. We have, however, turned up an interesting homicide.'

'I'm not interested in your damn homicides,' Lewis fumed.

'Oh, you will be in this one.'

'Let the man speak,' Appleby said, sitting up now and placing the ice bag on the low rosewood table in front of the divan. A crystal vase overflowing with yellow roses sat in the middle of the table.

'As I was saying,' Niel continued. 'Last Monday night there was a reported homicide at the medical laboratory of the Georgetown University not far from here. A night guard obviously surprised a burglar as he was leaving by the fire escape . . .'

Fitzgerald's ears pricked up at the mention of this similar means of escape.

'A rather professional job of killing, it seems. Cartilage to the brain; a clean kill, as the professionals would say. The burglar seemed to have broken into the chemical pantry. Officials at the laboratory say the only thing apparently missing is a vial of sulfuric acid.'

'The active ingredient for these German tube bombs,' Fitzgerald said, beginning to see the connection.

'Wild speculation,' Lewis said.

'Not so wild,' Niel said. 'A young assistant who conducts tours at the laboratory remembers a gentleman that very day who showed great interest in the chemical pantry and who also seemed quite interested in the view out an alley window. Our fellow probably unlatched the window while acting as if he was gazing out of it. This curious visitor matches the description of the assassin from the New National Theater.'

'Fine,' Lewis said, sitting down again, a pained expression on his face. 'So we know where M got his sulfuric acid. We know he made a bomb; we know he's a careful planner and ruthless as hell. But what does this have to do with you?'

'The night watchman,' Niel grinned at him. 'He was a government employee. That makes this federal business, you see?'

'I for one am happy to have you aboard,' Appleby said. 'It looks as though we could use all the help we can get.'

'Glad to hear that, Sir Appleby.'

Fitzgerald watched Adrian wince at the appellation and wondered if he would finally correct the agent, for Niel had obviously not picked up on his own attempts to do so. He felt himself agreeing with Adrian, however; perhaps they could use fresh help, and then he felt disloyal to Chief Inspector Lewis for having thought this.

Yet he had to remind himself that this was not a popularity contest they were running; it was a life and death struggle with a cunning and powerful enemy. It really was a wonder that no one had been killed tonight. The fellow had obviously been hiding in the wardrobe in that room on the third floor, waiting for them to charge on past.

I had the instinctive feel for him, Fitzgerald thought. I sensed he was in there. But Niel called; the police had mistaken a real bellhop for the killer, and we were all diverted just long enough for the man to make his escape via the fire escape once again.

But if I had opened the door to that wardrobe, he thought. What then? Who would have walked away alive?

'I'm sure there is plenty of room for both services on this case,' Niel was saying. 'And I strongly disagree, Sir Appleby—'

'Sir Adrian,' Appleby finally said, correcting Niel.

'Oh.'

Niel did not look embarrassed or put out, Fitzgerald noted. He simply noted the correction and filed it away for later use.

'I strongly disagree that this was a fiasco,' Niel went on. 'We didn't catch our man, but we're coming closer to him. We know a lot more about him than ever before. We know, for instance, what he looks like under his beard. We have several face-to-face encounters with him and can put together a new sketch of him to circulate. We also know that he has an injured left hand. The lady on the ninth floor may have a tendency to exaggeration, but the trail of blood the fellow left behind corroborates what she says. He's got a nasty wound there, may even have to see a doctor. And we know he left on foot. No getaway car waiting for him in the immediate vicinity. Maybe we'll be lucky; maybe the fool is taking public transport and somebody will remember him and his destination.'

From his chair Lewis groaned at this suggestion.

'All right,' Niel allowed. 'I said maybe we would get lucky. I don't bank on it, though.' He clapped his hands together suddenly, rubbing palms. 'It hasn't been a bad night's work, all in all. Though I do hope in future, Mr Fitzgerald, that you'll rein yourself in a bit. I had the killer in my sights until you ran into the field of fire.'

'It was damned brave of you, Edward,' Appleby said. 'I shan't forget it.'

'Brave and rather foolish. You're lucky to be alive,' Niel said, looking at him now rather curiously. 'What he said up there to you, that he was letting you live for now. It seemed almost that he knew you, or that he had some personal grudge against you. A rivalry or vendetta? You didn't, by any chance, recognize the man?'

Fitzgerald shook his head. 'I simply assumed that he felt I

had foiled his plans both times: at the theater and here at the hotel. That he was warning me off.'

Niel nodded. 'Interesting. It might be something we can put to use. A special animus for you.'

The room was silent for a time; traffic sounded from out the window, muffled and distant.

'We have work to do, gentlemen,' Niel said. 'The president will not return until Monday and there's no way to contact him, it seems. My boss has been on to the White House, as well, but it's no go. The president needs rest, is the reply we get. The president needs a break from all concerns.' He looked squarely at Appleby. 'It wouldn't do, I imagine, simply to see the vice president or somebody else in government?'

Appleby shook his head slowly and Fitzgerald was quick to explain that they had gone through that option as well, but it came down to the fact that Sir Adrian would need to talk with the president face-to-face eventually. That was the only way his 'business' could be conducted.

Niel shifted his gum from one cheek to the other and clucked his tongue. 'Must be some kind of business. The longer you delay, the more you put your life at risk.'

Appleby sank back down horizontal on the divan at this statement.

There followed another silence broken finally by Niel. 'So, where to now? It looks like we need another lodging for Sir Adrian. Some place right away from Washington, if possible.'

Fitzgerald brightened, pulling himself out of his defeatist thoughts. 'Of course,' he said. 'Why didn't I think of it before? I've got just the place.'

The phone rang then in the room, and Niel went to it. 'Yes?' He listened for a moment. 'Sorry, Mrs Fitzgerald. Yes, he is here.'

'Oh, lord,' Fitzgerald said. 'I completely forgot about Catherine. She must still be waiting for me at the restaurant.'

Max got off the nearly empty tram at Wisconsin Avenue. By now he was in bad pain. He had managed to staunch the flow of blood by pressing hard on the wound, but his entire arm was on fire and he felt almost as weak as he had after being wounded at Ypres. He kept his wounded hand tucked into the pocket of the jacket.

He knew, however, that he had to lead a circuitous route to his lodgings in case anyone could trace him this far, and so he began walking up Wisconsin past a saloon when a group of sailors came stumbling out, drunk and laughing. They saw him lurching along the sidewalk in his bellhop uniform and began teasing him.

'God, I love a man in uniform,' one of them, a huge ungainly man, said.

Another spun him around playfully, and Max tried desperately to keep from falling. He wanted to pull his gun and be rid of them all, but that would be suicidal. If nothing else, it would mean he'd be traced to this vicinity for sure.

'You oughtta trade that in, sonny, for a real uniform,' the big sailor said.

Max said nothing, and hunkered against the wall of the saloon for support.

'Ah, leave the little guy alone,' another sailor finally said. 'He looks like he's got problems enough already.'

'Fucking bellboy,' the big sailor said disgustedly. 'We're getting ready to fight the Germans, and he's humping rich bastards' suitcases around.'

He made to kick at Max, but the other sailors finally pulled him away.

'Come on,' one of them said. 'Let's find some women.'

Max waited for the sailors to be well up the street before proceeding.

They'll love war, he thought. Just let them get in their first sea battle; let them feel the floorboards underneath them rock from incoming shells; let them see their buddies blown to pieces by shrapnel; let them struggle in the freezing waters of the Atlantic with an oil slick all about them, praying it doesn't catch fire.

Oh, war will be a lovely adventure for them, all right.

His anger fueled him, and he was able to weave a crazy-quilt route back to the World Peace League House. The front door was unlocked and he went in, crossed to the stairs and reached the first landing before he passed out.

He had no idea how much time had passed, but it was still

dark outside his window when he awoke. He was in bed, and Annie McBride was sitting in a chair at his side.

'Hello,' she said.

He lifted his left hand; it was bandaged neatly. He was stripped to his underwear lying in clean linen sheets.

'Don't worry. I closed my eyes when undressing you.'

He felt himself smiling weakly. It was an unaccustomed feeling.

'I burned the uniform in the furnace. I don't suppose you'll be needing it again?'

He shook his head, not knowing what to say. 'Thank you,' he finally managed.

She shrugged, making the wooden chair creak as she moved. 'It's a nasty wound.'

He stared at a water stain on the ceiling over the bed, not replying.

'You want to tell me about it?' she finally said.

The water stain reminded him of an early abstract painting he had done, one of the first ever: a circular miasma like the ripples of cause and effect extending from an unintended action.

'You should not be involved,' he said, turning his head to look at her.

She nodded, half-smiling. 'I was wrong the other day,' she said. 'You don't really remind me of my son. That was only sentimental hogwash, remembering his death. John was a softy at heart. He carried a gun, but I don't think he would ever have used it.'

She looked at him closely, and again Max wondered if he could trust her.

'No. Who you really remind me of is myself. It's people like us who need to act to change this world before it imprisons us all in the lock-step of standardization, mechanization and materialism. Before the likes of Ford has us all working like drones on assembly lines and reading the illustrated magazines to see what we should be buying at Sears and Roebuck. John used to complain about the 35,000 men, women and children killed in this country each year in industrial accidents, about the upper classes who were only one percent of the population and controlled half the wealth. He was a great reader of Marx, was my John. I guess the difference between me and him is that I'm more fearful for our souls than our bodies. And the soul of this planet is being ground into the mud of Flanders, isn't it, Mr Voetner? You've been there, haven't you? I saw the scars on your leg when I was putting you into bed. Shrapnel wounds, by the looks of them. And I see the scars in your eyes, as well. Fey Annie.' She chuckled.

'You sound like an anarchist,' he said, attempting a bit of brightness to distance himself.

'Anarchist, Marxist, populist, socialist, pacifist, pragmatist. I'm any kind of "ist" as long as it means change.' She smiled at him. 'Why am I telling you all this? Now you've got your cornered animal look on again. And that's why I'm talking, to take the fear from you. To take it from myself. It's a fearful time, and only action can counteract fear. I figure you're doing the action. I hope you'll be giving as good as you get soon,' she said, nodding at his wounded hand.

'I should leave,' he said. 'They'll be looking for me.'

He did not need to explain to her who 'they' were; she understood.

'I run a respectable house,' she said. 'There's never been any trouble here. About that I've been cautious. I see no reason anyone would come looking for you here.'

'All the same . . .'

'You rest now, Mr Voetner. In the morning we'll talk about it further.'

She put her hands on her knees and got up from the chair with some difficulty.

'Your gun's under the pillow, if you're interested. I put your other things on the mantle over there.' She indicated the tile-lined fireplace opposite the bed, turned to go, and then suddenly looked back at him over her shoulder, a devilish smile on her lips.

'That was some to-do they had at the New National Theater this week, now wasn't it. They say some assassin was after a diplomat.'

Their eyes locked for several moments, and Max read trust and compassion in hers. His entire body suddenly relaxed, melting into the cool sheets, and he was asleep not minutes after she closed the door in back of herself.

'But you could have been killed,' Catherine said, touching her husband's cheek with the back of her hand.

They were sitting up in bed together, and she was extracting details of the latest outrage from Edward with some difficulty. Had she not spoken to her uncle at the hotel, she would never have known how heroic her husband had acted; how impulsively. Edward would not tell her about it.

'Were you awfully frightened?'

He smiled to himself. 'I'm getting rather used to it, actually,' he said. 'Twice in one week and all that.'

'You don't have to play the brave soldier with me, Edward.'

He grinned sheepishly, like a little boy with a secret. 'Niel is right,' Fitzgerald said suddenly.

'How is that?'

'The evening was not a complete failure. We have a very accurate description of the man now.'

'Am I allowed to hear?' she asked with a good deal of sarcasm in her voice.

He arched his eyebrows at her.

'All right,' she said, trying to rid herself of the bitter tone in her voice. 'What does he look like? Are his eyes large and white and does he foam at the mouth?'

'It's hardly a laughing matter.'

'Well, that's how you're treating it, isn't it? Just laugh the danger away. Make a joke about it. Be the brave man.'

He folded his arms over his chest.

'I thought we'd put this argument behind us,' he said.

She suddenly felt rotten for acting this way. Here Edward was, nearly murdered and she was climbing all over him for being his usual closed self. Perhaps now was not the time for confrontation.

'Let's go to sleep, Edward. Close the world right out for the time being.'

TEN

'I say, Edward. This was a damn fine idea.'

They continued walking down the sloping paths of Brantley, the country estate that old Mr Devereaux had settled on Fitzgerald and Catherine as their wedding present.

'Makes one positively want to don a riding costume and take to the hunt.'

Fitzgerald smiled. 'You've never been on a hunter in your life, Adrian.'

'Shh.' Appleby held a forefinger to his lips. 'Our little secret.'

'Besides, I shouldn't care to see this land run over by a flock of humans in hunter pink,' Fitzgerald said. 'I like it much better as it is.'

They stopped at the farthest southern slope of the four-hundred acre spread. To their back, northward, the manor house lay enfolded in a copse of sycamore, its chimneys clearly visible above the trees, its porticoed porch peaking through the bare limbs.

I'll have to trim the trees back soon, Fitzgerald thought, though he detested the idea of cutting the noble old trees.

All about them lay the rolling fields of Brantley's experimental gardens: though bandaged in snow now, underneath everything from roses to rutabagas were cultivated here; one thirty-acre patch was even set aside as a model forest, planted in European pine, a fast-growing variety that some agronomists were claiming to be the fuel source of tomorrow. The general impression was of the rolling bucolic English countryside.

Looking to the south they could just make out the broad gray swath of the Potomac in the distance. On a knoll above the river, Fitzgerald saw a tall sycamore under whose shade he loved to pass lazy summer afternoons.

I'll build a house there some day, he thought. Or have myself buried there. Make it the final resting place of the Fitzgeralds.

To spend eternity above the peaceful waters of the Potomac seemed a fine idea to him.

'It's quite amazing what you've done with this place,' Appleby said, bundling himself deeper into the heavy coat he wore.

A biting breeze was up off the river; the sky overhead was low and gray.

'It was a bit of a mess when we took it over,' he admitted.

Appleby laughed loudly. 'Why else do you think old Devereaux gave it away?'

Fitzgerald continued gazing out on the southward view, ignoring the implicit invitation to get digs in at his father-in-law. He cared not at all for the man, and thought him greedy and mean, but he was, after all, Catherine's father and was due familial loyalty.

It's so like Adrian, he thought, to involve me in a name-calling orgy that he can later, quite subtly, hold over me vis-à-vis Catherine. Some people are born to power, he thought; they are forever maneuvering. Give me these acres to manage, and I'm quite content.

In fact Fitzgerald would gladly give up the sordid world of shadow diplomacy to retire to the country and manage this small estate had Catherine shown any predilection for such a move. He would love to hear children's feet on the main stairs at Brantley, his own children's feet. He longed to walk these fields daily, examining the results of his labors, for the fields had been planted in the old manner, avoiding all use of artificial fertilizers which Fitzgerald believed to be a great danger. From the reading he had done, it seemed inevitable that the use of such substances would ultimately deplete the soil, allowing the fine top soil to simply be blown away. Someone had to hold onto the old agricultural methods so that they could be used again in the future: to such a mission Brantley had been dedicated.

Looking back on it, such a direction for his life seemed quite absurd. From a long line of Boston shippers, Fitzgerald hardly had the soil in his blood. But once seeing Brantley, he had been drawn inexorably to it. Which was a fine sort of irony, really. Old Devereaux had indeed settled the estate on him because it was so run down and mismanaged. The gift had been left-handed; almost an insult. But Fitzgerald had turned the land into a showcase: he had begun reading books on agriculture and horticulture; had hired a small crew of men to do the heavy work while he arranged the layouts of plots and decided on crops. The foreman, Ned Blakely, a farmer from upstate Maryland who had sold off his own farm to developers, had stared dumbly at him when Fitzgerald had announced his intentions of 'going about things naturally here'. The men took it as a bit of a joke that they should have to spread muck on the soil when other farmers round about were using the new chemical fertilizers with such amazing results.

But after the first two seasons, they had changed their minds. Blakely had even become something of a fanatic about the subject of what he called 'organic gardening' after seeing and tasting the yield from test fields sewn both ways.

A flock of winter crows flew overhead, landing on a field not far from them, black against the snow, strutting about like looters, pecking through the hard crust.

'Yes,' Appleby said. 'A little corner of heaven you've created.' His cheeks and nose were bright red from the cold, vapor bubbles appeared as he spoke.

'We should be getting back,' Fitzgerald said.

'Nonsense,' Appleby replied. 'I love the fresh air.'

'It wasn't so much the air I was thinking of.' He looked about them, suddenly remembering why they had come to Brantley in the first place. And perched on this bit of promontory with no cover, they provided marvelous targets.

Appleby took his meaning immediately. 'I'd almost forgotten that world,' he said, as they began walking back to the main house.

Two of Lewis's men had accompanied them on their little walk, but if a sniper should take up position, Fitzgerald thought, there are no police in the world who could stop him.

Suddenly the rolling fields took on a sinister aspect to him, and he hurried along the track.

'Only a few more days,' he said to Appleby, who was puffing along beside him. 'No use pushing our luck. It's inside for you for the duration, I'm afraid.'

Appleby grunted in reply.

Some two hundred yards from the house lay a duck pond in the cleft of two hillocks. In the spring Fitzgerald enjoyed the spectacle of the baby ducks learning to swim alongside their mothers. Now, however, it was frozen solid, the snow cleared away. Pairs of incised curved lines made an ornate, almost Celtic design in the ice. Local boys must have been skating on it recently, he thought, for he allowed the workers' children access to his lands.

Appleby stopped suddenly. 'Now there is a winter sport I love,' he said. 'Have you ice skates?'

The thought of Adrian on skates made Fitzgerald smile. 'I think we have some, yes.'

'Well, when this all over, I propose a skating party.'

'Grand. We'll bring Catherine down for it. She loves a good skate.'

Fitzgerald was happy to see Adrian talking of the future. After the capture of his intended assassin had twice been botched, he had seemed to become fatalistic, pessimistic even. Quite unlike the Adrian whom Fitzgerald knew.

As they neared the house, the dogs came running out to meet them, jumping up quite uncontrollably. Fitzgerald shouted at them, but the truth was he loved being around the animals, loved their obvious excitement at seeing him after long absences, for it meant that they should be taken on proper walks. Fitzgerald had hired a retired couple to look after the place in his absence, and the dogs got only the minimal amount of walking when he was not there. Mr and Mrs Monroe's greatest asset was that they were nearly invisible. Fitzgerald never had the feeling of being overwhelmed by servants here. In fact, they were pretty much on their own in the country: Mrs Monroe managed a bit of cooking, and her husband answered doors if need be, but generally Fitzgerald just looked after himself when in the country. That was the great fun of it for him. Perhaps it's that which keeps Catherine away, he thought as he pushed the big lab, Queenie, down from licking Adrian's face.

Perhaps if she could have her precious Thomas here, she would want to come more often.

They went up the wide arc of steps to the main door, the two policemen following a few yards behind. At the house were more guards, ten in all, and Chief Inspector Lewis promised near a hundred more from the local constabulary and home guards by tonight.

We'll have a regular fortress here, he thought, entering the front door and smelling rich stew smells throughout the house. Mrs Monroe is at her best when Adrian comes around, he knew. She likes to fancy things up for the 'English gentleman'.

Appleby smelled the fragrant aroma, as well, and began rubbing his hands together expectantly. 'What do you say to a large whiskey before lunch, Edward?'

'You're full of sound ideas today,' Fitzgerald said, heading for the drinks table in the paneled living room. Mr Monroe had set a fire in the huge fireplace and the room looked quite baronial.

Yes, it was a good idea to bring Adrian down here. It has cheered his spirits no end, and it's the safest place for miles around. By tonight we'll be like a little island quite cut off from the outside world by a cordon of police. Lewis has already posted men at the main gates and all around the house; the two personal bodyguards also lounged about inside. There's no way that M can get to Adrian here.

Fitzgerald poured out a stiff drink for Adrian, a lighter one for himself. After all, he would have to drive back to town after lunch to an interview with Chief Inspector Lewis.

Outside the bay window he could see blue-uniformed policemen on the grounds trying to keep warm with hands in their pockets and caps pulled low. Usually he disliked seeing people about the place, but not now.

'Here's to long life and prosperity,' Adrian toasted after Fitzgerald handed him his glass.

Max lay propped up in the single bed. He was tired, worn out, his hand throbbed painfully, and he was utterly confused.

The door to his bedroom opened and Mrs McBride bustled in, her hands holding a breakfast tray, a newspaper tucked under her arm.

'Please, Mrs McBride,' he said. 'You embarrass me. I'm no invalid.'

But in fact he partly was. Attempting to get up this morning to use the toilet in the hall, he had almost passed out. His head was dizzy and his body weak from loss of blood. It begged for rest and recuperation.

'You just lie there,' she said, plopping down the tray with a plate full of biscuits and gravy and a steaming mug of coffee. 'A day of rest won't hurt you any. Eat and get your body back in shape. You'll need it.'

He tucked into the biscuits, surprising himself with the appetite he had, and then she placed the newspaper, folded to page three, next to the tray.

He glanced at the headline of a story she indicated.

Outrage at New Willard

He read on hurriedly:

> The New Willard Hotel on Pennsylvania Avenue was the scene of an attempted assassination last evening when an armed assailant, apparently German, set upon the British envoy, Sir Adrian Appleby.
>
> Sir Adrian, in Washington for unspecified reasons, was residing under guard on the hotel's twelfth floor. The assailant, disguised as a bellhop, was at the envoy's door when police, aided by Mr Edward Fitzgerald, an old family friend of Sir Adrian, stopped him. The assailant, taking one of the police, Chief Inspector Hapgood Lewis, as hostage, managed to escape the premises via the fire escape, but sustained a wound to his left hand in the process . . .

Max stopped reading and looked up at Mrs McBride.

'You have been a busy boy,' she said. 'That bellhop uniform you came home in last night was from the New Willard, wasn't it? And that wound is to your left hand. So that's what you're about? Trying to knock off one of those damned meddling British who want to drag us into the war. Well, more power to you, son. I hope you succeed.'

He read on, realizing that there would be a city-wide sweep

going on to apprehend him. It would be impossible to get to
Appleby now. Or I'll surely die trying, he said to himself.
Why go on? Why keep proving yourself and devoting your
life to a country that despises you and your kind?

'I'll just leave you to your breakfast, then,' Mrs McBride
said, and closed the door softly behind her as she left.

He felt tired, exhausted, really. It seemed he had been planning escapes all his life.

The police would be after him with a vengeance now, he
knew. Is there any way they could trace him to here? He
thought of the tram ride home last night: some passenger may
have remembered him. The ashen-faced bellhop in the back
of the car? And then there were those sailors. With any luck
they were too drunk to remember him, or too hung over today
to bother reading the papers. But even with bad luck the police
would only be able to trace him as far as Georgetown, and
that was a sizeable community.

He finished the breakfast, sipping down the last of the coffee,
and leaned back against his pillows, feeling almost human
again.

A day of rest, he thought. Yes, I could surely use that. It
should be safe enough here. As safe as any place in Washington
for a man answering to my description. Mrs McBride is the
only one who knows I'm here, and I know I can trust her now.
Some pacifist, he thought. She's happy enough to have me
kill for peace.

As he drifted off to sleep, a troubling thought stirred him.
He could not put his finger on what exactly it was: something
to do with the bellhop's uniform. But that's all right, he reminded
himself. Mrs McBride said she burned it. That evidence has
been destroyed. Yet there was still something nagging at his
unconscious mind as he fell into a fretting and confused sleep.

Fitzgerald arrived at Metropolitan Police headquarters at one
thirty, returning from Brantley in his Cadillac. He had never
been in a police station before, and was surprised and amazed
at the plethora of activity going on there. Lewis's office was
on the fourth floor, but the bottom floors were, it seemed, a
normal precinct house with uniformed officers standing at a

counter booking several undesirable looking people: an old vagrant in a hole-riddled jacket and greasy cap; a youngish fellow dressed in the sort of flashy suit that Agent Niel sported, his fingers fairly filled with rings, and his left wrist handcuffed to an officer who was talking of 'safe-cracking' to the amused clerk behind the counter; and three rather gaudily dressed women with feathered hats and rouged cheeks.

Rouge in the middle of the day, Fitzgerald noted, as he went to the stairs. Only then did he realize that the three women at the booking desk must be prostitutes, and the thought astounded him. Prostitutes in Paris or London were to be expected, but that they should ply their trade on the streets of Washington was something unexpected for him, and he wondered how many other things about quiet old Washington he did not or would not know.

He took the stairs quickly, and caught Chief Inspector Lewis in his office having a late lunch. A map of the District of Columbia filled one wall, pictures of the current three police commissioners dutifully hung on another, and the standard profile of President Wilson was on the wall in back of his desk. Fitzgerald took all this in quickly, averting his eyes for a moment from Lewis with his cheeks full of sandwich.

'Come in, Fitzgerald. Make yourself at home. Sorry for the mess.'

He got up, taking his hat and coat off the only available chair and throwing them over an oak filing cabinet.

'Got to catch food when you can in this trade,' Lewis said, resuming his chair.

'Please eat,' Fitzgerald said, feeling the interloper. He'd already had his lunch in the quiet comfort of the country.

'Been a devilish morning,' Lewis said between bites. He tossed a newspaper across the desk to Fitzgerald. 'I suppose you've seen that?'

Fitzgerald glanced at the story of the attempted assassination of Appleby.

'No, I haven't. I thought we were keeping this sort of thing out of the press.'

Lewis chewed hard, bit the inside of his mouth and cursed.

Then: 'We were. But somebody leaked it at the Willard. Damn hard to keep this sort of thing from the newshounds for long. And it makes me look a complete fool. The only mention I get is as a hostage to our German friend.'

Lewis certainly looked abashed, Fitzgerald thought. He was not sure but that some of the man's chagrin came from the publication of his first name, which Fitzgerald had never heard before. It had always been Chief Inspector Lewis, as if the title were part of his name.

'The commissioner was on the phone this morning, I can tell you. But you don't want to hear of my problems. What about Sir Adrian? Did you get him neatly ensconced out in the country?'

Fitzgerald nodded. 'Safe as a nun, I should say. Your men have the place well-guarded already. When you bring in the auxiliaries tonight, the place will be like an armed camp. Even if this German agent finds out where Adrian is staying, he'll never be able to get to him. Not by Monday.'

He spoke more sanguinely than he felt. The German, he now knew, was a very resourceful opponent. He seemed to be able to guess their moves even before they made them, as if he had inside knowledge of some kind.

'I'll just be very happy when the president returns and this is all over,' he added.

'Won't we all,' Lewis said effusively. 'And meanwhile, we do have leads.'

He picked up a sheet of foolscap, and read the brief messages there.

'Seems our friend the bellhop was seen riding a Georgetown streetcar last evening at about the right time.'

A sudden knock at the door interrupted them.

'Enter,' Lewis said in an alarmingly loud tone. A sergeant meekly looked in. 'Sir? Sorry to interrupt, sir.'

'What is it?'

'It's about that clothing found in the employee locker room of the Willard last night.'

'Right. What about them?'

The sergeant glanced at Fitzgerald. 'Get on with it, sergeant,' Lewis boomed.

'Yes, sir. The bellboy the German assaulted confirms they were the clothes our man was wearing before he took the bellboy's uniform. The pants and sweater came from a haberdashery shop in northeast Washington, purchased only a few days ago. We got on to that lead, but the shop owner couldn't really remember the customer. We were luckier with the jacket. We managed to trace it through a laundry stub found in one of the pockets. Belongs to one John McBride, deceased. A labor organizer, we discovered. His mother is a known radical and runs this library and boarding house for international pacifists. It seems a likely hiding place for our man. He may have borrowed some of John McBride's clothes.'

'We need a warrant and a dozen men.'

The sergeant smiled sheepishly. 'The warrant's in the works, sir. And we've got fifteen men in the cars already.'

'Good man,' Lewis said. Turning to Fitzgerald, he grinned broadly. 'This could be it. The break we've been waiting for. You want to be in on the kill?'

'I wouldn't miss it for the world,' Fitzgerald said.

ELEVEN

By early afternoon Max was up and dressed. Annie had brought him a charcoal gray suit that John McBride had only worn twice before being killed; the collars of her son's shirts were too big for Max, so he wore a collarless white shirt under the jacket. It was increasingly a bizarre feeling for Max to be dressed in a dead man's clothes, and whatever Annie McBride said to the contrary, it was as if he were more and more expected to take the place of the dead man. She had even mistakenly called him John when she brought lunch.

Max was not up to being a surrogate anything to anybody.

But this will be solved soon, as well, he thought. For he now had a plan. One more night and he'd be gone from this room, from this city, from this country forever.

He heard a knocking at the front door downstairs, and pricked up his ears. Annie McBride finally answered it and he could hear muffled voices. Suddenly he felt on guard once again, laid the sketch down on the small table where he was working, got up and went to his door. She was talking now, but he could not make any sense out of the conversation. Opening his door slowly, he half stepped out into the hall. The voices carried up the stairs to him.

'No,' Annie McBride was saying. 'We don't need any of those here. No call for them.'

'It's a trial offer, ma'am,' a man's voice replied. 'Nothing to lose. We install the units free of charge, and you use them for ten days before deciding. You don't like them, we take them out free of charge. No risk to you. Just let me get a look at your rooms and I can give you an estimate on the spot. All the rooming houses hereabouts are installing them. What do you say?'

'I say you should shove off and stop bothering me. I don't want any of your so-called intercommunications systems. God gave us a healthy pair of lungs for a purpose. To be able to shout up the stairs if need be.'

Max smiled at the comment, his tension slackening. He moved back in the room, closing the door behind him. Below, he heard Annie slam the front door shut in the salesman's face.

Now there's a hard sell, he thought. I'd hate to be the salesman who knocks on the door of this house.

Fitzgerald sat in the idling police car next to Chief Inspector Lewis, watching with his mouth agape as Agent Niel skipped down the steps of Annie McBride's house.

'The silly son of a bitch,' Lewis said, his jaw clenched. 'How the hell did he get onto this?'

Fitzgerald simply shook his head, for it was obvious that the Bureau man had traced the lead before them. This could not be a matter of coincidence.

'I'll carve out the heart of any man in my command who is tipping off the Bureau,' Lewis said.

Niel now noticed their car parked down the street and on the same side as the McBride house. He grinned at them, approached the car, and stuck his hatless head in the back window.

'Fancy you being here, Inspector Lewis.'

Fitzgerald felt Lewis next to him tense as if to attack, then control himself with a heavy sigh.

'What in the name of Jesus were you doing at that house, Niel?'

Niel grinned back at him impishly. 'Let's leave the Lord out of it, inspector. I was merely ascertaining the lay of the land. I was hoping to gain entrance posing as a salesman of intercommunication systems, but the good lady was having none of it. I did, however, see enough from the stoop to figure things out.'

'And just what the hell have you figured out?' Lewis blustered at him.

'The dining room cum library and sitting room are off the hall to the right. Unoccupied. The kitchen is to the left down the entrance hall. The stairs are at the end of the hall. Our man will most likely be above stairs.'

'Our man?'

'Come on, inspector. The German agent. He's been traced here.'

'Listen, Niel. I'm going to ferret out your little informer in the police department if it's the last thing I do. And if you've managed to compromise this raid by your silly melodramatics—'

'Hardly silly,' Niel interrupted. 'And hardly melodramatic, either. Have you got the back garden covered?'

'Of course I have,' Lewis barked at him. 'Do you take me for a fool?'

Niel only smiled in response to this.

Fitzgerald was beginning to have a bad feeling about the raid. Nothing seemed to be going smoothly, he thought. Every step of the way on this hunt for M the unexpected had turned up, the surprise element. And I am damned tired of surprises.

'Shall we be at it, then?' Niel said.

'This is my operation,' Lewis said, shifting in his seat to climb out the back door. He opened the door and uncurled his long frame out of the car; Fitzgerald followed from the other side.

The street was alive with blue-uniformed police. Theirs was the only car in the block; the other police had left theirs in the next streets, out of sight of the McBride house. They were all converging on the dwelling on its side of the street, as well, to avoid detection from the windows above. Fitzgerald saw a pair of uniformed police manning the intersections at either end of the block, their vans turned crosswise in the street as barricades, sealing the street off to traffic.

'If he's in there, we'll get him,' Lewis said, signaling for a sergeant near the McBride door to station men at each corner of the house.

Lewis turned to Fitzgerald. 'You can see it all from here, Mr Fitzgerald. It'll be over in a couple of minutes.'

Fitzgerald understood that he was meant to remain behind at the car like some incompetent civilian whom the professionals did not want getting in the way. He momentarily bristled at this, but kept his tongue, leaning against the car in feigned repose. He and the driver of the car remained behind as Lewis and Niel moved toward the house. The car, left running, was vibrating in rhythm to the rapid beating of his own heart.

*   *   *

'What was strange about him?' Max was saying inside the house. His entire body was alert suddenly, tingling.

'He wasn't a salesman, that's all,' Annie McBride said, still out of breath from negotiating the stairs to Max's bedroom. 'The minute I closed the door on him I knew something was wrong. He was dressed too flashy for a door-to-door salesman. He wasn't carrying a samples case; he didn't even offer me a pamphlet on his product.'

'So he's a rotten salesman.' Yet even as Max said this, he knew he was indulging in false optimism. 'Besides, how could the police have got onto my whereabouts so soon?'

Mrs McBride did not bother listening to his protests. She crossed the room to the window and, standing to one side and slightly lifting the lace curtain, she glanced out at the street below.

'Look at that,' she said.

He went to the other side of the window and looked through a fold in the curtains. 'I don't see anything.'

'Exactly,' she said, letting the edge of the lace flutter back against the window. 'This time of day there should be all sorts of activity outside. Cars going by, pedestrians. But now there's nothing.'

'Christ!' he hissed, feeling automatically for his gun where he had earlier strapped it under his left arm.

'We've got to get you out of here.' She thought quickly. 'The attic. It's the only way. Then out the roof and through the back garden.'

'They'll have it cordoned off, as well,' he said, thinking out loud.

If they really are there, he thought.

But of course they are there. Now stop wishing and start moving.

'I'll stall them somehow,' Annie McBride said. 'You've got to get out of here.'

A loud rapping sounded below at the front door, and they both froze momentarily. Then a shout came: 'Police! Open up. We have a warrant.'

This galvanized them both: Annie ran screaming from the room, crying out at the top of her lungs for help, like a frightened animal. Max thought of stopping her, of silencing her, but figured she was only trying to save herself now, and he bolted out of the room on her heels, but turned up to the stairs for the attic as she ran down the stairs to the front door. He remembered something suddenly. It would be a long shot, the final gamble, but there was no other way out.

Annie's screams followed him up the stairs: 'Help! Help! He's a killer! He imprisoned me. Please help. He's getting away through the back!'

Max heard the front door crash open and then this last bit was repeated by Annie even as he lunged against a tiny locked door to the attic, ripping it off its hinges.

She hasn't betrayed me, after all, he thought. She's sending the police on a wild goose chase instead, giving me a few minutes to make an escape. Bless you, Annie McBride.

The attic was a clutter of old trunks and wooden boxes filled with books, periodicals, and old clothing. Max made his way through these to one of the dormer windows and looked out.

Wrong one, he thought, and then moved to the one to his left. From this window he saw what he was looking for: his memory had served him right. He unlocked the lower sash of the window and tugged on it, but the window was stuck.

Christ! Come on, he said to himself, putting all his might and effort into pulling the window up, but the wood was sealed tight and the sash would not budge.

Let's just hope that all the police have followed Annie's false lead into the back garden, he thought as he drew the pistol out of its leather holster, reversed it to hold it by its barrel, and began smashing the glass and frame.

Fitzgerald and the driver had both automatically raced for the house at the sound of cries from within, as had all the other police stationed outside. By the time Fitzgerald had reached the hall, he could see Lewis and Niel following a squad of police out the back door to the garden. He was suddenly alone with a large and frightened looking woman in a bulky cardigan who he figured must be Mrs McBride.

'Are you all right?' he asked, and she nodded dumbly at him, closing her eyes.

'Did he harm you? Do you need a doctor?'

'Out the back,' she said, her hand to her heart. 'Hurry. He's getting away.'

Suddenly Fitzgerald heard the distant tinkling of glass being broken. The sound seemed to be coming from upstairs, and his eyes went upward automatically, not understanding. Then, looking at Mrs McBride, he saw her eyes flick nervously toward the stairs and a look of absolute despair crossed her face.

'He's up there, isn't he?' he shouted at her, but did not bother waiting for an answer. He dashed to the stairs, taking them two at a time, drawing his revolver from out of his overcoat pocket.

It's going all wrong again, he thought, reaching the first landing and rushing headlong up the stairs to the second floor. All wrong. It's like a bad dream.

He reached the second floor and saw a door open down the hall, but the sound of breaking glass was now more distinct, coming from the floor above, and he kept to the stairs, climbing as fast as he could.

He can't get away, he told himself. Not again. I won't let him. He tripped on a step, falling heavily with his cheek against the cold steel of his revolver, but quickly got up and kept moving to the top of the stairs. At the dormered third floor, he immediately saw the small door torn open and made for this opening. Across the cluttered attic space he saw the German, crouched in the frame of a window.

'Stop or I'll shoot!' he yelled.

The German looked back at him with an intensity that penetrated Fitzgerald like a knife blade; it was a look so full of hate and contempt that he was momentarily mesmerized by it, just long enough for the man to leap from the window.

Fitzgerald shot at the empty space, not believing his eyes.

The man's committed suicide, he thought. Thrown himself out of the window.

Max felt the wind go out of him as his chest struck a limb of the tree outside the dormer window: the escape route he had noticed his first day at the house. His grip failed for an instant, for his left hand was almost useless, but he held onto the small branch with all his might even as a burning pain shot up his left arm. The branch swung and he held on, swinging with it. Below he could see people congregating in the street, pointing up at him.

Not police, he thought. Neighbors, most likely; curious at the sound of the shot and all the police activity, and all coming out now to see the excitement.

But he had no more chance to think as the branch he was gripping suddenly bent double and cracked. He felt himself slipping down through other branches that tore at his face and ripped his clothes. He grabbed frantically at branches, and suddenly his fall was broken when his right hand caught in the fork of a branch and he was able to wrap his legs around the limb next to it, securing himself. He quickly and deftly shinnied down this limb to the main branch of the tree, the people below getting closer and closer to him, their eyes wide in amazement.

But now he saw men in blue uniforms approaching from both ends of the street. Climbing down, he looked around desperately for some means of escape once he was on the ground. He dangled from the lowest branch for an instant, expecting another shot from Fitzgerald above at any moment, but none came. Damn his soul, Max thought, as he dropped the last five feet to the ground and instantly pulled out his revolver again. Damn him forever. I've got to kill him; that's clear.

The neighbors, startled and screaming at the sight of the gun, provided Max with cover from the approaching police for an instant until he became orientated. No one tried to stop him as he ran first to Annie's electric car parked under the tree, only to discover that there was no key in it. He then bolted out of the crowd toward the police car at the curb down the street from the house, exhaust fumes pumping out of its tailpipe into the cold air.

'Stop right where you are!' one of the policemen running after him shouted.

Max turned toward the voice, crouching at the knees and holding the pistol in a triangle from his body. He pulled off two fast rounds and the cop who had yelled for him to stop suddenly tumbled over in the street, crying out and grabbing his shattered lower leg. The other stopped for a moment to help his fallen comrade.

Max leaped into the driver's seat of the police car as shots rang out, one smashing into the side of the door in back of him. He put the car into gear, released the parking break and headed directly for two policemen coming at him from the other direction. One of them, red-faced and portly, managed to get one wild shot off before Max nearly ran them both down, their bodies diving to either side of the car as it lunged forward. Only then did he see that the street had been barricaded by a police van.

Nothing for it, he thought, pushing the accelerator to the floor and swerving to miss the front bumper of the van parked at the intersection of O Street. He miscalculated, smashing into the van and tearing off its left front wheel in the process. His lighter car ricocheted from the collision, bouncing up onto the sidewalk and smashing through piled snow and a street lamp. For an instant his vision was blocked by snow on the windscreen, and the car lost traction, fishtailing out of control. He threw the wheel into the spin and the car righted itself, its tire treads finally catching the cobblestone of the sidewalk beneath the snow. Another shot rang out, passing through the back window and whistling inches from his head to shatter the glass in front of him, and he again floored the accelerator and sped around the police van, lurching off the sidewalk and heading south down 31st Street toward the river.

The car was limping but still operable, he realized. Looking back through the side mirror, he saw a flurry of activity behind him as the police tried desperately to clear the crippled van out of the way so as to be able to give chase. But he had already turned off 31st before they were able to clear the street, heading west and again south into narrow lanes near the river, and still there was no pursuit.

Fitzgerald watched it all from the dormer window. By the time he reached the window and realized that the German had not jumped to his death, but had used a tree outside to attempt an escape, it was already too late to shoot. Crowds of neighborhood people were gathered beneath the tree, and Fitzgerald was afraid to shoot for fear of hitting one of them. He watched helplessly as the German swung down the branches and leaped to the street; watched unbelievingly as the man raced to the very car he and Lewis had come in, stole it and made his getaway, disabling a police van in the process and thereby blocking the path of pursuit until he had such a head start that no one would be able to follow him.

He's done it again, Fitzgerald thought, slamming his fist against the window sill. The bastard's outdone us. Will this never end? Fitzgerald left the attic and walked down the stairs despondently to the second floor. He heard movement in the room there, approached the open door, and saw Agent Niel searching the room.

'He's got away again,' Fitzgerald said.

Niel looked up, his small white teeth baring through his drawn lips.

'Yes,' he said. 'He's made us all look like fools. But for the last time. I swear that.'

Max bumped over railroad tracks and then parked and left the car amongst freight cars at the deserted side railings. No one was about to see him as he headed off on foot south, soon coming to a barge canal that he followed to his right, west, along the pathway upriver. No one was following him, and after half an hour of walking he left the towpath to hide in the dense greenery edging the canal. He was far enough away from the car now that it did not matter if the police found it. They would not be able to track him. Perhaps they might even think he had hopped a train out of town. With his boot he scuffed snow away from a boulder and sat, hidden in the bushes.

How did the police track me to McBride's? Who could have tipped them off? he wondered anxiously to himself.

And then it hit him, finally, what had been nagging him since the fiasco at the Willard Hotel. The clothes he had left in the locker room. Of course. They found those and somehow traced the jacket to Annie McBride. And now what? He was alone, injured and half the city was after him.

But they would not stop him. No.

TWELVE

'Yes, sir. We are doing everything possible to catch him. No. That won't be necessary. We're putting all uniformed patrolmen out on the beat tonight. If he's in Washington, we'll ferret him out.'

Chief Inspector Lewis choked the black phone stand in his massive left hand as he held the mouthpiece close to his lips. The earpiece was all but lost in his right hand. He frowned at Fitzgerald as he spoke to the police commissioner.

'I realize that, sir. And I do not exactly like being made to look like a monkey, either. No, I'm not being facetious. I am taking this seriously. Now, just a moment, commissioner. I never said that.'

Fitzgerald felt uneasy overhearing this phone conversation, but the call had come in the midst of their discussion back at Lewis's office, and the chief inspector had given no sign for him to leave. Agent Niel sat next to Fitzgerald in a captain's chair.

Lewis now set the phone stand down, continuing to cup the receiver to his ear. He shook his head as he listened. Fitzgerald could hear the commissioner's voice from where he sat. He and Niel exchanged glances, Niel raising his barely visible golden eyebrows and switching the toothpick he was chewing on today from one corner of his mouth to the other.

Lewis suddenly leaned over the mouthpiece again. 'No, I would not care for that eventuality, sir,' he said, anger and belligerency in his metallic tones. 'My record here speaks for itself. But if you are not satisfied—'

More chatter came through the earpiece, high and shrill. Lewis moved the instrument away from his ear, his eyes squinting.

'Very good, sir.'

He thumped the earpiece back into its holder on the stand. 'The bugger's given me until Sunday to catch our man.'

'And if no luck?' Niel asked.

'Then I'm off the case.' Lewis glared across the desk at the Bureau man.

'But this is absurd, chief inspector,' Fitzgerald finally said. 'You've been doing all that's humanly possible to catch the man.'

'The commissioner doesn't want to hear of hard work. He wants to hear of success. He says the newspapers are going to give us a good beating over this latest fiasco. The preparedness boys are already screaming bloody murder. If we can't catch one German in our nation's capital, then what the hell are we going to do with the whole nation of them when and if we go to war?'

He slumped back in his chair, deflated. 'My God! That was the worst dressing down I've had since cadet school.'

'I suggest we get on with the search then,' Agent Niel said brightly. 'This Damoclean sword should spur you on no end.'

Lewis let the comment go. 'Where the hell were we?' He began shuffling through the mess of papers on his desk. Fitzgerald could see he had been flustered and unnerved by the call. His career was on the line with this case.

But more than careers are at stake with this, he thought. If we do not find M soon, he may very well succeed in getting to Adrian somehow. The thought chilled him. It seems impossible, but the fellow has been resourceful enough to elude us at every turn. He is surely resourceful enough to track Adrian to Brantley.

'The McBride woman.' Agent Niel prompted Lewis back onto the course of their discussion before the commissioner's call.

'Yes, that's right. I'm not sure we'll be able to hold her past tonight.'

'She's an accomplice,' Niel said forcibly.

Lewis shook his head. 'There's only circumstantial evidence to that effect. Nothing in her version of events can be disproved.' He glanced down at the transcript of her interview with several police interrogators which had taken place in the late afternoon. 'She claims that our man was posing as a South African representative to the World Peace League. One Maximillian Voetner. According to her, she believed him, trusted him even. By all accounts our M is a personable boy when not seen from the wrong end of a revolver barrel. She even loaned him some of her dead son's clothing to attend his supposed meetings. Her first suspicions, so she says, were aroused last night when he came home stumbling up the stairs. She said she thought he'd been drinking, and it was only this morning, after reading the newspaper accounts of the attack on Sir Adrian at the New Willard Hotel, that she discovered bloodstains on the carpet of the stairs leading up to her tenant's room.'

Lewis stopped speaking, his eyes tracking back and forth across the page on the desk as he read on. 'No,' he said finally looking up. 'Her story holds together. She reports that she discovered he'd been cut somehow, but at that moment he drew a gun on her and held her prisoner in her own house until we came this afternoon. It's her word against ours.'

'And what about when I went to the door?' Niel said, aroused now, his cheeks red. 'She wasn't any captive then, I tell you.'

'She says the man had a gun on her the whole time.'

'She's lying!' It was almost a scream; the first time Fitzgerald had seen Niel lose control. He calmed himself after a moment. 'And what about how she told us he was escaping out the back when all the time he had gone up to the attic?'

His voice was evenly modulated again, but there was anger and a sort of childish petulance at being thwarted, Fitzgerald thought.

Lewis smiled at him, and this seemed to fan the flames of Niel's ire.

'Mrs McBride reports that he forced her to say that,' Lewis read. 'Said he would have her in his sights the whole time. That he would shoot her if she told us where he'd gone.'

'Nonsense.'

'She did seem awfully nervous,' Fitzgerald said. But it was more than that, he knew. Yet he held his tongue. Lewis is right, he thought. Her word against ours. And maybe I am wrong about her; maybe she really had been held captive; maybe her nervous glance toward the stairs was simply her way of telling me where M had gone, and not a guilty flicker of the eyes at all.

'So you're going to let her walk.' Niel said it with great contempt.

'Hardly that. We'll have her followed, her house watched. Until we round up M, Mrs McBride will be under the closest surveillance.'

This appeared to mollify Niel, who crossed his right leg over his left, hitching the pants up at the knee so they wouldn't bag.

'There's scant little to go on from what we found in the room,' Lewis went on after a momentary pause and more referral to the papers on his desk. 'Nothing to tell us where M might be, who his contacts are, when he might strike again.'

Fitzgerald was growing impatient with this discussion. Looking outside he saw that the evening had come on without him even realizing it. He would go out to Brantley first thing in the morning. For now he was hungry and tired and wanted to go home to Catherine so that she would not worry.

'That's all fine, chief inspector,' he said. 'But what are we doing to stop him from striking again?'

Niel smirked at the question, Fitzgerald noticed, and Lewis gave him a 'not-you-too' look of semi-disgust.

'We're doing all we can along those lines, Mr Fitzgerald,' Chief Inspector Lewis said. 'As I told the commissioner, we have all our uniformed men out there tonight. M has got to sleep someplace. We have men turning out every flophouse in the city; every known German sympathizer will be inter-viewed; M's description is being given out to each and every hotel and rooming house in Washington. Our spotters at the German Embassy have been doubled, but I don't figure he's dumb enough to go back there. We've got men at the train station and at the steamers. M won't be able to scratch without us pouncing on him. I tell you, we're running the biggest sweep this city has ever seen. We'll have him in our nets by morning.'

'And what about Brantley?' Fitzgerald said, unconvinced.

'The place is like an armed camp, for God's sake,' Lewis said. 'I just hope M does show up there. We'll use him for target practice. I'm going out there myself tonight to coordinate operations. Does that satisfy you, Mr Fitzgerald?'

'I'll only be satisfied when Sir Adrian has spoken with Wilson.'

The meeting broke up soon thereafter and Niel accompanied Fitzgerald down the stairs and through the precinct house to the street. The night was absolutely clear and bitterly cold. Orion was high in the southern sky already; Fitzgerald took a long deep breath of the chill air. It cleansed him.

Niel pulled up the fur collar of his overcoat around his neck, took fur-lined gloves out of his coat pocket and put them on, fastidiously pulling down each finger snugly.

'You'll be going to Brantley, as well?' Niel said.

'Tomorrow,' Fitzgerald answered.

'He's floundering, you know. Lewis. Quite hopeless.'

Fitzgerald found himself defending the man. 'He's doing everything possible. What else is there?'

'Search out the man's contacts. If we can't find him, we can at least find his base of operation. No one acts in a vacuum.'

'We've scared him off now. Lord knows where he'll go. Besides, I get the feeling this fellow is the lone wolf sort. The maniacal type who is out to prove something; who does not want anyone else sharing the glory.'

'You speak from experience, Mr Fitzgerald?'

Fitzgerald reddened at the comment. 'Merely indulging in amateur psychology.'

'You may be right, though. Our M might just be one of those maniacs, all right. Stands to reason, if he keeps coming after Sir Adrian with all the odds against him.'

Fitzgerald remained an instant longer out of courtesy. 'Well, I really must be going. My wife will be frantic with worry.'

Agent Niel touched the brim of his hat as adieu and Fitzgerald got into his Cadillac and headed toward his home. Soon the lights of Poplars came into view up the long drive off Massachusetts Avenue, and Fitzgerald shifted down to make the turn. Lights were on in the house. She's waiting for me up there; Catherine is waiting patiently and perhaps with some trepidation. I'll have a warm dinner and pleasant conversation with the woman I love sitting opposite me.

He thought of the assassin for a moment: where will he be tonight? He surely cannot find refuge indoors with all of Washington on his heels. It will be a cold night for him. No warm food, no loving companionship. What must the man be thinking of? Fitzgerald wondered. What motivates him so that he will continue on this mission even after realizing that the odds are so greatly stacked against him?

I wouldn't be in his shoes tonight for anything, he thought

as he drew up in front of his house, and the outside light went on to the right of the tall Georgian front door.

Max crouched in the bushes like an animal. There was no place for him to go; no place to hide but here in the woods above the C&O canal. They would be scouring Washington for him; this was the safest place, he knew.

Cold bit at his hands and feet until they had gone numb. He thought he would soon die. Darkness closed around him like a shroud and suddenly an unfamiliar smell made his nose twitch; a sort of tar-like chemical scent wafting on the freezing night air.

He looked up out of the thick undergrowth where he was hiding. An orange glow throbbed in the sky just northwest of him. A fire. Whose fire?

But he no longer cared. Max forced himself to his feet, standing uncertainly, and began moving out of the thicket and back onto the canal's towpath, following the beacon of warmth.

He knew only that he must find warmth, must defrost himself or die. And I cannot die, he thought. I have a job to do, a mission.

In ten minutes he discovered the source of the fire. Up a narrow track north of the canal, he saw a group of men huddled around the licking flames of a bonfire. The firelight threw shadows on the faces of these men like pagan face-painting that danced and rippled as the flames moved. It was a large fire made from old creosote-soaked rails discarded along the lines, and it burned intensely and with the faintly chemical smell that had attracted Max. All around these men he could see the accoutrements of the tramp's life: the precious cans used for cooking; the crude shelters made of cast-off wood and corrugated tin clustered around the little opening in the woods. The men were scattered about the fire, lounging in its warmth in all manner of mismatched clothing, both begged for and stolen off of clotheslines up and down the eastern seaboard.

The men did not see him at first, standing just out of the ring of fire, but he was happy to see them. There could be safety in such numbers, he knew. Warmth, as well.

A big man with a shock of red hair was the first to see him, looking casually at Max as he rolled a cigarette, licking the paper down.

'Come on over, buddy,' he called out, and Max moved to the fire, crouching low to it to warm his icy body.

Following the time-honored tradition of the road, there were no immediate questions, though Max could see the men were curious, looking him up and down as he extended various parts of his body to the fire. The large one who had called to him was especially interested, he saw, in the bandage on his left hand, and in the gray suit he was wearing which was ripped at the knee and arms from his escape via the tree at McBride's. The communal stewpot was bubbling over the flames, and Max had smelled its delicious aroma from several hundred yards away.

'You got a can of your own?' the big man said.

Max merely shook his head.

'Here.' One was thrust under his nose, and he followed the arm holding it back to its owner's face: a big-eyed man about Max's own age and size who grinned quite idiotically at him.

'Now you're a real gentleman, Karl,' the big man said ironically. 'Karl's the gentlemanly type, ain't he, boys?'

'Aw, knock it off, Red,' one of the men in the shadows behind Max said. 'Let the little German alone.'

Max almost jumped at the word until he realized they were describing Karl as a German, not himself.

Max took the tin can gratefully, smiling at Karl who truly seemed to be mentally impaired now that he continued looking at the man. He filled it with some of the hot broth from the big pot, and sipped it slowly, happily. Nothing had ever tasted so good before in his life.

A half an hour later, after sitting with the men and listening to stories of great coups in begging and thievery, he was beginning to feel human again; beginning to feel at ease.

'So, you don't seem much of a fellow for the road,' Red said finally. Tradition had been mollified; now the men would find out about him. 'You don't even carry a can with you; no bindle. What brings you here?'

Max hesitated. I'll have to give them some sort of story, he knew. If only in repayment for their hospitality. To say nothing would be an affront to their implied camaraderie.

'Women troubles,' he said.

'Ooh!' Red slapped his knee. 'I knew it. Kicked you out

for the night, did she? You're no tramp. Anybody could tell that. Why not go to a hotel?'

Max stared at the fire, saying nothing.

'Say,' Red said, a worried expression on his large face now. 'You're not wanted by the cops or anything, are you? We don't want any trouble with the police.'

Several of the men around Max mumbled assent to this.

'No,' Max said, taking his eyes from the dancing flames. 'No police. I just wanted to get out in the fresh air and think things through. It got cold.'

Red again slapped his knee. 'Well there's plenty of fresh air out here, buddy. You come to the right spot. Do you have any money with you?'

Max's alarms tingled into action. He got up suddenly, moving to the edge of the crowd of men, his back protected.

'Easy, buddy,' Red said, palms up peaceably. 'No one's going to hurt you. It'd just be nice if you contributed something. If you've got it, that is. We all do our bit here, you see. This ain't no free ride.'

Max dug in his pocket and pulled out a silver dollar, and flipped it to Red. 'That enough?'

Red turned it over, examining both sides before pocketing it. 'Great, brother. You got a name?'

'Max,' he said.

'Welcome, Max,' Red said.

He had found a home.

In the middle of the night, Max, bedded down near the dying fire in an old blanket the other German had shared with him, was awakened by the sounds of voices coming from one of the corrugated metal shelters. He could just make out the gruff, threatening voice of the big man, Red, and the pleading voice of the German, Karl.

Drawing close to the shelter he heard Red: 'I know you got some tobacco in here. Now hand it over.'

Then Karl, whining: 'But it's mine. I've been saving it up.'

'You want a crack on the head? Maybe it'd do you good, you silly son of a bitch.'

There was the sound of scuffling and Max crawled quickly through the low opening. His eyes were already adjusted to the darkness, and he instantly saw Red crouched over Karl preparing to strike him. Max's teeth bared like an animal's and a sharp hiss exploded from his mouth as he lunged for Red. He surprised the big man and grabbed his right arm, twisting and pinning it in a lock grip he had learned at the Marburg training camp. Red yelped with pain and frustration as he tried unsuccessfully to break the grip, for the greater he exerted, the more pressure he put on his own arm, pinioned over Max's forearm and locked in place by Max's chest.

'So you were going to steal from him, were you?' Max hissed in his ear. 'You swine.' He twisted the arm further back, bringing another cry of pain from Red who clawed at him with his left hand. Another twist and Red stopped struggling.

'Stop, please! Stop. I wasn't going to hurt him, I swear.'

'He's defenseless and you were beating him. I should break your arm off.'

'No, please God! Stop. You're breaking it. I promise.'

'Promise what?' Max said, not letting up on the pressure despite the pain he was causing to his own wounded left hand.

'I'll never do it again. Honest.'

Max's mind raced. I should kill him, he thought. I know I can't trust him. He's suspicious of my wounded hand. What if he goes to the police and reports me once I'm gone? I have to kill him.

Only then did he notice Karl who had crawled off to a corner of the shelter and was hugging his knees to his chest, shaking with fear, his eyes bulging with terror as he watched the scene of violence unfolding before him.

And Max knew he could not kill Red: not here, not now, not with Karl looking on.

'Red, I'm going to let you go in a moment, but I want you to listen carefully to what I'm going to say first.' Max put his mouth right next to Red's ear, whispering low and fierce. He could smell the sweat of fear on him, feel his body quiver in pain and fright. 'If I ever discover you've hurt Karl, or that you tried to play me false, I'll kill you. You understand?'

Red's entire body shook as he vigorously nodded at this.

'You tell anybody about my presence here and you're a dead man. I'll break your body in half, just like I could your arm now. You'll die slow, I'll see to that. You've never seen me, never even heard my name.'

'Yes, yes! Now please, you're tearing my arm out of the socket.'

'Please, Max,' Karl said, still huddled in the corner.

Max slowly released pressure on the arm, and Red, finally freed, rolled away rubbing his arm and shoulder and emitting small groans.

Max watched him for several minutes in the dimness of the shelter until he finally got to his knees, holding his limp right arm in his left hand. Max was looking for signs in Red's face, signs that would tell him that the man would have to die: the evil vindictive slitting of the eyes; the drawn mouth; the veil drawn across his face.

But he saw none of these.

'You're a fucking wild man,' Red said. 'You could've just told me to lay off Karl. I can hear, you know.' He rubbed the socket gingerly.

Max said nothing, continuing to peer into Red's face for signs of duplicity.

'OK, OK,' Red said finally, unnerved by the stare. 'I heard you. I never seen you, never heard of you. But you –' he poked his left forefinger at Max – 'don't go bringing the police down on us, hear? I don't care what you're up to, just leave us in peace.'

Max nodded slowly at the big man. This statement saved his life, convincing Max that the man would not go to the police on his own. After Red left, Max turned to Karl.

'You all right?' he said in German, and the man's face lit up.

'You saved me,' Karl said.

'It's nothing.'

'You saved me. Nobody's ever saved me before. You really are my friend, aren't you?'

Max felt a knot in his stomach at the question. He didn't know if he could be anybody's friend ever again.

'Sure,' he said finally. 'I'm your friend.'

Karl scooted over to him suddenly on the earth floor and clasped Max to his breast, sobbing in his ear. 'My friend. My friend. You must stay in here tonight. Where it is warm and safe.'

Karl and he talked a while before going to sleep, and Max learned the bare outlines of Karl's life: his miserable childhood in Kiel, beaten by an autocratic father, once until he had become unconscious. His mother had tried to protect him, but had died when Karl was only nine. There had been sixteen more years of abuse after that – which could explain Karl's simple-mindedness, Max thought – before the young man had jumped ship bound for America. A stowaway, he had been discovered mid-voyage, whipped and then made to work like a slave to earn his passage to America. He had arrived in New York five years ago, penniless. And penniless he had remained for many months until one day in New York he had been recruited into the army, quite without his consent. He thought he had been signing a voucher for a free lunch. But his stint with the army had not worked out, either.

'They wanted me to always sleep inside,' he had told Max, as if this were the silliest request imaginable.

Finally, Max gathered, Karl had been given a medical discharge: the army had no more use for him than did the rest of society. However, he had kept the uniform that the army had issued him; his one treasure from that time. He showed it to Max, taking it out of the bindle he kept under his blanket with something like reverence, unfolding it as one would a nation's flag.

Once out of the army, Karl had fallen in with the homeless vagrants of the country who formed a large sub-culture and an ever-ready job pool for manufacturers too greedy to pay an honest wage. He had wandered up and down the east coast, from one hobo jungle to another, a pitiful, simple, but loveable human.

Max shared little information with Karl, only that he was a ship's representative of a German line, down on his luck: he had lost his job and his woman. Just enough to satisfy Karl's curiosity. It was not a very deep curiosity.

They continued talking until the light began breaking in the east, showing pearly gray through the chinks in the shelter. Again Max was struck by a resemblance between them despite their age difference: they both wore their brown hair close-cropped; their faces both had a sort of high-boned sharpness. Max felt a momentary kinship with Karl, as if he were the younger brother Max had never had.

'Sleep now,' Max finally said, and Karl obeyed like a dog, curling up against Max's flank and quite quickly fell into a deep sleep. Max felt his warmth against his leg and almost smiled at the man's simple trust.

THIRTEEN

President Wilson watched the antics of a hummingbird almost lost inside the massive hibiscus blossom. The bird's needle beak was at work gathering nectar as the bird hovered, its wings a blur of motion. Wilson loved the little birds, the seemingly defenseless ones. So inventive they had to be, so plucky.

He was seated in the veranda of the presidential suite at the elegant old Miramar in St Petersburg, Florida. The air was thick with the fragrance of jasmine, a lattice full of which covered one of the high walls of the veranda. He had just finished a solitary and meager breakfast of chamomile tea and Melba toast. His digestion had been off for the past few days despite the fresh air, sunshine and exercise out on the links. It was often like that for him: ideal conditions could unnerve him, making him wonder when things were going to go wrong again.

Man is a funny creature, he thought, pushing the hotel plate away from him and leaning back in his chair to enjoy the morning sunshine. The sun shone directly into the veranda at this time of the morning and he closed his eyes, feeling it warm his face. Gentle sun; healing sun. Motes of light danced in front of his closed eyelids.

Of course he knew his indigestion was more than a simple result of his normal fatalistic approach to life. It had more to do with the situation in Washington. He felt guilty about having run away as he had. There had been the appointment on Wednesday with Sir Adrian Appleby, a man whom he personally knew and respected. But his instincts had told him not to meet with the man; not at this juncture at any rate. He feared the news the British envoy might be carrying. Wilson still felt badly about it, however; he was not a rude man. Authoritative and overbearing, perhaps, but not intentionally rude as a rule.

The hummingbird swooped low over his head with a flurry of wings, and he opened his eyes again.

In front of him, next to his cup and saucer on the table, were the newspapers. He knew he would have to tackle these. He had not seen a paper in three days.

I should be feeling lighter than air; I should be feeling relieved and contented. Truth is, a rotten shank has plagued my golf game the whole time I have been here; dear Edith has been out of sorts with some female problem; and I have been as skittish as a cat on heat, desperate to know what has been going on in the capital.

So much for rest and relaxation; for the therapy of vacations.

It was with mixed relief and anxiety then, that President Wilson opened the newspapers this sunny Saturday morning. He examined the day old copy of the *Post* first. Within two minutes he had discovered the article about the attack on Sir Adrian Appleby at the New Willard Hotel. He felt the blood rising in him; felt that somehow he must be responsible for this outrage. It was unclear from the article if the attack had anything to do with the message he was carrying; after all, diplomats incur the hatred of all sorts of people all over the world. All the same, he felt somehow responsible, as if his absence from town had allowed such an outrage to occur.

Colonel House should have told me last night on the phone, he thought. He and Edith are being too protective of me. A glance at the second paper, today's edition of the *St Petersburg Times*, completed the job which the *Post* had begun.

Its front page screamed out at Wilson in two-inch headlines:

Horror at Sea

Yesterday, Wilson discovered by a quick perusal of the numerous subheads and the article itself, German U-boats had sunk two merchant ships: the *Essex* out of Falmouth bound for New York, and the *Aguire*, from New York and bound for Liverpool. Both ships had been carrying Americans on board, and there was a heavy loss of life. The newspaper, within the confines of the news story itself, was crying out for reprisals and wondered out loud what the president of the United States could be doing vacationing in their fair city at such a time of crisis.

Who has leaked my presence? Wilson wondered with real venom. But he knew that it was impossible to keep such a thing quiet for very long. The security set up at the Glen Haven Country Club alone was enough to make people curious.

Well, it is patently clear what I must do, he told himself. I must get back to Washington. The afternoon train will see me there by tomorrow morning. I know Edith intended for us to stay until tomorrow, but this is clearly an emergency. The reporter for this town's small newspaper has asked the apposite question: what am I doing here at a time like this?

That's settled then, he said to himself. I'll return to Washington by tomorrow, see Appleby and find out just what he so urgently wants to tell me, and then I shall deal with these Germans. They leave me no recourse but to ask Congress for a bill authorizing the arming of our merchant ships. Damn the Germans, anyway. It's as if they actually want to draw us into war with them. Well, it shall be kicking and screaming for me all the way. A reasoned response is what is needed.

He began writing out on a pad of legal paper his plan for arming the merchant fleet, still hopeful that he could continue walking the tightrope of neutrality.

Yet for the first time since the hostilities had begun in 1914, Wilson began to despair of the future. For the first time he began to feel he was losing his balance on the tightrope.

Edward came out of the half-bath attached to their bedroom wearing a light woolen under vest and his comical shorts that hung to his knees. He thought Catherine was still asleep, but she could see him through tiny slits in her eyes as he danced from foot to foot climbing into his tweed trousers. He then put on a freshly starched white shirt and collar, fidgeted with his tie in front of the mirror on the dresser, and brushed his hair with two silver boar's hairbrushes. The final items of apparel were boots, vest and jacket, and he tugged on the lapels of the latter for just the right fit.

He suddenly came to the bed and pecked her cheek innocently and softly so as not to wake her. For an instant she wanted to reach out to him. But instead she kept her eyes closed and smiled languorously at the kiss, as if still in half sleep. Then she rolled onto her side and he tiptoed out of the room.

Later, she got up, brushed her hair and dressed in a long green skirt and a charcoal roll top sweater and lace-up boots. She was planning to work in the dark room this morning, and it was chilly back there. It was Mrs Greer's day out of the house, and Catherine would have all to herself the back pantry where her dark room was located; she would not have to creep to and fro through the kitchen.

She hurried downstairs in time, like a dutiful wife, to see Edward off to Brantley. He was just coming out of the dining room as she came down the stairs, and he looked happier than she had seen him in days.

'Morning, dear. You didn't have to get up for me.'

'I've got developing to do this morning,' she explained.

'We've had great news,' he blurted out, cheering up again. 'Colonel House was just on the phone. Wilson is coming back to Washington earlier than scheduled. We're to meet with him tomorrow afternoon. Isn't that splendid?'

'Marvelous,' she said. 'Uncle Adrian will be so relieved.'

'I've got to be going.' He crossed to the hall closet, fetching an overcoat and hat. 'They're expecting me this morning. You're sure you'll be all right here without me?'

'Absolutely,' she said. 'I've got loads of work to do, and Thomas is here to keep me company if I get lonely.'

Fitzgerald was distracted, only half-listening as he slipped on his hat and coat.

'Only one more day,' he said. 'By God! I think we've done it. There's no way the German can get to Adrian at Brantley in so short a time. It's an armed camp out there.'

'I am happy,' Catherine said limply. She was happy that her uncle would be safe, but still there was a nagging hollowness in her over his mission to send her country to war.

Just as his car was pulling out of the driveway, there came a ringing from the telephone in the hallway. Catherine went to it, picking up the receiver and telephone stand.

'The Fitzgerald residence,' she said.

'Is Mr Fitzgerald there?' It was a young man's voice with a heavy languid British accent.

'Sorry. He's just gone.' She almost said to Brantley, forgetting Edward's admonitions to give his whereabouts out to no one she did not know.

'That is a shame,' the man said. 'This is Gaston from the British Embassy. We have a message for Mr Fitzgerald to convey to Sir Adrian.'

She knew Gaston, had met him at an embassy party just the month before. She thought the voice had sounded familiar; it fit the horsy face she put it together with in her memory.

'This is Mrs Fitzgerald,' she said. 'Could I be of any assistance? You know that Brantley is on the telephone, don't you?' She figured it was safe enough to tell Gaston the whereabouts.

'No, we did not,' he said, and his voice sounded relieved. 'It is rather urgent that we get this message to him. Do you have the number handy?'

She thought for a moment: it was as if everything that had to do with Brantley was held at arm's length by her. Too many associations with her father. Edward loved the place, but she could not be bothered with it. That she did not offhand know the number of her own country house was embarrassing to her and she tried to cover it over as she pulled out their black leather address and phonebook, flipping through the pages hurriedly to B.

'It's been so long since I've phoned myself,' she laughed. 'Just a moment.' It was the only number on the page, next to the name of the house. 'It's Capitol 2345,' she said. 'The Cabin John exchange.'

There was a pause on the other end of the line as Gaston obviously copied down the information, then: 'That's lovely, Mrs Fitzgerald. Good of you to help.'

'Not at all,' she said, hanging up the earpiece and looking down at the open address book once again. I should be there with them, she thought, and to hell with what the police suggest. I feel guilty not being there to share any danger that Uncle Adrian may be facing.

Max had borrowed the army uniform and gloves from Karl and bought the cane off of Red this morning before leaving the hobo camp. He hoped his military disguise would make him anonymous, faceless to the police. He had also stolen a Chevrolet Model 490, the competitor to Ford's Model T, picking it out of a parking lot near the railway. It was hardly the car of his dreams, better a roadster, but the Chevrolet was unassuming enough, and also quite simple to steal by manipulating a few wires by the ignition.

He drove to Massachusetts Avenue and had parked the car a safe distance away from the Poplars and took up watch early this morning. When he saw Fitzgerald leave in his Cadillac in the escort of two police cars, he knew this was his chance. He would follow Fitzgerald, assuming he would take him to where Sir Adrian Appleby was now ensconced. The fact that only one policeman was left to guard the Poplars confirmed his belief that Appleby was not staying there anymore.

He watched as the big car chuffed out onto the road and the police cars hugged closely behind him. Max gave them thirty seconds, and then he pushed the ignition button on the Chevrolet.

The car refused to start. He pushed and pushed but the beastly machine only spluttered and gasped. Fitzgerald's car was now out of sight. Max slammed the steering wheel.

What now? How to find his way to Appleby? Ahhh, perhaps the wife?

First he had to get past the one remaining policeman. Max knew that the wound to his left hand and his limp would now be focal pieces of any description circulating on him. From training at Marburg he'd learned there were two ways to beat a description: disguise and accentuation. He had disguised the wound to his hand by wearing Karl's gloves which went along with the uniform; with the aid of the cane, he had accentuated the limp, making an elaborately pained procession straight up the drive to where the policeman stood watch, tipping his hat at the man. When asked his business, Max had said in a muffled unaccented voice that he was collecting for the military preparedness committees, one of the pet projects of America's rich.

The policeman had looked him up and down quickly and waved him on, wishing him good luck. At the door he repeated the story to an old colored servant, explaining how important it was that he see Mrs Fitzgerald personally, and the servant had looked over his shoulder warily to the policeman to make sure all was in order.

The servant let him in, leaving him in the hallway near the phone for a time while he went into a sitting room. The servant came back out of the room.

'Sorry, sir. The mistress must be in her dark room. Isn't there some way I can be of service?'

'I was told by my superior to speak with Mrs Fitzgerald herself. Tell her it's also to do with the Belgian relief fund.'

The servant nodded his head slowly, looking Max up and down. 'Just wait a bit, sir.'

Again he left Max standing in the hall. Now he looked down at an address book open on the table by the phone. Only one number on the entire page, Brantley Hall.

Max quickly memorized the name and number. It could be a lead.

Suddenly he realized how stupid this was, coming to Catherine Fitzgerald in this military outfit. Whereas it was meant to disguise him from the police, to put them at ease, it would only serve to make Catherine Fitzgerald suspicious. As far as she knew he was a representative to the World Peace League, a pacifist and not a soldier. How would she react when she saw him?

It might be another thing to pay a visit dressed in civvies, maybe even return her journal – though that was long gone now. But he could chat her up, perhaps she might let something out. A slip of the tongue, for he could tell the other day that she had enjoyed his company.

But this? It was all wrong. One look at the uniform and no telling what she would do. She might even scream for the policeman.

And now another thought. Max did not know how much Fitzgerald told his wife. But if he told her about the raid last night at Annie McBride's, perhaps she already had made the connection between her 'South African' savior and the man trying to kill her uncle.

Altogether this was too risky. He moved quickly to the front door and then went down the steps, glancing at the policeman still patrolling the drive. Max nodded at the man, and then took out a scrap of paper from his tunic pocket and hurriedly scribbled the word and number which he'd discovered inside, then stuffed the paper back into the pocket and went down the steps slowly to the gravel drive, the cane in obvious use.

He pulled his hat down low and put his right hand in the cargo pocket of the tunic.

'Any luck?' the big policeman man said cheerily.

Max shot him what he hoped was a broad grin. 'Maybe.'

'Good.'

Max continued on a few paces.

'Hey, buddy.'

Max froze at the sound of his voice. His right hand tensed in the cargo pocket, ready to grab for the pistol in his shoulder holster. He turned slowly, looking for cover nearby, a place to dive and roll while he pulled his gun out.

The cop sauntered up to him, reaching into his pocket, and Max drew his right hand out of his own pocket slowly, deliberately. Then he let it inch up to the top button on his tunic as if absent-mindedly scratching his sternum.

'Didn't you forget something?' the policeman said.

Max attempted a smile, but all he could feel was the sweat breaking out again on his forehead.

The cop pulled his hand out of his trouser pocket and held a palmful of change.

'You didn't even bother with me. What kind of salesman would you make?' He grinned and Max was momentarily confused. The policeman shoved the fistful of coins at him. 'Here. I want to help out, too. Anything to kick the Kaiser's ass.'

Max felt the wind rush out of him in relief. 'Great,' he said with real meaning, taking the money and putting it into his cargo pocket.

He turned and headed back down the drive, looking back once to wave at the policeman, and reaching Massachusetts Avenue, he turned west to head downtown. He would leave his stolen car behind.

So preoccupied was he with his thoughts that he did not even notice the watcher on the other side of the street.

* * *

Agent Niel had arrived at Poplars a few minutes before and was still seated in his car. There was something about the Fitzgerald woman that did not ring true to him. And he had waited for her husband to leave before visiting with her. There were questions he had: specifically why her journal should be in the possession of a German agent. Correction: why it should be in a room recently frequented by a German agent. For Niel had found the journal at the scene last evening, before Lewis's men had a chance to search the room. There could be an innocent enough explanation, or maybe not. But it was not something he wanted to discuss with Edward Fitzgerald present.

But I must watch what I say, he told himself as he sat hunkered behind the wheel in his Ford. For she is a powerful woman, or at least a woman with a powerful husband, which amounted to the same thing. Niel knew about power in Washington: it was reserved for the right crowd from the right part of society with the right sort of friends. Niel had none of these. He was just a spunky little Irishman in the eyes of people like Catherine and Edward Fitzgerald. An oddity, an annoyance perhaps. Born in Washington, Niel had none of the advantages of people like the Fitzgeralds or Applebys of the world: he'd put himself through school, going nights mostly, working days as a newspaper compositor. His parents had no fancy Rhode Island homes; his accountant father had died when he was seven and his mother taught school to support the four children. They had grown up in far from genteel poverty in southeast Washington, on the borders of the Negro ghetto.

Oh, yes, he said to himself again. I know about power and people with power.

His sophomore year in college he had dropped the 'O' from the front of his name so that he would be more like those who ran things. And after graduating second in his 1908 class at American University – he had been one of the university's few token scholarship boys – he had quite literally stumbled into the Bureau of Investigation. Answering an ad he saw one day at his work at the newspaper, he soon discovered that the 'bright young men' the ad was looking for were being given the chance of a lifetime in Washington: to come in at the birth of a federal agency, to shape it, to grow with it.

Niel definitely meant to get ahead, and to that end the Bureau needed to get ahead, as well. No more southeast Washington for me, he thought. Niel's entire life was a battle for and against power. The Fitzgerald case could prove a turning point in that struggle, but only if he played it correctly.

So he continued to sit in the seat of the Ford and try to figure out how to handle the difficult and imperious woman named Catherine Devereaux Fitzgerald.

He was still thinking of this when a soldier came limping down the drive from Poplars, turned west and began walking toward downtown.

Niel had no chance to get a look at the man's face, for his hat was pulled down low over his forehead and they were at an awkward angle from each other.

He didn't give it much thought at first, for the policeman on duty at the house would have checked the man out, Niel figured. For a few moments he continued to think of the right approach with Mrs Fitzgerald, then a sudden flash of insight made him shoot bolt upright in the car seat.

The soldier had a limp. Which leg had it been, left or right? But even as he was mentally answering this question, he was getting out of his car. Our man's a clever one. He'll know that we're looking for a man with a limp. Why not play up the limp rather than hide it? he thought. A soldier with a distinct limp, just like the assassin.

Niel waited long enough to ensure that the man remained on foot and was not heading for a car, then he quickly left his own car and followed.

I've got you now, M, he thought. You're mine. All mine.

FOURTEEN

Fitzgerald arrived at Brantley around ten-thirty Saturday morning and was truly amazed at what he saw there. Chief Inspector Lewis had promised an armed camp, and an armed camp the estate had become. At the tall wrought iron gates to the long drive there were four policemen, heavily armed with shotguns and carbines, who stopped his car and gave him a thorough questioning before Lewis himself appeared and waved the officers off. Lewis got in the Cadillac and they drove up the drive, between rows of bare sycamores, spotting men at intervals of twenty yards or so on the drive and spread throughout the grounds. In fact, as far as Fitzgerald could see in all directions around the house, were blue uniformed and khaki uniformed men against the white of the snow-covered park.

'We've brought out the local home guard, as well,' Chief Inspector Lewis said, with real pride in his voice. 'Our man would have to be a regular Houdini to get past all these boys. And there are a dozen more in the house.'

'So we just convince Adrian to lay low until tomorrow,' Fitzgerald said. 'What about getting him back to Washington to see the president?' He shifted down for a second barricade checkpoint halfway up the drive, but the police there recognized Lewis and waved them through.

'Shouldn't be a problem,' Inspector Lewis said, nodding at the police as they passed the roadblock. 'We'll have a regular motorcade for that; shield Sir Adrian in and out of the cars. That's the danger point with assassins. Getting in and out of cars and buildings. But there will be men all around him during both operations. Thank God he's a short man. We'll keep him below the window level on the drive in and have three identical cars to confuse anyone lying in wait. But there won't be anyone on the route into Washington, I guarantee. My men are busy now securing it, checking every derelict building along the

way. I tell you Fitzgerald, there is no way this M can get to
Appleby now.'

Fitzgerald could see the two dogs out in front of Brantley,
and though he could not yet hear their voices, he knew they
were barking by the way they lurched forward with each yap,
bouncing stiffly on strong front legs. Soon they pulled up in
front of the house and three more policemen on duty at the
front door, new since yesterday, had their weapons at the ready,
relaxing only when they saw Lewis unfold out of the car.

'It's all right, boys. This is Mr Fitzgerald, owner of the
house. I want you to take a good look at his face and remember
it. Besides me and the servants, Mr Fitzgerald here is the only
other man you let in. Understood?'

The men were eager, Fitzgerald saw. They eyeballed him
with great intensity, almost scowling as they did so. Big men;
big and brutal, he thought. I would not want to go up against
these.

Monroe, the caretaker and part-time servant, opened the
door as he and Lewis mounted the broad front steps, the dogs
swarming around them.

'It's very good to see you, Mr Fitzgerald,' he said. His thin
pinched face was white and his hand trembled on the door.

'What is it, Monroe?' Fitzgerald said, entering the main
hall and leaving the dogs outside to plague the policemen on
duty. 'You look as though you've seen a ghost.'

'It's all these men about, sir,' Monroe said, helping Fitzgerald
off with his coat in the hallway. 'They've got me and the
missus spooked, they have. They all talk about a crazy assassin
who's coming to blow the house up. We didn't bargain on this
when we signed on, sir.'

Fitzgerald smiled at him consolingly. 'I know you didn't,
Monroe.'

'Is it true, sir?'

'That an assassin is after Sir Adrian?' Fitzgerald said. 'Yes,
I'm afraid it is. But look at the protection around here, Monroe.
No one is going to come near here, I assure you. It will all
be over by tomorrow, and there shall be a special bonus in
store for you and your wife for your loyal service through
such a difficult time.'

Monroe's glum expression brightened perceptibly at the mention of a bonus. He half-bowed as if to accept, then showed the two into the main sitting room with its ten-foot-high fireplace, a roaring blaze filling the entire room with its warmth. Appleby sat in a chintz-covered armchair sucking on his extinguished pipe. Looking up at their entrance, his face bore a concerned expression. His brows were as furrowed as a bulldog's jowls.

'How goes it, Adrian?' Fitzgerald said as he went to his friend, clapping him on the shoulder good-naturedly. 'It's almost over now.'

Appleby remained seated, nodding at this comment. 'Let us hope so, Edward.'

Fitzgerald quickly informed him of President Wilson's early return to Washington.

But Adrian was unimpressed. 'Yes, I already know. Chap from the embassy called this morning.'

'Have you planned what you'll say to Wilson?' Fitzgerald said.

As Appleby pursed his lips, considering this, the phone began ringing in the hall.

Max listened as the phone rang once, twice, three times. On the fourth ring, someone picked it up. Max looked around the busy phone room of the city post office in Washington: let's hope this leads to something, he thought. In his bones he felt that it would; he was sure that the number he had copied from the open phone book at Catherine's would take him directly to Appleby.

'Capitol 2345,' a man's voice on the other end said.

Damn, Max thought. He'd hoped there would be some named identification from the person answering, a way to trace the phone number.

'Hello,' he said, thinking quickly. 'Is John McGuire at home?'

As he spoke he could hear snippets of the conversations from other people in the large marble-paneled room who were using the public phones: plans for trips; emergency calls announcing a death; a young woman whose face had gone red all over as she talked in hushed tones to her lover.

There was a pause on the other end. Finally: 'There is no John McGuire at this number, I'm afraid.'

Quick before he hangs up, Max told himself. 'I'm sure that this is the correct number. And you say it's not the McGuire residence?'

'No, sir. This is Brantley Hall, the Fitzgerald residence.'

Max wanted to shout for joy. Instead he said, 'I am sorry. Please pardon the intrusion.'

'Not at all,' the man said on the other end and then hung up his receiver. Max stayed on the line for several instants more, listening to the crackle and pop of the open line.

You can't outmaneuver me, Appleby, he thought. Now to trace the Capitol prefix; to find out just where this Brantley Hall is located. He finally hung up the receiver and turned to walk back to the directory assistant.

Niel had tracked the soldier all the way downtown, hopping a streetcar when he had, and then descending just near Union Station. He had tailed the man into the City post office and watched him as he had gone into the phone room off the monumental main hall. While the man had been arranging to make a call and waiting his turn for one of the phones, Niel had made his own call from the porters' office near the front door, calling Bureau headquarters and requesting backup.

Now, even as Niel, stationed by one of the marble pillars in the main lobby of the post office, watched the soldier place the call and speak to somebody on the other end, he tried to plan a course of action. He was not so sure the soldier was M anymore: after all the man had continued to use the cane all the way downtown. If he is in disguise, then it is a very convincing one.

But he actually has a limp, he had to remind himself. He actually could use such an aid. And his disguise is needed anywhere in Washington, Niel suddenly realized. As far as he would be concerned, his description has been circulated all over the city. Every cop on the beat will be looking for him.

As the suspect hung up the phone, Niel saw from his vantage point two Bureau cars pull up in front and six men pile out of them. He hurried to the front entrance to meet them. Randall, one of their best field men, was among the six, Niel was happy to see. You could count on Randall, he thought.

Niel reached the door just as the men had climbed the steps to the building.

'You got here fast,' Niel said.

Randall nodded only, awaiting instructions.

'We take him outside,' Niel said. 'If it's the German, we don't want to try to rush him in there.' He nodded to the cavernous interior of the City post office, just across 1st Street from Union Station. 'He's a plucky customer. Who knows what he'd do. It could turn into a real bloodbath with all those people in there. So we cover the exits. I take up watch again inside and follow him out, you men cover each side of the main entrance. We squeeze him between us like an insect.'

The six men, young and fresh from training school, listened to him with rapt reverence.

'You're all armed?'

Six nods.

'Stay out of sight if possible. We don't want to alarm him or give him any advance notice we're here.'

'You're sure that it's the German?' Agent Randall finally asked.

'I haven't gotten close enough yet for a hundred percent read on him, but we work on the assumption that it is him. That he is armed and extremely dangerous.'

The youngest of the agents, Miller he thought the fellow was called, went absolutely white at this suggestion.

'This could be the biggest coup for the Bureau to date, men. Something to tell your children. Just remember your training.'

But Niel was not sure that basic training covered anything remotely like this operation.

'Randall, you keep two men with you here at the front entrance and three more of you go round to the back entrance and set up watch there. I've got to go inside and shepherd him. Good luck, men.'

Niel went quickly back in before they could ask any more questions; before their fear had an opportunity to make further inroads on their courage. He could see the soldier at the phone directory desk now, talking to the middle-aged woman there. What's he up to? Niel wondered.

'It must be a fascinating job,' Max said to the directory assistant, a woman with dark circles under her eyes that she tried to hide with pancake make-up. She succeeded only in making her face look like a mask, brittle and coarse. Her bright red hair was colored, Max noticed, and everything about her spoke of a quiet desperation to look younger than she was. She sagged in the breasts and middle, and had the beginnings of jowls.

'Oh, yes. Never two days alike, you know. Just the other day we had a call come all the way from San Francisco.'

'Imagine that,' Max said. 'It's not like a soldier's life. Mine's all routine.' He smiled at her winningly.

Suddenly the assistant, noticing others in line, became all business. 'So you placed your call, then. That'll be fifteen cents.'

Max dug some change out of the pocket of the unfamiliar and scratchy uniform, still feeling conspicuous in the puttees. He laid the coins on the shiny wooden counter between them.

'You know, I've been awfully foolish. I just called my friend and arranged to meet with him, but did not find out where exactly his house is located. It's in the Capitol prefix area.'

The assistant had already turned from him to serve a little lady in fur hat and muff. She looked like a forest creature: all that poked out of the fur was her tiny pink nose.

'Sorry?' the assistant said turning distractedly back to Max.

'The Capitol prefix area. Where exactly is it?'

'Oh, that's way out of town. Up the Cabin John area just north of the Potomac.' She turned back to the little lady, completely ignoring Max now.

That's it, then, he thought. You've got him. Your luck is holding. More than luck though, he knew. You make your own luck; you keep pushing, keep working.

Max left the phone room and passed into the main hall of the post office building, remembering to use the cane, to keep up the disguise at all times. As he moved toward the entrance, he began figuring out how he would trace Brantley Hall.

Pity I got rid of my guidebook, he thought to himself. The map in it of suburban Washington would probably have shown him where the house was. It's sure to be an estate with land around it. The name has most likely not changed from colonial times, regardless of who owns it. He'd have to go to a book-shop and thumb through one of their guides. The Cabin John area, the assistant said. Funny name.

Out the corner of his eye he caught a glimpse of a man half hidden behind one of the marble columns. Max did not think anything of it for several steps, until approaching the front entrance he noticed another young hatless man loitering on the steps.

Alarm bells sounded in his head: the man in the lobby behind the pillar. The loud yellow vest he wore. Where have I seen that before?

Even as he thought this out, Max abruptly changed direc-tions, turning to his left and heading back into the main lobby toward a wide arc of stairs ascending the upper stories.

It came to him in a blinding flash of remembrance: the red-haired agent at the New Willard who had been trying to get him in his sights. The one Fitzgerald had been fool enough to get in front of.

Max casually looked over his shoulder, as if scratching his cheek on the rough wool collar of the tunic. He caught a glimpse of the man in the yellow vest at the front entrance now. Red hair.

Christ! It *is* him. Max had to control himself, to stop the feeling of panic overcoming him. He must have followed him from Fitzgerald's.

He looked around quickly. The other man at the front entrance: he was with yellow vest. There will most likely be more at the back entrance. Think.

He kept walking back into the main hall, heading for the stairs as if drawn there. Slowly, he told himself. Just pray they don't try to take you inside with all these people about. Keep among people; do not give them a clear shot at you.

The stairs seemed the busiest part of the post office just at this moment; arrow signs pointed upward toward the cafeteria. It was midday, and many of the workers and customers were availing themselves of the food in-house. Max joined these people going up the marble steps, jostling into the midst of a knot of several men and a woman, obviously employees of the post office, who were talking heatedly about a projected pay raise.

'Two cents an hour is nothing, I tell you,' a hawk-faced young man was saying as Max managed to insert himself within their group. He looked at Max strangely, but Max smiled in return, limping along with them as they mounted the stairs.

He looked back quickly and now saw yellow vest, along with three other men, entering the main hall and moving to the stairs. Think, he ordered himself again. He could remember from his external view of the place that it was a four-story building, but could not remember seeing emergency exits on the façade of the building. Reaching the first floor, he desperately scanned his visual memory of the building for anything; any means of escape.

Yes! It came back to him suddenly. When he had come here on Wednesday morning to find the address of Fitzgerald's city house, he'd noticed an enclosed overpass for ease of mail transport connecting the City post office and Union Station, crossing over 1st Street. It must be on this floor, Max thought, and he left the group of workers as they reached the shadows of the first-floor corridor.

Max flung caution aside now, and no longer affected a worse limp than he actually had. The bridge was on the east side of the building, he knew, to his right. He made his way down a corridor in that direction, past private offices. This is a wild gamble, he thought, as he raced down this corridor. I have no way of knowing whether or not this is a blind alley, whether or not the overpass is even accessible, he thought to himself.

But he moved on, never looking back, reaching the end of the corridor and then looking left and right where a narrow hall continued perpendicular to the main corridor, running along the east side of the building. Which way? he wondered, his heart pounding in his throat. At that moment an employee wheeled an empty mail cart from a room to his left and he raced for the door before it closed.

'Hey! You can't go in there,' the man said, startled as Max hurtled past him and into the tunnel overpass.

Max felt his lungs biting, felt the muscles in his left leg ache and cry out for rest as he raced along the narrow corridor. From in back of him he heard echoing voices. Move! he told himself. Move or you're a dead man in this tunnel. There's no cover. You're a perfect target here. Lights overhead lit the narrow, white-walled passage. No windows gave to the outside.

Racing along, Max drew his gun out and began leaping up to strike at the naked bulbs, exploding them and leaving the space in back of him in darkness.

Just as he reached the other end of the overpass a voice rang out behind him: 'Stop or I shoot!'

Max did not slow his pace one bit as he hit the door to the station and turned the knob. It opened just as a shot rang out in back. Max was through the door and out onto the concourse, the brakes of a recently arrived train spewing steam at him. He looked around quickly and found an empty porter's cart, and jammed it against the door, under the knob. That will stop them for a few moments, he thought, as he once again set out at a run down the long concourse toward the main hall.

Should I jump a departing train? he wondered. I've got to cover my tracks quickly, before yellow vest and his men reach the concourse. Ahead of him he suddenly saw his salvation. The train that had just arrived was disgorging a large contingent of soldiers, all dressed in the same khaki color as he was. He looked down and suddenly saw he was holding not only the cane, but also the gun. He quickly slipped the gun inside his shoulder holster as he approached the group of soldiers. He tossed the cane out onto the tracks and melted into the mass of other khaki-clad men as they moved toward the main hall.

Don't look back, he commanded himself. Don't give yourself away. His tunic was soaked with sweat; his stomach turned into a knot. Blood pounded at his temples.

Soon the soldiers overtook other passengers from the same train, passing porters' carts piled high with suitcases and over-coats. As they passed one of these, Max picked a likely looking black camel hair overcoat and derby from an unattended pile of leather luggage monogrammed in brass with FDR, and quickly put these on.

He slowly filtered to the edges of the mass of soldiers pouring into the main station, walking listlessly as if he had not a care in the world. Soon yellow vest and his men came racing past, grabbing first one, then another of the soldiers as they were just reaching the main hall. There was absolute confusion and pandemonium as the agents were gruffly shoved aside by the soldiers, here in Washington on leave and not wanting to be messed with. An altercation broke out with one of the soldiers, a little man about Max's size, and yellow vest. Max passed unobserved out of the main hall just as the soldier was threatening to cave in yellow vest's nose.

Outside three men similar in appearance to those with yellow vest mounted the steps two at a time right past Max, dashing into the hall.

Max continued down the steps, climbed calmly into a waiting taxi, and drove away.

FIFTEEN

'Man to see you, Miss Catherine,' Thomas announced later that morning.

Agent Niel entered, his face screwed into a grimace. 'Could we speak,' Niel said. 'In private.'

Catherine caught Thomas's eye and nodded at him. Niel's tone made her nervous.

'What is it, Mr Niel?' she said as Thomas closed the door. She did not offer him a seat, but he took one anyway, on the chintz couch. He picked up the novel she had been reading, Lawrence's *The Rainbow*, examining it as if for clues, then dropped it back casually onto the cushion.

He said nothing for a moment, then suddenly he stood once more, staring straight into her face. He was a couple of inches shorter than Catherine and so had to look upward. Still his presence frightened her. She involuntarily moved backward a step.

'You had a visitor this morning, didn't you?'

'No. Not that I recall.'

'Come off it, Mrs Fitzgerald. I saw him coming out of here myself. The officer on duty let him go by.'

'You mean the soldier?'

Niel bared his teeth; he obviously meant it as an ironic grin, but it made him look like a ferret and Catherine felt herself shivering.

'Yes, the soldier.' He continued to fix her in his gaze.

'He came for contributions for the preparedness committees,' she said.

'I'm sure he did. And did you contribute?'

'Nothing. He left before I could speak with him. I was in the dark room.'

'Are you sure?' the agent said.

'I beg your pardon.'

He suddenly drew a notebook out of his pocket. 'Do you recognize this?'

'Wherever did you find that? That's my journal.'

'I know what it is,' Niel said. 'This was found in the room of M, the man who is trying to kill your uncle.'

'Impossible.'

'I myself found it under the man's mattress at the World Peace League house.'

The name stopped her for a moment. 'The World Peace League?'

Niel smiled, nodding his head.

'It can't be.' She remembered now that the journal had gone missing the day of her attack, the day the man named Maximillian Voetner saved her. And she had been unconscious for several moments.

'He must have taken it then,' she said out loud.

'You're not making much sense, Mrs Fitzgerald. Do you admit you know the man who had this journal?'

'Yes. I think I do. I met him quite by accident several days ago while photographing in town. He was . . . most helpful to me.' She was damned if she was going to tell this little worm the whole embarrassing tale.

'How convenient,' Niel said with a smirk.

'I tell you the man was a complete stranger to me. His name is, I believe, Maximillian Voetner. He said he was the South African representative to the World Peace League. Ask him yourself, if you don't believe me.'

'I would ask him if I could, Mrs Fitzgerald. But the man gave us the slip at Union Station.'

'That was most unfortunate for you, Mr Niel. But I again tell you the man was a total stranger to me.'

'Then why come here today?'

'I don't know. As I said, he did not wait for me. He was gone by the time I got out of the dark room.'

'I must tell you, Mrs Fitzgerald, I do not like this.'

'And I do not like your insinuations, Mr Niel. I believe it is time you left.'

'Not until you tell me your connection to this assassin.'

She felt an uncontrollable rage overcoming her and wanted to physically attack the man. Instead she shouted at him. 'What right have you to come into my home and accuse me? This is still a free country.'

Again the ferret smile came across Niel's face, and he shook his head. 'Oh, no, Mrs Fitzgerald. That's where you're wrong. Freedom.' He suddenly laughed high and quite wildly. 'There's a time coming when we won't be able to afford your sort of freedom and individual privacy anymore. Those concepts will have to go the way of the dinosaur. Our great country is beset upon by enemies from every quarter. We have revolutionaries threatening us on all sides. Negroes, suffragettes, Wobblies and socialists who want to do in our form of government. Free love people, like that filth you're reading.' He nodded scornfully at the novel on her couch. 'Enemies everywhere you look. And we're building files on all of you, I tell you. On Emma Goldman and the Negro socialist Philip Randolph and Max Eastman and Big Bill Haywood. Files on all of them, including you, Mrs Fitzgerald. And you think you're so special that we at the Bureau can't touch you? Think again.'

He suddenly fell quiet, breathing rapidly. It was as if he realized that he had said too much, and suddenly his menacing grimace was transformed, replaced by the plucky little Irish grin. This transformation chilled her more than his ranting had.

'Of course,' he said calmly, 'if you say you did not see the soldier who came here this morning, I'll have to take your word for it. Just one thing I would like to know: how did he get the phone number of your country estate, then?'

'What?'

'Capitol 2345. That is the number at Brantley Hall, isn't it?'

She nodded dumbly, her mind racing.

'And that's the number our man called from the City post office. He went straight there from here and placed a call. I checked with the clerk afterward and got the number.'

She knew Niel was not lying about this, and suddenly she remembered how she had left her address book out on the table after talking with the young man from the embassy that morning. It was open to the number at Brantley.

'He must have looked at my address book while waiting for me.'

'Most unfortunate,' Niel said. After his outburst, he now was calm again, almost solicitous, as if afraid that he had so overstepped his position that he was in danger.

Catherine was filled with sudden fear. Both Adrian and Edward are at Brantley, she thought. Is this German agent on his way there now?

'Have you alerted my husband?' she said.

He nodded though he had not yet. 'I'll be leaving then, Mrs Fitzgerald,' Niel said. 'Don't be too hard on yourself,' Niel said ironically, as he opened the door. 'At least we know where our man is headed now, don't we?'

Max paid the cashier with his last five-dollar bill, and received $4.15 change. He was not concerned about money; after killing Appleby he knew he could somehow make his way back to New York, and from there Manstein would have to see to getting him out of the country. Besides, America was filled with rich people. If I need more money, I will simply rob somebody, he told himself.

Leaving Brentano's bookstore with the guide to suburban Washington under his arm, he felt powerful and unstoppable. The cold air braced him. Slanting rays of low winter sun filled the street with a rich golden light, throwing massive shadows across the street. Shoppers, busy with their Saturday purchases, did not notice Max as he made his way down the street.

'What do you mean, at my home?' Fitzgerald heard his voice thunder in the narrow hallway of Brantley. 'My God! Catherine.'

'She's quite all right,' Agent Niel said, smiling brightly.

What the hell has the man got to smile about? Fitzgerald wondered.

'It seems the fellow was posing as a veteran collecting for preparedness committees to gain entrance.'

'Wasn't Thomas there? Didn't anyone get suspicious?'

Niel shrugged. 'I only know what your wife told me. Luckily, the man was gone by the time she came from the dark room.'

'But what in God's name did he hope to achieve by such a stunt?'

Appleby sauntered into the hall now, followed by Chief Inspector Lewis, both curious to see who the visitor was. Lewis sighed with his eyes when he saw Niel; Appleby nodded curtly.

'What brings you out here, Niel?' Chief Inspector Lewis said. 'I thought you were coordinating things in Washington.'

'He's spotted the German,' Fitzgerald blurted out. 'At Poplars.'

Appleby's face turned white. 'Christ! Is Catherine all right?'

'I was just explaining to Mr Fitzgerald that everything is fine at that end. I tailed the fellow to the City post office where he went directly after leaving Poplars.'

'Don't tell me,' Fitzgerald said. 'You lost him.'

Niel sucked air between his front teeth making a rather unpleasant sound. 'Yes. He gave us the slip at Union Station.'

There was a communal groan from the men in the hall.

'But we did discover something quite important. What he was doing at the City post office at all.'

Niel paused momentarily, seeming to enjoy the attention his pronouncement had made on them.

'Well, get on with it then, Niel,' Lewis finally spluttered out. 'What was he doing at the post office?'

'Making a call.' Niel looked at the three each in turn, stopping at Fitzgerald. 'It seems he had a chance to go through your wife's address book. It was the number here at Brantley he phoned.'

'No.' Appleby said it with a rasping moan at the end.

'Afraid so, Sir Adrian,' Niel said.

Fitzgerald felt his heart sink, remembering having heard the phone ring earlier. How could Monroe have been so stupid as to give the man any information? Couldn't he hear the accent? But even as he thought this, he knew it was pointless to blame Monroe. After all, the man had signed on as a caretaker, not a warder.

'Why the hell didn't you alert us by phone?' Lewis demanded. 'The bastard could already be here by now.'

'Oh, I don't think there's much worry on that score,' Niel said, again smiling.

The smile was beginning to irritate Fitzgerald. It was the sort of cockiness he did not at all like. His thoughts went momentarily to Catherine. A sudden and paralyzing fear overcame him. What if the fellow had harmed her? Kidnapped her? Attempted to force the whereabouts of Appleby from her? How ignorant I've been, leaving her virtually unguarded in Washington while we sit here at Brantley surrounded and protected by over a hundred police and soldiers.

'What's not to worry about?' Lewis said.

'I mean simply, Inspector Lewis, that I have seen to laying roadblocks on every conceivable entry route to Brantley. The local constabulary here on the grounds have been alerted as to a new description: our man is possibly wearing an army uniform.'

'Won't that be a bit confusing?' Fitzgerald said, stirring himself from his evil thoughts. 'Seeing as how we have a unit of the home guard here as well?'

'What would you have me do, Mr Fitzgerald? Tell the men to strip down to their skivvies? It may be warming up outside, but underwear is still far from seasonable attire.'

Fitzgerald noticed only now that in fact it had been getting warmer outside. The dripping sound he'd been subliminally hearing this afternoon was obviously the melt from the roof.

'We've got to move Adrian again,' Fitzgerald said. 'We can hardly risk staying here now that M knows our location.' He found himself discussing Adrian as if he were not present; in fact Adrian was only marginally there, standing apart from Lewis, Niel and himself almost in a daze. The news had sent a film over his eyes; his jaw was slack.

'Hold on now, Mr Fitzgerald,' Lewis said. 'We don't want to go off half-cocked scurrying for a safe house about the countryside. That's exactly what M would want. Give him the opportunity that he needs. We keep Sir Adrian under wraps and inside the house with all these men outside and inside, and there's no way the German is going to get to him.'

'Unless he torches the house,' Niel said.

'My God!' Fitzgerald said.

'Or bombs it,' Niel added cheerily. 'Though there is really little likelihood for either of those circumstances. After all, the man would have to gain proximity for either maneuver. And if our men posted outside remain alert—'

'If?'

'They're only human, Mr Fitzgerald,' Niel said.

'We're not talking about an eternity of vigilance. All we need is one night! I say we move Adrian. Now.'

'It's just not on, Fitzgerald,' Lewis said, obviously warming to his argument.

'Stop!'

The three turned to Appleby.

'I believe I have some say in these matters,' he said, regaining his poise. 'And I have had enough of running. I'm damned if I will allow one German to send me scurrying any longer. Here I make my stand. I want a gun, Edward.'

'Certainly.'

'Do you think that wise, Sir Adrian,' Niel said.

'I was handling a shotgun while you were still at your mother's teat.'

Which was patently a lie, Fitzgerald knew, but it was good to see Appleby regain his bluff façade.

'I take it you have a root cellar in this old house, Edward.'

'Yes, but I hardly see—'

'Fine,' Appleby went on blithely. 'I shall make my bed down there tonight. Let the rotter burn us or bomb us. I shall be below ground impervious to his assaults, like my fellow countrymen when the Zeppelins fly over London. Here I am and here I shall remain. Besides, we have to finish our rubber. Are you a bridge man, Niel?'

'Afraid not, Sir Adrian. I have my work cut out for me outside, anyway.' He looked meaningfully at Lewis.

'I guess I might as well join you,' the inspector said to Niel. Then turning, he called down the hall, 'Scott, Paxton.'

Two blue-uniformed policemen who had been designated personal bodyguards to Appleby came out into the hall from the sitting room doorway where they had been respectfully waiting.

'I'll be in the grounds for a time,' Lewis said. 'What are your orders?'

'To stick with Mr Appleby here like glue,' said Scott, the

shorter, thicker of the two, who was built like a wrestler with a neck stouter than Fitzgerald's thigh muscle.

'And where have you been for the past few minutes, then?' he demanded, and Scott's face went red.

'We were just by the door, sir,' the other policeman, Paxton, protested. His voice was surprisingly high for a man so large; everything about him was massive, even his fingers which now played nervously on the leather twine around his neck holding his whistle.

'From now on there are no private moments. Even at the toilet, I want one of you inside with Sir Adrian, the other stationed at the door outside. Is that understood?'

'Yes, sir,' the two said in almost exact unison.

'If anybody you have not been introduced to thus far attempts to approach Appleby, you two shoot first and ask questions after. And that is not just Wild West hyperbole, but an order.'

Lewis turned abruptly from the two to glare down on Niel. 'Shall we be going? I want to double check our men before nightfall.'

'Not to worry, Lewis,' Niel said in his most ingratiating faux Irish brogue. 'We're after having this under control.' Then his roguish smile vanished suddenly, replaced by a determined and menacing squint. 'Let the fool come near here tonight. It'll be the end of him.'

Fitzgerald watched the two bundle up and go outdoors to check on the deployment, and as the door closed in back of them he looked at Appleby. It was as if his old friend were someplace else once more; his unfocussed gaze drifted out through the narrow hall window to a strip of crimson light low on the western horizon. Sunset.

Max waited patiently outside the offices of Western Union Telegraph Company at 1401 F Street in Washington.

He knew that having tracked him to the City post office, yellow vest most likely knew Max had discovered Brantley.

So what? he thought. They won't move Appleby, not at this late date, and they won't risk moving him at night, not if they fear I may be lurking about in the bushes with a sniper's rifle.

The worst that has happened because of yellow vest is that

they will be expecting me, but then they have always been expecting me. I'll have to be careful on approach roads, but I'll get through whatever obstacle they put in my way. After all, this is now a matter of wills. Mine against theirs. So they have a cartload of police out there at the estate: how many of those will be willing to lay down their lives to save Appleby? That's the real algebra involved here: not a hundred of them against one of me, but my will and willingness to die to accomplish this mission, against theirs to simply do their job and live to put their feet up on the hob at the end of the day.

A shiver passed through him; he had never made this ultimate calculation before, but knew now that he was willing to give up his life in order to stop Appleby from getting to Wilson with the Zimmermann telegram; in order to stop further carnage in Flanders and all up and down the eastern and western fronts.

He watched a motorcyclist in leather helmet, uniform, and goggles pull up outside the telegraph company, dismount like an equestrian, pull the motorcycle up onto its stand, and dash into the office. Lights were coming on now throughout downtown Washington and the streets, wet from thaw, shone translucently with the incandescent light cast through hundreds of windows. Max watched through this particular window as the young leather-clad messenger went to the back desk of the telegraph office and talked to an older clerk there wearing wire-frame glasses and a black suit.

The messenger's motorcycle coughed in the evening air, running ragged. In his haste he had left it going, something Max had been waiting the last hour for. He quickly moved to the motorcycle, mounted it and pushed forward off the stand. Revving the engine once with the hand throttle, he quickly took stock of the configuration of brake and clutch. The machine throbbed between his legs like a living thing. He stepped the gear into first, slowly fed the throttle and sped off down F Street to the west, toward the strip of sunset glimmering like a streak of blood on the horizon.

Step one accomplished, he thought, smiling at the ease of it all.

SIXTEEN

C atherine and Thomas sat in the red roadster at the main gates to Brantley, a surly home guard sergeant leveling his carbine at them.

'I tell you,' she insisted once again, 'I am Mrs Fitzgerald. This is my home.'

'They'll be along presently, ma'am,' the sergeant said. 'You just sit tight. No sudden moves, please.'

'But this is absurd.'

She felt a hand at her arm, and turned to face Thomas.

'This is no time for decrees, Miss Catherine. You don't reason with a gun; you just sit tight like the man says.'

Thomas was right, she knew, but still it rankled that she should be denied entrance to her own home. They sat for a few more moments in relative silence, the car engine still running and the headlights casting twin antennae into the night. The grounds of Brantley looked as if there were hundreds of fireflies flittering about, and she only slowly came to understand that these were campfires and hurricane lanterns of police and army men who had come to protect her uncle. The roads leading to the estate had been guarded as well; she and Thomas had had to go through two separate sets of roadblocks just to reach the main gates. They would all have a cold night outside, she thought, and then felt badly for her complaints to this sergeant. After all, the man was only doing his job, trying to keep Uncle Adrian alive. I should be grateful rather than complaining, she castigated herself.

Yet she could not help it: she was anxious to get to the house, to see her husband, to find out exactly what Agent Niel had told him. She could hear footsteps coming down the drive; saw the bouncing beams cast by hand-held lanterns and a group of legs illuminated in their globes of light.

'Sergeant Carson?'

Catherine recognized Chief Inspector Lewis's gruff tones.

'Over here, inspector,' the sergeant answered, never taking

his eyes off Catherine or Thomas. 'Lady here says this is her house. Got a colored fellow with her.'

'Catherine?'

This was her husband's voice, and as the men approached she could make out his tall, straight form.

'Yes, Edward,' she called out to him. 'Do please save us from execution in the morning.'

'Open the gate, sergeant. It's my wife.'

She could see him clearly now, illuminated in her headlights along with Lewis and another policeman, and the sergeant fitted the key in the huge lock. There was a clinking and clanking of metal against metal and the gate opened. Edward trotted out to the car.

'What are you doing here?' he said. 'I've been worried sick trying to call you at Poplars all evening and getting no answer.'

'I wanted to be with you,' she said simply and honestly. Then teasingly she added, 'I brought Thomas along for protection.'

'The police on duty in Washington should never have let you leave,' he said. 'After what Niel told me today about M being at Poplars, I didn't know what to think.'

'I couldn't stay at Poplars alone. I belong here, with you.' And saying it, she suddenly realized that it was true.

'Yes,' Edward said reproachfully. 'But all the same, it was damn silly of you. You shouldn't have let her do it, Thomas.'

'Don't blame Thomas,' she said sharply.

'How in the name of God did you get by the guards at Poplars?'

She smiled. 'I told them we were off to an embassy party.'

A half smile crossed his lips at this, she noticed.

'May we get to the house now, or do you want to search us first?'

'Don't be ridiculous,' he spluttered. Then turning back to the gate, he called out to Lewis, 'We've got a couple more visitors. Best alert the men in the house.'

Catherine put the roadster in gear. 'Hop on the running boards,' she said, and to her surprise, Edward did. They traveled up the drive like that, with Edward hanging on for dear life as she drove along. Lights were everywhere, she noticed again. There were men scattered so thickly about the grounds that not even a field mouse could get into the house tonight.

There seemed no way for Max to be able to get to Adrian.

'I could use a nice hot toddy,' she said, turning off the engine and climbing out of the roadster.

'You need a good firm reprimand,' Edward said, jumping off the running board and suddenly hugging her to him. 'But it was marvelous of you to come,' he whispered in her ear.

Later, after freshening up, Catherine sat at one end of the dinner table, Edward at the other. In between, on opposite sides, were Niel and Lewis. Appleby sat next to Lewis. Dress was country casual. At the door to the dining room were two massive policemen introduced to Catherine as Scott and Paxton, though she was unsure which was which. It was a relatively quiet meal, at least as far as Catherine was concerned. When meeting Niel again she nodded but turned away before he could make polite talk.

She smiled prettily for the men and picked desultorily at her roasted potatoes and veal.

'This is a quite decent bottle of claret, Edward,' Appleby said.

Fitzgerald looked up from his plate distractedly. 'Pardon? The wine. Yes, it is drinkable, isn't it?'

Catherine was surprised at his distraction; Edward is usually so attentive, she thought. Clearly all this has been affecting him as much as any of us. She cut a small chunk of the veal and forked it into her mouth. It had no taste for her; neither did the potatoes or the wine.

'What is it?' Appleby went on. 'St Emilion? It has that sort of lime soil aftertaste.'

'Californian, actually,' Fitzgerald said. 'The Napa Valley.'

Appleby held the wine glass out at arms length in shock. 'You've got to be joking.'

'No,' Fitzgerald said, smiling. 'They're beginning to put out some fine wines there.'

Appleby shook his head, holding the glass in front of the candles in one of the silver candelabra on the table, and examined the deep red color in the flame's light. 'Incredible,' he said. 'Next they'll be making wine in Australia. Gold diggers and convicts become the great vintners.'

Thomas entered the dining room quietly, surprising them all by a sudden question: 'Shall I clear for desert now, Miss Catherine?'

She quickly surveyed the plates. 'Not yet, Thomas. I'll call.'

'Very well.' He backed out of the room, a faint smile on his lips.

A violent pounding at the front door suddenly sounded. Scott and Paxton on duty in the dining room drew their weapons. Suddenly another policeman from the hallway rapped on the door to the dining room and Scott opened it carefully. The policeman at the door had wide eyes and was out of breath. He sucked in air and said excitedly, 'They've got him, sir. Down by the front gates.'

Max drove north out of Washington on Connecticut Avenue, suspecting that the roads leading more directly to Brantley Hall, either along the Potomac or via River Road, would be closely watched, perhaps even blocked. He was amazed at how quickly he reached the countryside of Maryland. Here and there along the roadside were lights in the windows of the great estates, brick-pillared entryways in front. An occasional car passed, heading south into the city. No other traffic seemed to be going his way. The moon, low on the horizon, came out from behind a haze of clouds and lit the winter landscape all around.

Max was not dressed for a motorcycle, wearing only the army tunic and breeches he'd borrowed from Karl at the hobo camp. He had discarded the coat and derby he'd stolen this afternoon at Union Station, opting to keep the military uniform. After all, he reasoned, Washington is full of service men, and there are sure to be more at Fitzgerald's estate. Why risk buying or stealing a new set of clothes when the military uniform could still be my best disguise?

But it did little to keep the chill out as he sped along the nearly deserted country road. A rabbit skittered across the road in front of him at one point, and he gripped the brakes, skidding across the road into the opposite lane. No traffic was coming, but the incident brought him out of his planning reverie and he realized he had traveled far enough north. He then headed west on small back roads, using the moon as his direction finder. In his mind was a fair reproduction of the road systems leading to Brantley Hall from the northeast, a direction from which the police would not, he hoped, be expecting him.

He was wrong about that, however. Some three miles above
Brantley, Max caught a glimpse of brake lights ahead of him.
He pulled over, cutting his engine immediately. It could just
be a cautious driver, he thought. A sharp curve ahead. But he
could take no chances. The night silence became profound after
the noise of his engine died and his ears took a moment to
adjust, like eyes to night vision. He heard the slamming of a
vehicle door up the road, voices, then the gunning of an engine
and the slow grind of a truck pulling away and going through
its gears. More silence as the truck got further and further away.
Then the sound of voices again from just up the road.

Max pushed the motorcycle off the side of the road into a
thicket of bushes and concealed it under branches. There was
nothing he could do about his footprints in the snow leading
in and out of the thicket, but by the feel of the air temperature
now that he was not moving, he knew there would be a melt
tonight. Besides, he reasoned, who will be coming along with
a light tonight to search for footprints in the snow? They're
looking for me on the roads, not in hiding. By the time it's
light, I'll be long gone from here.

He made his way along the side of the road for a time, the
puttees quickly becoming soaked in the calf-high snow. Ahead
he caught the glimmer of lantern light, and the sound of voices
was even more distinct. As he approached the light, he maneu-
vered further off the road, making his way now through a copse
of bare trees that provided a modicum of cover for him. The
moon was in front of him; there would be no backlight to
silhouette him. He moved cautiously through the snow, careful
not to step on branches or stumble in the dark. Soon enough he
could see the source of the light: two policemen with a roadblock
effected by their car turned sideways to halt traffic. One of the
police was stumping up and down the road in front of the car,
while the other crouched near a fire built out of scrub brush.

'Crazy son of bitches at the Bureau,' the one walking
suddenly called out to his partner.

The man by the fire said something so low that it was
unintelligible to Max.

Then the first one continued his complaint: 'Nobody's
coming along this road, for God sake. Not even Santa Claus.'

More grumbling from the one by the fire and Max made his way around the roadblock, following the road at a distance of a hundred yards or so. He would have to go the rest of the way on foot. If there were a roadblock this far from Brantley, then the roads closer to the estate would be crawling with police, he figured. He kept the moon to his left as he made his way; the rough layout of roads was in his head. He should come to an intersection soon and then he would have to head directly south.

After an hour of walking, he skirted the intersection he was looking for, bypassing yet another roadblock, this one manned by six police. They do mean business, he thought, and grinned into the night as he continued walking stealthily off the roads. The game pleased him: to win against all odds, that would be a lovely thing.

After another hour he had to leave the road systems completely and head cross country, for police were stationed at odd intervals along the roads and he could not risk being seen. He reckoned Brantley was, in fact, just over the next rise. It was hard going up the hill and the moon went behind dense cloud cover for a time. He floundered off course and before he realized it he stumbled into a barnyard, the great black hulk of the barn looming up suddenly in front of him.

A dog nearby set up a staccato barking and a door opened suddenly to his left. Max dove to the first cover he could find, which turned out to be a muck heap, but at least it was warm. He watched as a tall reedy man in a wool shirt and baggy work pants came out onto the porch of a small farmhouse, carrying a lantern in front of him. The timid light lit up the whole of the darkened barnyard, and Max quickly took note of his surroundings: the barn; the ramshackle house; a plough he had almost dived onto just by the pile of muck he was hiding behind; a dog kennel next to the barn with a short-legged dog setting up a racket still.

'Quiet, Brutus,' the man on the porch called, and the dog stopped barking, but still whined as it looked directly at Max not fifteen feet distant.

Max then noticed that the man carried a shotgun in his left hand. He held the lantern up to the night, peering into the darkness, and Brutus gave another yap.

'Shut up, you mongrel!' the man growled, and the dog obeyed, its tail curling under its rump.

The man looked to right and left once more, sniffed the night air, then went back into the house, slamming the door in back of him.

Max sat still for another few minutes, breathing shallowly, not making a sound. Then finally he got to his feet and the dog began to whine at him again.

'Shh, Brutus,' Max whispered, and he could see the dog's ears in silhouette perk up at the sound of its name, and its tail began to wag. Max passed out of the barnyard unmolested, reached the crest of the hill, and began the downward ascent. He could see a house in the distance with lights on and surrounding it seemed to be an army of more campfires.

Jesus! he thought. They do have Appleby protected. He moved on stealthily, half bent over to the ground, for there was little cover now as he approached the gates to the estate.

As he reached a safe watching position just across the road from the main gates and hid in a clump of bushes, all hell broke out across the way from him. There was confusion and shouts and lots of motion. A pair of policemen even ran by the bushes where he was hiding to aid in the disturbance at the main gates. Soon he saw a car driving down to the gates and saw in the light illuminated now by more than a dozen torches and lanterns Fitzgerald himself get out of a black car along with a big rough looking fellow, the one who he had taken as a human shield at the Willard, and also by yellow vest. Max stilled his thoughts, listening to what was going on across the way.

'Good job, men,' the big one said to the officers at the gate who Max now could see were holding a man by his arms, a gun to his head.

'For God sake!' Fitzgerald shouted. 'You fools. That's not the German. That's my land manager, Ned Blakely.'

'I told 'em, Mr Fitzgerald,' the lanky man whom the police were holding called out. 'But they wouldn't believe me.'

'Your what?' the big man said, exasperated.

'I told you, Lewis. It's Blakely. He was coming over tonight to discuss spring planting. I thought it would help to pass the time.'

'Brilliant,' yellow vest said in a voice full of irony.

Max was beginning to enjoy the show.

'Well, you heard what Fitzgerald said,' Lewis told his men. 'Uncock that gun and let the fellow go.'

The men did as ordered and Blakely shook his rumpled coat free of their hands.

'Come on Blakely,' Fitzgerald said. 'I'll give you a stiff drink back at the house. Sorry about this.'

Max continued to watch as the men got back into the car, first Blakely, then Lewis, and then yellow vest and Fitzgerald as they were caught in a silly male dance of 'No, you first' and vied for last position. Fitzgerald won, but not without a clumsy sort of brushing against each other, mistaking who would go first. But finally the car was packed and set off back to the main house, the police on duty chastised for being too quick on the draw.

Max stayed in position for several more minutes. I know two things now, at any rate, he thought. One: Appleby is still at Brantley. And two: there is not a chance in hell for me to get through the police lines to him.

Feet moved by the bushes where he was hidden and stopped. He could see the scuffed toes just inches from him; see mud splattered on the blue serge cuff. His entire body tensed. So busy had he been watching the scene and plotting his next move, that he thought he would be invisible to all watchers. Now he was not so sure. He reached silently for his gun. They won't take me without a fight, he determined. Perhaps I should feign sickness; pretend that I'm just one of them who had to sneak off into the brush to relieve himself.

The policeman lit a cigarette, and Max could now see his face in the yellow globe of flame: hawk nose, long black moustache, thick fingers curling around the cigarette as he breathed smoke in deeply and then let it trail out slowly through his clenched teeth.

Max had his gun out now and eased the safety off.

Another deep inhalation, and then the guard moved away.

Max breathed deeply; his racing heart began to calm down.

I can't stay around here hoping for a chance meeting; for a lucky shot if and when Appleby makes an appearance outside. That would be pure stupidity. I have a matter of hours to get

to the Englishman now. How to do it? There were some
uniformed soldiers at the main gate, Max now noticed, but
their uniforms were different than his. The tunics were longer
and they wore no puttees.

I could ambush one of them, he thought. Kill him, hide his
body and take his uniform and get close enough to the house to
. . . To do what? he wondered. There are sure to be more inside:
bodyguards who will let no unauthorized person close to Appleby.

Max waited for the smoking policeman to walk further
away, and then moved out of his hiding place in a crouch,
heading back up the hill. Several hundred yards from the road,
he turned and surveyed the scene again. Maybe I'm going
about this the wrong way. He thought of the silly incident at
the gate and smiled at the incompetence of the police.

Suddenly a plan came into his mind, complete and perfect;
all of a piece. It was as if he had been planning it all along.

I'll need to go back to the hobo camp for this, he told
himself. I'll need help. He turned the plan around in his mind's
eye quickly again, like a jeweler examining a diamond before
making his cuts.

It had been a long day for Fitzgerald. The grotesque mix-up over
Blakely had capped it off. He had spent an hour with the land
manager in his downstairs office once he'd calmed the man with
a stiff whiskey. But neither of them had really felt in the mood
to go over planting schemes after all the turmoil. They had sat
silently for the most part, listening to the wall clock tick. He
and Blakely had an unspoken sort of male friendship in which
words played little part. They had hunted grouse together on the
estate and plotted fields. They talked for a time of Mrs Blakely
who had been recently ill, and then of the European war, and
Fitzgerald had felt himself going mute on the subject. He was
no longer so sure about anything, the necessity for war included.
But it was much too late for such second thoughts.

By ten he was on his way upstairs to join Catherine who
had retired half an hour earlier. Adrian, true to his word, had
had a bed made up for him in the root cellar off the basement.
His watchers, Scott and Paxton, were keeping post down there
with him.

Yes, a long day, Fitzgerald thought as he reached the first landing and headed for their corner bedroom. He knocked lightly before entering the room. Catherine turned from the mirror of the low make-up table where she was seated. She wore a white muslin nightgown cut high to her throat. A brush was in her hand.

'I think I'll let my hair grow out again,' she said, smiling at him as he entered. 'What do you think?'

'I think that would be a lovely idea. If you want to.'

'But what do you want, Edward?' She pulled the brush through her short thick hair, looking at him now in the reflection over her shoulder.

'I like it long.' He took off his jacket and let it drop on the bed, watching her as she fidgeted more in front of the mirror.

'What are you looking at?' she said.

'The woman I love.'

He thought he saw tears come to her eyes; her hand trembled as it brushed her hair. 'Edward . . .' she began.

'Look,' he said at the same time, their voices sounding together.

He nodded at her, but she said, 'Go on. What?'

'I haven't been quite truthful with you,' he said. 'And it makes me ashamed. You've put your life at risk for your uncle, for his telegram. At the theater, now here again you've come to be with me. Expressly against my orders, may I remind you.'

'Don't be a stuffed shirt, Edward. What is it you want to say? How have you been untruthful?'

'The damned telegram. There, I said. At first I had my doubts about it. The British government is not above forgery. But initially that did not matter to me. And I lied to you about that. I let my political goals take precedence over my oath to you as a husband. I apologize.'

'And now?' she said. 'Any more doubts?'

'Absolutely none at all.'

There was a moment of silence. 'Thank you, Edward. I am grateful to you, more than you will ever know. That was important for me.'

It was as if he blushed at such praise, she thought.

'And what is it you were going to say?' he asked.

And then she told him about the mysterious 'South African' who had saved her from rape. His face went white when she recounted this. She told him of losing her journal and how she suspected that this was the same man who came dressed as a soldier to Poplars this morning.

'He was very kind to me after . . . after the incident. Talked to me. Helped me work through the shock.'

'But you never said a thing about it to me.'

'No, darling,' she said. 'I suppose I was too embarrassed, too angry at myself for being caught in such a weak position.'

'How awful it must have been for you.' He came to her, cupping her head in his large hand tenderly.

'I do believe Niel suspects me of some relationship with this M as a result. He behaved quite strangely this morning. I had to ask him to leave the house.'

'He's a jumped-up corner policeman. If he's bothered you, I'll have his badge.'

'No, no, Edward. Just to let you know. The man is very ambitious. I do believe he hopes to make his career with this case. With or without our cooperation.'

He looked at Catherine with deep affection.

'Maybe we've both dealt in half-truths with each other long enough. Maybe it's time for a new beginning.'

It was as if she gave herself up at that moment, he thought, let her body sag completely into his, and he picked her up, took her to the bed, and lay her down like a rag doll.

'You're exhausted from all this. You need a good night's sleep. I'll bed down in the spare room next door.'

She grabbed his hand as he was backing away. 'No. Stay. Stay with me. Make love to me.'

Later they slept curled together like spoons as they had when first married.

Outside, the wind came up out of the south, blowing warm, and the moon appeared again from behind the clouds, buttery yellow on the snow-covered fields. An occasional clicking of rifle against bandolier and the rustle and creak of leather belts sounded from the men on duty outside the house, but Fitzgerald and his wife did not hear: they slept together deep and dreamlessly, almost innocently.

SEVENTEEN

I t was a solemn breakfast. Mrs Monroe had laid on her best approximation of the English country house extravaganza, even down to the kippers on the groaning sideboard in the dining room, but Lewis was the only one with any appetite.

Fitzgerald never ate large breakfasts, but was feeling damn fine this morning, as if a new life had been granted him. Catherine and he had rekindled the love that had been smoldering all these years: it was a wonder. Yet as usual he hid behind a controlled facade, restraining himself from smiling or from acting as happily as he felt. Old habits die hard.

He looked across the table at Appleby who had obviously had a rough night: dark pouches hung under his limpid eyes. Appleby nibbled on a golden brown slice of bacon, sipped on tepid tea, wearing his best diplomatic gray morning coat for the meeting with Wilson, but seemed far from confident he would ever get to meet with the president.

Niel had joined them, as well, and he ate toast and drank coffee, eschewing any of the animal fat. He had treated them to a long disquisition on the evils of same, and the healthy joys of vegetarianism, to little of which any of them had listened. Now Niel had resumed silence, except for the crunch of his unbuttered toast between his tiny white teeth.

Catherine had not yet come down, and Fitzgerald found himself wishing he could simply remain in bed with her all day long. He loved the feel of her skin next to his; the warm yeasty smell of their lovemaking coming from under the blankets. He felt as if last night were the beginning of a new life for them; as if he should give up public life and devote himself to this farm and his wife. Perhaps there might even be children. That would be a lovely thing, he thought. Children in this old house.

'God, that is a chilly root cellar you've got, Edward,' Appleby suddenly said, breaking in two the bacon he was holding and dropping both pieces disgustedly onto the blue and white china plate in front of him.

Fitzgerald could no longer restrain himself. 'I don't know why you're acting so glum, Adrian. You're out of the woods now. You'll be meeting with Wilson in a few hours and on your way back to England by tomorrow evening.'

'Let's not get over confident,' Niel said, looking up from his toast once again.

'Do you really think so?' Appleby looked at Fitzgerald with real hope.

'Yes,' Fitzgerald said, then caught a reproving look from Lewis whose mouth was full of eggs and cottage fried potatoes at that moment, but whose eyes squinted coldly at the suggestion.

'We won't let down our guard, of course,' Fitzgerald added. 'But it seems to me if our German were going to strike, he would have done so last night. He would never risk approaching Brantley in broad daylight.'

He glanced automatically out the window to the back orchard, its trees bare, but dappled now in sunlight which reflected warmly off the melting snow. A pair of policemen patrolled by the window at that moment, their cheeks red in the morning air. What a day! he thought.

Rein in your emotions, man, he told himself. Don't get slipshod and fuzzy like a schoolboy in love at this juncture. Save it for tomorrow, or even this afternoon. For now concentrate on keeping Adrian alive. You've begun something with him and you, as a man of your word, must finish it.

He heard Lewis begin to speak about the arrangements for Adrian's trip to Washington, and how he would be meeting with his commissioner later in the morning to personally fill him in on the progress of the case, but he did not really attend to it.

Catherine suddenly entered the breakfast room, looking crisp and fresh in a pale green cashmere sweater and matching skirt. Fitzgerald rose with the others and noticed with a queer pride how their eyes followed her as she piled a plate high with eggs and bacon from the sideboard, filled a cup with dark steaming coffee and joined them, smiling as if this were her graduation day.

'Did you all sleep well?' she said, as the men sat again.

'Adrian has complaints about the root cellar,' Fitzgerald said lightly.

'Poor Uncle,' she cooed, buttering her toast.

'It's no laughing matter,' Appleby said. 'I might have caught pneumonia down there.'

'More likely that fate will befall poor Scott or Paxton,' she said. 'Their faces still looked blue from last night's chill as I passed them in the hall.'

She smiled at them all, and saved a special warmth for Fitzgerald, looking him directly in the eyes and then suddenly winking at him. He found himself flustered and embarrassed at this.

He heard the jangle of the phone in the hall and then creaking footsteps on the floorboards as Monroe went to answer it. There was the muffled voice of a one-sided phone conversation followed by footsteps coming to the door of the dining room. Everyone's eyes were on the door as it opened. Monroe, accompanied by a sleepy looking Scott, entered.

'It's for you, chief inspector,' Monroe said. 'A call from Washington.'

Lewis rose and went to the phone. Again all eyes followed, and he left the door open as he picked up the receiver. No one made a pretense not to listen in.

'Lewis here.'

There was a long pause, and Fitzgerald, who could not see Lewis, could hear him shifting from foot to foot by the phone stand, making the floorboards squeak. Fitzgerald sought out his wife's eyes, but they were averted, as if trying to look in back of her as she listened closely to Lewis.

Finally: 'You're sure it's him? He's a tricky devil.'

Fitzgerald met Catherine's eyes at this statement.

'There was a cut on his left hand. You're sure? That's marvelous, sergeant. Great work. There'll be a promotion in order for you . . . No, no. Hold him there. I'll be in town soon anyway to meet with the commissioner. Whatever you do, keep him stuck where he is until I get there. Right.'

Fitzgerald heard the receiver click back into its hook. Lewis entered the room with a smile from ear to ear on his beefy face.

'It's all over. We've got the German.'

Lewis sat back down into his chair and drained his cup of coffee, leaving the rest of them open-mouthed at this pronouncement.

'How? Where?' Niel finally demanded.

Lewis leaned back in his chair, sticking thick thumbs into his vest pockets. 'An anonymous tip, it seems. Ironic how these things ultimately work themselves out. Someone calls our boys at the Georgetown precinct house to tell them this German reported on in the papers is hiding out in a hobo camp off the C & O Canal. Our boys don't think much of it at first. They get a lot of such calls. Sometimes it's even one hobo snitching on another just to get them in trouble. But they check it out anyway and they find our man sleeping in some corrugated metal lean-to.'

'Are they absolutely sure?' Fitzgerald said, hoping that this would all finally be over.

'Oh, they're sure all right. He fits the description exactly, right down to the army outfit our boy was wearing yesterday. And he's got the wound on his left hand, to boot. He protests his innocence, of course. But then he would. He's our man, though. The wound proves it.'

Lewis sucked in air proudly, but Niel was still skeptical.

'I'll have to see him face-to-face before I believe it,' he said.

Lewis grinned broadly. 'Don't worry, Niel. You'll get plenty of chances to see him when we begin questioning.'

'I mean now,' Niel said standing and tossing his napkin onto the table. 'Which precinct house?'

'We'll go in together,' Lewis said. 'But first I need to step down security here.'

'Step down security!' Niel said. 'Don't be crazy, man.'

Lewis now stood as well, towering over Niel. 'I hope you're not forgetting who you're talking to, Agent Niel. The men at this house are under my command. We've got over a hundred of them roaming these grounds with bullets in the breeches of their rifles and safeties off. They're men from different services unused to working together in concert. It's a wonder no one was shot during the night by accident. These men are tired and cold after a night out in the open. Nerves are on edge and tempers short out there. I know. I've been out to talk with them this morning. So yes, I am going to step down security now that the German has been apprehended. To do otherwise would be insanity. Someone will be hurt needlessly if I don't. I don't intend to gut the protection here, merely avoid confusion. I'll leave, say, fifteen men to patrol the grounds, and of course Scott and Paxton will remain as personal bodyguards until Sir Adrian leaves this country.'

This did not mollify Niel who was about to start out on another tirade, but Appleby spoke up finally. 'I think that will be sufficient, chief inspector,' he said, his voice proud and full.

Fitzgerald looked at him closely and was amazed to see that he had performed yet another chameleon performance, Lewis's news having galvanized him. He sat stiffly in his chair now like a noble elder statesman. Even the bags under his eyes seemed to have diminished instantly, his face becoming taut and confident looking.

'I must prepare for the president. How does this news affect our meeting?'

'No change, Sir Adrian,' Lewis said. 'We'll still seal off the route to town; give you a little motorcade. We won't have to lay on as many men now, that's all.'

'*If* this is the right man in custody,' Niel emphasized.

'I'll re-confirm with Colonel House for you, Adrian,' Fitzgerald said, getting up from his chair and moving to the hall phone. Meanwhile Lewis and Niel departed together, an odd couple if ever there was one.

Catherine continued eating, happy that things would be getting back to normal. She had to confess that she felt a twinge of sympathy for Maximillian Voetner, or whatever his real name was. He had been kind to her and she had felt a certain attraction to him. But she realized now that was all artifice on his part. It was all a ploy to get to Uncle Adrian.

Edward rejoined them, saying that all was in order with the upcoming meeting with the president.

'Fine, fine,' Adrian said. Then, he suddenly exclaimed, 'I know what! Why waste the last bit of winter weather lounging about in the house? That pond of yours still has ice on it, Edward.'

'What are you getting at Adrian?' Fitzgerald said, suspicion in his voice.

'Why, a party, of course. This calls for a celebration, not for more skulking about like the persecuted. I am proposing a skating party, my boy. With champagne all around. In moderation of course, for I must play the restrained diplomat this afternoon. But for now, let us cut up a bit. What do you say?'

'I say what Lewis and Niel would if they were here. Keep up our guard. Stay inside.'

'Oh, nonsense, Edward. You've got not one ounce of gaiety in you.'

'Besides,' Fitzgerald went on. 'The weather is warming up. Ice can be dangerous in a thaw.'

Appleby turned to Catherine and said, 'Why you married this old stick in the mud, dear niece, I will never understand.' Then to Fitzgerald he added, 'We're as safe outside as inside, my boy. Didn't you hear Lewis? They've caught the fellow. Time to kick up our heels and shout out loud. We'll take our bodyguards along, if that's what's worrying you.'

'I still don't think it's a good idea,' Fitzgerald said.

Appleby turned to her and said, 'What do you say, niece?'

'It's a marvelous idea, uncle.'

Edward shot her a reprimanding look, then saw it was no use. He was outnumbered.

'Let's get the skates out from under the stairs,' Catherine said like a child on winter break. 'We'll have Thomas bring the champagne down later.'

Niel sat in back with Lewis as they bounced over the rough country road back toward town. Mud slapped on the chassis beneath them, the thaw was turning the roads into quagmires. His doubts about the miraculous capture had diminished and he was allowing himself to gloat.

By the time they pulled up to the precinct house on M Street in Georgetown, Niel was more than ever determined to make the German talk.

The precinct house was alive with activity; word had got

round of the coup they had made with the capture of the
German and the police there were congratulating one another,
clapping Lewis on the back as he entered. Niel tagged along
behind, making his way through the host of brawny police
as best he could. Lewis stopped at the booking desk to first
check out the sheet on the German. Looking over his
shoulder, Niel could see that they had not got much information down.

'He keeps yelling in his thick accent about how it's all a
mistake, chief inspector,' the sergeant who had made the arrest
said, taking the sheet back from Lewis. 'He must think we're
a bunch of fools.'

'Let's see him, sergeant,' Lewis said. 'I want to tell this boy
exactly what I think of him.' He rubbed his head, remembering,
Niel suspected, the blow the fellow had given him at the New
Willard.

The sergeant led them in back to the holding cells, smelling
damp and stuffy. There was no natural light back here, only
naked bulbs hanging from the ceiling of the hallway between
two rows of cells. Most of the cells were occupied by drunks
and vagrants.

'We kept him by himself back in the last one so he couldn't
get up to any mischief,' the sergeant was saying as they moved
by the cells.

Niel was planning how he would deal with the man even
as they came to the cell.

The German was sitting on his bunk, his head in his hands
looking at the floor. His left hand was bandaged, and the way
his shoulders slumped, Niel knew he was a broken man.

This should be easy, he thought.

'Hey, buddy,' the sergeant called to the German. 'I got some
men here want to talk to you.'

At this, the man raised his head and looked questioningly
from Lewis to Niel.

'Oh, Christ!' Lewis blurted out.

Niel felt his stomach do a flip-flop. It was not their man.

Max grabbed the top metal footrest of the climbing rungs on
the telephone pole and hoisted himself up level with the wires.

He looked quickly around the estate through the limbs of the tree that partially concealed him.

Make it quick, he told himself. He could see one of the guards doing his perimeter rounds several hundred yards to the west, his back turned toward Max. He would get to the furthest reach of his rounds at the copse of trees some three hundred yards from where he was now, Max knew, for he had been watching him all morning, since returning from Georgetown. He felt the taut telephone wire under his hand: it was thicker and stronger than he thought it would be. You'll never be able to break it with your hands, he told himself. Improvise. The policeman was still headed away from him, but for some reason had picked up his pace, moving briskly now as if to stay warm.

Quickly, man, he ordered himself. Think.

He had brought no clipping tools along with him. His plans had not gone that far ahead. He tugged again at the wire: it would take too long to crimp it and split it in that manner. Once the policeman finished his rounds and turned back around to face the pole, the game would be up, Max knew. He'd see him immediately.

With his feet on different levels of the pole footholds, and his left arm wrapped tightly around the pole, he reached under his jacket and drew out his gun. He quickly opened the chamber and knocked out the rounds into his left hand. Then he cocked the gun, fitting the wire between trigger and chamber. Let's hope this works, he thought. And that it doesn't ruin your firing mechanism in the process.

He pulled the trigger and the wire bent into a geometric 'U' shape under the trigger. He cocked the pistol again and pulled the trigger, then repeated the process three more times until the wire was so weakened that, re loading and putting the pistol away, he could work it with his hands. The policeman below was nearing the copse of trees as Max continued to work the wire.

Hurry. Break, damn you.

He was about to climb down the pole, hide in the trees below until the policeman had done his return walk, then climb back up, when the policeman's back was to him again. But

time was of the essence, he knew. How long ago had he seen
yellow vest and the other bulkier cop drive off from Washington?
Forty-five minutes? An hour? Long enough, he knew, for them
to discover that the jailed German was Karl and not he. Long
enough for them to be rushing to a phone, perhaps at this very
moment, to warn those at Brantley about the trick.

He rolled the ends of the bent wire more vigorously, the
pole shaking with his exertion. A quick glance at the policeman
told him he had only a matter of seconds not minutes to finish
this job and get down the pole. Sweat broke out on his forehead and his mouth was dry from nerves and exertion.

At that instant, the wire broke in his hands. He quickly
wrapped the loose end around the guide wire above it so that
it would not dangle down and give him away, then scooted
down the pole so quickly that he drove slivers into his legs
several times. Just as he hit the ground, the policeman made
his turn and headed back toward the pole and tree where he
was hidden.

As Max lay crouching in the bracken by the tree, watching
the policeman draw near, he thought about Karl. Clearly the
police had bitten at his anonymous tip, he thought. The lowering
of the security proved that. And with the old couple going out,
and then yellow vest and the other cop driving off, it all
signified that they'd arrested Karl, thinking he was their man.

It had not been easy for him to ask the other German to
help him in this manner; he knew he was putting the man into
extreme danger, but Karl, once he'd heard Max's story, had
half-suggested it himself, even down to the bit about the wound
on the left hand. Karl had cut himself, smiling at Max as he
had done so.

A stupid damn lapdog, Max thought. A brainless wonder.

He loves you, Max told himself. You protected him and he
loves you for it. He'll sacrifice himself for you.

He's a half wit. He'd sacrifice himself for a stick of chewing
gum.

And he remembered Mrs McBride and how she had taken
care of him, how she had covered for him at the house, allowing
him to escape and placing herself in jeopardy doing so.

A sentimental old woman who mistook me for her dead son.

The policeman neared his hiding place and Max put all such thoughts out of his head.

'Try it again, operator,' Niel said almost frantically into the mouthpiece. 'There must be some mistake.'

He gripped the earpiece in his right hand, his heart pounding and teeth grinding.

'We're not able to get through, sir. There must be trouble on the line. We'll have to send out crews tomorrow.'

He slammed down the earpiece. 'He's cut the lines. The bastard's there, I tell you.'

Lewis came roaring out of the shock he had been in since discovering the wrong German in the holding cells. 'I'll get on to the local police at Cabin John and have them send out anybody they can to get word to Brantley. Meanwhile we gather a contingent and get back there as quickly as we can.'

'Why not get in radio contact with your men at Brantley?' Niel said, feeling damn stupid he had not thought of this before.

Lewis looked suddenly sheepish.

'Don't tell me that was part of the security you stepped down?'

Lewis shook his head. 'We were relying on phone lines the whole time.' He looked squarely at Niel. 'We didn't have time for thorough planning, and we don't have time now for post mortems.'

Niel flexed his jaw at Lewis. 'I told you it wouldn't be our man. I told you!'

He controlled his anger only with great difficulty. Lewis had backed away from him, he noticed, shocked by the wild sound of his voice.

'Have your officers call the local police,' Niel said, taking charge. 'We're going back now.'

They were at the main desk and the sergeant called to them as they moved off, 'What do we do with the Dutchman in the cells?'

Lewis turned abruptly. 'Hold the bastard for questioning. He's in on it for sure.'

*   *   *

Max had made his way slowly and stealthily almost up to the house now. Hidden by the dense growth of trees surrounding the building, he wanted to maneuver to the back, figuring he could gain entrance more easily there. If his reasoning was right, the old couple that had left earlier in the morning and had not yet returned were the domestics. There would thus be no one about in the kitchen. He would enter the house there and make his way through the rooms until he somehow tracked down the Englishman.

He had a disguise now, his last one. It would serve him from a distance, but not up close. He would need to act quickly, efficiently. There was no chance to map out an escape route this time. He was a trapeze artist without a net. This thought filled him with a momentary exhilaration.

Suddenly the front door to his right opened and several people came out. First were two large men in police uniforms. Then came Fitzgerald in a winter coat. Max put his hand on the butt of his pistol in its shoulder holster.

Could I be this lucky? he wondered. Is Appleby actually going to make an appearance outside? If so, they really did buy the story of my capture. He began pulling the gun out, readying himself. If it is him, I'll simply take him at the door. There is still a good chance for escape that way. He could see the shadows of another person coming to the door and he pulled his gun out now, ready to fire.

Catherine walked out into the bright sunshine of the porch, accompanied by Appleby, both dressed in long coats. She hugged the dumpy old man, then wrapped an arm around him as they moved down the front steps.

Max could not get a clear shot at Appleby with Catherine Fitzgerald so close to him.

Don't be absurd, man, he told himself. Shoot the bastard. Here's your chance. He's a big target; you've got the advantage of surprise and cover. Your chances will never be so good again. And damn the woman.

He aimed the pistol through the branches of the trees, catching Appleby in the front sight; fixing on the buttons of the man's coat just to the right of his heart.

Catherine suddenly hugged the old man again, playfully rumpling his hair.

'What a fine idea,' he heard her say. 'A skating party.'

The sound of the woman's voice took Max back for an instant, back to his first love, Erika, and he hesitated for a moment. The tone of the voice was happy, child-like, as if from another time or from another epoch, at any rate, in Max's life.

He felt his finger begin to squeeze the trigger almost automatically, without him willing it. Slowly, slowly squeezing.

'Hey, you!'

Max had not noticed that one of the bulky watchers was taking up the rear, scouring the grounds for any possible trouble. The man had spotted him in the trees; was looking straight at him.

Just down river from Cabin John, Niel and Lewis were stalled on the road when a local farmer decided to lead his cows in to the barn, using the macadamized surface to avoid the mud. Lewis, now at the wheel himself, honked his horn furiously at the animals and they began scurrying every which way, the farmer shaking a stick at them as they sped past.

He won't walk away from this one, Niel promised himself, sitting rigidly in the passenger seat, his hand on the door handle. The bastard won't do it again to us.

'Hurry up, Lewis.'

Max stood apart from the skating party, his disguise protecting him for the time being.

He had attacked the guard at the telephone pole, knocking him unconscious and taking the uniform and tying and gagging him with his own clothes. The disguise had allowed him to get close to the house, had even saved him when the bodyguard had spotted him, ordering him to join them on watch at the pond. But he knew he had to act quickly now. Soon either Fitzgerald or his wife would recognize him.

They were busily putting on skates near the pond; Catherine was the first to get hers on.

'Careful,' Fitzgerald warned Catherine as she headed onto the ice. 'Watch out for thin spots.'

Out of the corner of his eye Max saw the colored servant, Thomas, picking his way down the slippery and slushy drive toward them, bundled in an improbable fur-collared black overcoat, a tray holding a champagne bottle in an ice bucket and glasses in his hands.

The rest happened so quickly that it stole choice from Max and he could only react as his training had taught him to do. Fitzgerald looked up from lacing his boots, staring squarely into Max's face. Recognition was immediate.

'Get down, Adrian,' Fitzgerald shouted, and drew a pistol from his coat pocket.

Instead of ducking, Appleby sprang nimbly to his feet from the crouching position he had been in putting on his skates, and he too drew a pistol from his coat. The two guards were looking in the wrong direction for attack: to them Max was still another policeman on duty at Brantley.

Lewis stopped momentarily at the main gate, calling to the guards on duty there, 'Have you spotted him?'

Their blank faces told both Lewis and Niel that they were ignorant of the German's ambit.

'Open the gate,' he shouted at them. 'We've got to get to the house.'

One guard opened the gate quickly and his partner, a young and intelligent looking officer, caught the desperation in Lewis's voice. 'They're not at the house, sir. They went down to the pond. Ice-skating.'

He pointed off to the left, and Niel could see the entire tableau: the woman on the pond; what looked to be Fitzgerald and Appleby side by side at the edge of the pond, their backs to it; the colored servant coming down the hill toward them, champagne in hand; Paxton and Scott watching over it all, and another police officer in back of them.

'The fools,' he said. 'Get going, Lewis. We've got to get them inside before the German shows up.'

And then they heard the first shot.

Fitzgerald could not believe his eyes. The German, here. He felt the gun in his hand before he even realized he'd drawn it. He sensed rather than saw that Adrian was not seeking cover. His eyes were on the German as the man suddenly produced his weapon, shooting instantly through the two body-guards who had not yet figured out what was going on.

He continued thinking in shocked surprise even as the bullet struck him full in the chest, throwing him onto his back in the snow. He could hear screaming, and realized it was his wife, Catherine. Screaming his name, over and over.

Why is she screaming so? he wondered.

'Edward! Edward!' She could hear her own voice shrill in her ear, piercing and cold. She watched horrified and helpless from the ice as she saw the guards turn toward another policeman who she suddenly recognized as the man she knew as Maximillian Voetner, but now dressed in a uniform a size too large for him.

She watched in horror as the German agent shot the closest man, who sat down hard on his rump, holding his stomach. Then there were more shots and she saw the German dive, roll, and shoot.

She came alive and started skating as hard as she could toward Edward. Her arms pumped as she glided over the ice, and suddenly she heard a loud crack beneath her as the ice began to break.

'Edward!'

Max rolled in the snow, the pain in his left arm intense where the second guard had shot him. Another crack of the pistol sounded and a bullet splattered into the soft earth by his head. He stopped rolling, held the gun straight out ahead of him lying flat on the ground, and pulled off two fast rounds. The first took the guard in the shoulder, and the second one hit him in the middle of the chest. The man fell to the ground like a dead weight.

Max got up slowly. Time had lengthened for him and his left arm dangled uselessly at his side. From the pond came Catherine Fitzgerald's scream once again.

He looked toward her and her attention fixed on her fallen husband as she skated over the ice.

To his left the colored servant had dropped the tray and was running toward him. On the far side of the pond he saw yellow vest and the big cop racing through snow up to their knees. Only then did he fix on Appleby. The Englishman stood defiant and angry, the gun held in his pudgy hand like a cricket bat.

'Damn you to hell,' Appleby yelled, then pulled off a round that whizzed past Max's head like a pesky bee.

Max felt absolutely no anger as he leveled his gun at Appleby. The crack of his pistol left his ears ringing. A dark splotch blossomed on the front of Appleby's light gray dress coat, and for a long moment the man continued to stand as if riveted to the earth.

'Help!'

The woman's scream from the frozen pond seemed to topple Appleby; he fell like a statue, flat onto his face.

Then Max saw Catherine Fitzgerald sinking through the ice.

It was all like a dream to Fitzgerald. He could hear his breathing, a wet sounding whistle. The sky above was incredibly blue and still. Champagne corks were popping all around him.

A piercing scream brought him momentarily out of his stupor, and he rolled onto his stomach, facing the pond, and saw Catherine's fur coat billowing up around her as she slid down through the ice.

How strange, he thought.

Then, seeing her hand clutching at the ice as she began to sink beneath the water's surface, he finally realized what was happening. He began painfully and slowly to crawl out onto the ice to her.

Once again, events overcame him. Training, instincts, yes, and his basic humanity took over.

Max gave no thought to escape, but ran instantly, automatically toward the pond. Shots rang out from in front of him: yellow vest was shooting at him, but was too far away to be anything but an annoyance.

He ran past Fitzgerald who was laboriously pulling his way to his wife, and the moment he hit the ice he knew it was breaking apart. There will be no safe spot here, he thought. Anyone who goes out on it will be lost.

Catherine's hand clawed frantically as she went below the surface, and then she bobbed up again momentarily, spluttering and choking.

'I'm coming,' Max yelled out. 'Don't panic.'

But he could see that the heavy coat, now soaked, was dragging her down. To his left, Thomas was just reaching the pond.

'Stay there,' he ordered the servant. 'The ice won't hold us both. I'll get her.'

But Thomas continued to edge onto the ice, and Max ignored him as he dashed for Catherine's hand as she was going under again.

Everything was a blur and confusion. She felt the sting of water in her lungs and the freezing cold of it all over as she floundered in the water. She wanted desperately to get her fur off: it was pulling her down like some fierce animal. But she had no control over her arms. All she could do was flap them helplessly in the water, lost in panic and fear. Her lungs felt like bursting and she knew she was going to die.

Suddenly, out of this chaos, came a firm hand gripping hers, and she felt herself being hauled out of the icy water. She gasped for air as her head broke the surface, and finally her cheek was laying against the brittle surface of the ice. She could feel someone pulling her up and up, out of the water to safety, but could do nothing to help.

Opening her eyes, she saw the German leaning over her, giving one last desperate jerk to push her back away from the ice hole she had created.

There was another loud crack and she thought it was a gunshot, but was mistaken. It was the ice all around Max giving way, crumbling beneath his weight.

'Get her away from here!' he shouted. She looked behind her and saw Thomas reaching out to pull her by the collar of the fur along the ice to safety.

She saw the hole widening and Max sliding into the cold water. Thomas, letting go of her collar, crawled to the edge to Max, extending his arm as far as he could. Max bobbed to the surface once again and Thomas was able to barely grip his hand.

'Get him! Pull him out. He's mine!' Niel was shouting at them from the far edge of the pond, then stopped and began circling to their side.

'Let me go,' Max said, and Catherine watched numbly as Thomas seemed to nod at him in understanding.

Thomas gripped Max's hand more tightly for an instant, black on white over the icy water. Suddenly Max's hand escaped the grip, and he cast a quick glance Catherine's way. Then his whole body slipped underneath the water. She watched and watched, but he did not re surface.

A hand touched her side and she saw that Edward had pulled himself to her, leaving a trail of blood in the snow behind him. Turning him onto his back, she cupped his head in her hands and rested it in her lap.

Please don't die, she prayed.

A shadow loomed over her. 'Where is he? Where's the German?' Niel demanded.

Thomas slid back off the ice, stood and wiped snow from his front.

'It's over,' he said. 'All over.'

EPILOGUE

There were no winners.

History leaves no record of Maximillian Volkman. He died as anonymously as he had lived.

There was nothing linking Max to Germany – nothing but the British intercept, and London was loath to bring that up and compromise their secret Room 40. There was no posthumous hero's ceremony for him in Berlin. In fact, Berthold, his master, had aborted the mission soon after losing contact with Max.

But his mission was a success – for a time. Sir Adrian Appleby was mourned in America and England, yet as Berlin had calculated, his death prevented immediate transmission of the Zimmermann telegram. Moreover, the assassination was attributed to a personal vendetta, and President Wilson, swamped by more pressing matters, accepted this explanation.

Whitehall initially accepted this loss. After another week, however, and desperate to bring America into the war before Germany totally destroyed her shipping, Lloyd George's government decided to approach Wilson through normal diplomatic channels. They would hold their breath and simply hope that the US president did not ask too many compromising questions about the provenance of the telegram.

President Wilson, when finally presented with the Zimmermann telegram at the end of February, was first shocked and then horrified by its contents, for Mexico had long plagued his administration. Ultimately, however, he did ask the compromising questions that London feared. When the British showed themselves to be reluctant to prove the authenticity of the telegram, and thereby reveal the existence of Room 40 and its code-breaking secrets, Wilson, like many others, became convinced that the telegram was a hoax.

Again, Berlin had calculated on this.

Yet one thing that Max, the spymasters, and diplomats in

Berlin and London had not reckoned with: the arrogance of Foreign Minister Zimmermann himself. Zimmermann honestly believed that his Mexico gambit had been simply an extension of diplomacy; that there was nothing underhanded about it and thus no reason to deny the telegram when asked about it by the press.

The telegram, once authenticated by Zimmermann himself, had its hoped for and feared effect: on April 6, 1917, the United States declared war on Germany.

Meanwhile, Edward Fitzgerald slowly recovered from his wound. By the time the first American soldiers reached France, he was finally beginning to put on weight again. But he'd had enough of the half-truths of diplomacy. He and his wife Catherine ultimately retired to the hills of Brantley, Edward to create a model farm, and she to pursue her photography, eventually publishing in 1921 a photographic study of poverty in Washington that shamed the federal government enough into cleaning up the alley dwellings in the capital.

The Fitzgerald's also had three children: two boys and a girl. The first boy, a golden-haired and warm-hearted child, they named after Adrian. The second son, Edward. The daughter, a rangy and inquisitive creature even as a baby, was named after Catherine's servant, who died the year before the girl's birth in 1923. Thomasina – Tommy to her friends – grew into a long-legged beauty, not unlike her mother.

Chief Inspector Lewis had no easy retirement: as a result of his failure with the case, he was demoted to a precinct chief in southeast Washington, finishing out his career dealing with domestic violence and small-time crime.

Agent Niel was more fortunate, for his name was not officially linked with what became known as the Appleby Affair. His star rose in the Twenties with the advent of the Red scare, and he ultimately became one of the top officers of the Federal Bureau of Investigation. He never forgot Catherine Devereaux Fitzgerald. Upon his death, a file code-named St Jude was found in his safe: a dossier on Catherine. In it was everything from a detailed exposition of his suspicions of her connections with Maximillian Volkman in 1917, through her growing involvement with the Left through the Thirties and Forties.

Throughout all the following years, until Edward Fitzgerald's death in 1951, Max Volkman's name was never mentioned in the Fitzgerald household. His act of bravery in saving Catherine was commemorated, however. On a knoll overlooking the Potomac, well within the property line of Brantley Hall, stands a simple lichen-covered gravestone under an old sycamore tree. The inscription on the stone is short and as anonymous as events of the time forced it to be:

If you have come,
You know me.